THE
HABIT
OF
FEAR

THE HABIT OF FEAR

...

DOROTHY SALISBURY DAVIS

CHARLES SCRIBNER'S SONS
NEW YORK

CHARLES SCRIBNER'S SONS
Macmillan Publishing Company
866 Third Avenue, New York, NY 10022
Collier Macmillan Canada, Inc.

This is a work of fiction. Names, characters, places, and incidents either
are the product of the author's imagination or are used fictitiously. Any
resemblance to actual events or persons, living or dead, is entirely coincidental.

Library of Congress Cataloging-in-Publication Data
Davis, Dorothy Salisbury.
The habit of fear/Dorothy Salisbury Davis.
p.   cm.
ISBN 0-684-18887-2
I. Title.
PS3554.A9335H3   1987   87-16013
813'.54—dc19   CIP

10 9 8 7 6 5 4 3 2 1

Printed in the United States of America

for
CHRISTIANNA AND ROLAND,
who shared a part of the journey

THE
HABIT
OF
FEAR

PART ONE

...

1

...

"I really don't understand," Julie said. "I just don't."

Her husband frowned and screwed up his eyes as though searching his mind for another, no more unkindly way to explain something that ought to have been accepted without explanation. Explanations were not going to help.

If only she could do that, Julie thought, if only she could say, "Okay," and get up and walk out of the room. What she said was, "Why don't you start from the beginning? I want to be sure I heard what I think I heard."

"You heard what you heard," Jeff said: a gentle voice, a message of stone. When Julie shivered in spite of herself, he put out his hand to her. She pulled away, and he turned the gesture into one of flicking dust from the arm of the chair. Despite all her housecleaning, a tiny cloud of dust rose and shimmered in the beam of early summer sunlight that angled across the living room.

"I'll bet there's no dust in her house," Julie said. "Or is she a slob? Am I too fastidious? Too much like you?" She didn't want to say the things she was saying. They simply spurted out. To forestall any more of them she pressed her knuckles against her mouth.

"You must have known," Jeff said, his sad eyes coaxing her to agree with him.

"How? Tell me how I was to know."

"Something. You must have known something."

"Is it my fault that I didn't?"

"No. It's not your fault. We don't communicate very well. We don't pick up on one another. You want me to explain, but how can I explain the inexplicable? I've fallen in love. I didn't plan to, but it happened."

"And what am I to do?" More words to regret. And underneath the pain and panic was the feeling that she had never been in love with him. Lacking in variety of experience she might be, but she knew there was more to loving than occurred between them. And yet there had been love.

"I don't intend to leave you destitute."

"I'm not talking about money," she screamed, and then in self-disgust, "Oh, why can't I shut up? Christ! Words don't mean anything. Not to a child, and that's what's wrong with me. I'm retarded. I refused to grow after hitting twelve." She got to her feet and stretched until her bones crackled, trying to break the tension. "Maybe we're onto a cure now. How about that?" She moved from place to place in this sacred room of his, this so-called living room in which she had not been able to live in all the nine years of their marriage. She was looking for the single object she had added to his exquisite collection of Victoriana, a china giraffe.

"I consider myself at fault there," he said. "I liked you that way."

Would it have choked him to say that he had *loved* her that way? Having found the ornament and taken it in hand, she forgot her purpose, if any, in looking for it, and put it back on the shelf. "You're not at fault, I'm not at fault, my mother wasn't at fault . . ."

"Your mother?"

"Phyllis wasn't at fault either, was she?" Julie ranted on with the pointless mention of Jeff's first wife. "What you want is a no-fault divorce. Right?"

"Since you put it that way, yes. I suppose that is what I want. I want to be fair to you, certainly."

"Yeah."

2

"I mean by that that I shall always provide for and take care of you."

"Always?" Julie whirled around on him. "I can't believe what I'm hearing, what we're saying to one another."

"I know," he said soothingly.

"Let me say something to you, chum. Before I let you take care of me, I'll find a jumping-off place and celebrate my independence."

"If that's to be construed as a suicide threat, it's not allowed."

"It's not a suicide threat! It's a survival plan."

"Then I'll be the first to celebrate your independence. I'm sorry, but you set yourself up for that. I think it's demonstrable that self-support with you is a recent and tenuous accomplishment. Look at matters squarely, Julie. You finally have a paying job, a column under your own byline . . ."

"Half a column," Julie said of "Our Beat," the *New York Daily* column she coauthored with Tim Noble. She sat down, but on the edge of the chair, the easier to be off again if sitting became unbearable.

"Would you like it any better if it were all yours?"

"No. I don't see a gossip column as my life's work."

"What do you see?"

She gave an angry shrug and said nothing. It was mad, unreal, discussing her so-called career at this moment.

"You're almost thirty, Julie."

"Is that why you're divorcing me? How old is the new one? Getting on toward puberty?"

"I'm not amused."

"I'm not either. And you don't have the right to lecture me."

"I do love you, Julie."

"So why? . . . Strike that. I know why. You love her—differently."

"We're very good together," he said, not looking at her.

That hurt deeply, a scalding splash of pain. But she managed, "And at your age you don't have that much time."

"Touché." A little twitch of nostrils showed the bristling: She had wounded his pride.

3

Julie sat up straight, feeling starched and stretched. "Why should I make it easy for you?"

"It's not easy for me. The whole thing is a torment. Easy? Half the time I feel like an idiot, this happening to me. I dream of castration. I dream I'm impotent and it's a relief."

"And the other half of the time?"

"When I'm with her . . ." Jeff started slowly.

Julie stopped him. "Never mind."

"So," he said, cat-cradling his fingers.

Why marriage? she wondered then. If that was his intention. And otherwise, why divorce? Was the woman pregnant? After two childless marriages, Jeff might like that. There was some faint solace in the idea, but she put it out of her mind when it began to rankle: Already she was twisting it into something with which she could reprove herself.

"You'll want a little time," he said. "I didn't think it would be such a shock to you."

Julie snapped her fingers: a mere bagatelle. That was a phrase of her mother's she hadn't thought of for a long time. The pressure of tears she was determined to hold back bore down between her eyes. "A little time for what?"

"It might be helpful for you to see Doctor Callahan again for a few sessions."

"That's my business, Jeff."

"She could give you some support, that's all."

"She's not that kind of therapist."

"That's ridiculous. All psychiatrists are supportive when the patient needs it. But as you say, it is your business. . . . I thought I might return to Europe and stay for a year this time. Since I have a book contract, I may take a sabbatical from the paper. . . ."

Her first thought was: In a year the affair could be over. "No! Let's get on with it here and now. You've got a lawyer. I'll get one. I don't think they're in short supply."

Jeff raised his hands placatingly. "I hoped we could manage a sensible arrangement before bringing in the lawyers. I intend you to have half my worth, do you understand?"

4

Conscience money. She gave each word a cutting edge: "I'm not sure half your worth, Geoffrey Hayes, is worth having."

Two patches of color tinged his cheeks. "You are probably right." He looked at his watch—as though it mattered that it was half past ten of a Sunday morning in June. "Would you like me to move to the club?"

"It's something I haven't given much thought to, Jeff."

"No. Of course not." All softness again. "I'm very, very sorry. I know I've hurt you, but I think in time I'd hurt you more if I didn't take this step now."

"Oh, shit." A glorious flood of anger finally released whatever clogged the tears. On her feet she said, "No, I don't want you to move to the club. This house is so much yours it can't wait for me to get out. And I want to be the one to go. It isn't as though I haven't a place of my own to go to. . . ."

"Julie, you're not in a fit state to go anywhere," he called after her as she started from the room. "Come back and let's talk sensibly. I can make some coffee."

And drink it, she thought. To hell with him and Queen Victoria and whatever little flick was waiting to share his sabbatical. Running, half-blind with tears, she bumped against the pedestal and tumbled a marble bust of a woman masked in nineteenth-century gentility. She broke the fall of the sculpture with her leg, but left it where it landed, intact. She hauled the heavy sliding door closed behind her. It was still closed a few minutes later when she went out of the house.

She walked quickly, unheeding of pace or appearance, her raincoat swinging open, a duffel bag slung from a shoulder strap from which she struggled to free her hair. Let it go, let everything go. Only her anger was real, a rage fueled by her helplessness, humiliation, and something that had to be jealousy. Not to have known . . . Not to know now where or why or when it happened. Along Sixteenth Street and up Sixth Avenue, she strode through the flower district, where spent roses and irises and baby's breath lay wilted on the curb. She crossed the street because the light was with her and she could keep on moving. She turned uptown again toward Forty-fourth Street, where she had an office with a hot plate and a cot and chairs and a bathroom to throw up in. Virginia Woolf and her goddamn room of her own. The relief of a moment's amusement before the pounding anger took over again.

She found herself striding along a street she was pretty sure was in the thirties and too far west for where she wanted to be. The skeletal steel structure of a monster building project crisscrossed the sky. At street level was a wall of boards; in the street itself the giant cranes sat idle, like long-necked beasts dipping their heads to somewhere beyond the reach of her eye. And across the street, wheeled into place where the rubble had not been entirely cleared first, was a caravan of trailers that serviced the construction-site workers. So complete was the Sunday shutdown not even a security guard was in sight. The West Side Highway traffic provided a mobile border to that swatch of deserted city.

The Hudson River lay beyond the highway and, time no longer mattering, she set the river as her immediate destination, wherever she could gain access to a pier. Sky and water and ships that were going out to sea. She thought of an Irish seaman she had known who spouted poetry although he could barely write his name . . . and she thought of her Irish father, whose very name had been taken from her. . . . And Jeff with his year abroad—to write a book, et cetera.

She stopped, hearing something at once familiar and, in that setting, strange: She thought she heard an infant crying.

2
...

Or was it a cat, perhaps, or a kitten, and what would she do about that? But the cry persisted, and she knew that it was human. It came from behind the nearest trailer, a whimper, then a series of gasps, then silence, then it started over again. She took a few cautious steps among the broken bricks. Nothing about the trailers suggested that some of them might be residential, but that didn't prove it wasn't so. Something, someone was alive there.

She stopped and listened for sounds other than the crying. None nearby. She took stock of how far she had come from the street, uneasy. But it was far from a cul-de-sac she was heading for. Beyond the trailers a long vista lay over the leveled rubble, climaxing with the lower-Manhattan skyline, its totems of trade etched into the horizon. A lone figure scratched among the debris with what looked like the shaft of an umbrella. He—or she—turned up bits of treasure and bent an already stooped back to where he could collect his finds and deposit them in a shopping bag. The crying grew more frantic, yet the solitary reaper paid no attention. Deaf, perhaps. Julie moved into the open on the far side of the trailer.

The trailer door was wide open, but there were no steps up to it. In the doorway, bundled in a blanket, the little bald head just visible, was the helpless figure that sounded barely able to cry any longer. And it was about to tumble out onto the ground.

Julie ran, her arms outstretched, to catch the child before it fell. The instant she saw that it was a doll, not a child, she tried to stop. But it was too late.

A man's hand shot out from the side and caught hold of her hair before she could pull back. He made a twist of it round her neck and at the same time compelled her forward and clapped his hand over her mouth. The scream was stopped in her throat. A second man clutched her arm, her bag, her clothes, whatever he could hang onto. The two of them dragged her up and into the trailer. She kicked and swung out at them and tried to use the karate she'd studied years before. But there was no time, no way she could position herself. Panic. She could not even swallow. Fear was stuck, a lump in her throat. She couldn't breathe. She was flung to the floor, facedown. One man jumped astride her and again clapped his hand over her mouth. The hand was soft and sickening with a putrid smell—vomit, stale medication.

"If you promise to shut up you won't get hurt. Hear me?"

He was leaning over her, his face close to hers. He was wearing a stocking mask, but she could smell stale beer and more vomit, and she tried to turn her head away.

He spoke to his partner: "For Christ's sake shut the door. What's the matter with you?"

"The lock's broke. We broke the goddamn lock."

"Get something you can tie it up with. Jesus."

Julie tried to beat on the floor. He raised himself and then thumped down on her back. She moaned at the pain in her ribs and breasts. That made him do it again, riding further up on her. He took his hand away from her mouth, but only to grasp her throat with both hands. She gagged with the pressure and the pain. He let up the pressure. "Promise you won't scream?"

She nodded. She couldn't scream if she tried. She opened her eyes and saw his hands: white, very white, with little clumps of black hairs on the fingers. She could see the open door, but no more of the outdoors than a fringe of distant skyline. Eye level was the doll where it had been kicked aside. She saw the other man for a second or two against the sky. He, too, was wearing a mask, and he waddled

8

or was lame. He made a slipknot around the knob with an electric extension cord. She could not see where he fastened the other end in the near darkness.

She said the prayer of her childhood, the Lord's Prayer, and closed her eyes, waiting. Her mouth was dry, and the foul taste had to be of fear. But the panic had passed. She was able to remember a detective she'd heard lecture on rape and how he'd driven home the point again and again: Don't fight it. Don't resist. It's your life that matters most. Save it. . . . Don't fight. Don't resist. . . .

The lame one, if he was lame, had a knife. While they pulled off her clothes, he slashed through buttons, straps, whatever obstructed them. To make her shape up, to take whatever position suited them best, he kept pricking her with the small sharp blade. They helped one another clumsily, obscenely. One sodomized her. The pain bolted into her head, all that way, with every thrust. When she passed out, they revived her. The knifer raped her, the pain just as bad, its source so close to the other wound. When conscious, she feigned unconsciousness and tried to concentrate on color, sunsets, Cézanne, oranges.

When they were finished with her, they bound and gagged her with pieces of her clothing they pulled out of her duffel bag. The smell of semen and sweat made her retch and choke under the gag. The sodomist removed the gag to let her vomit and get her breath. Then he gagged her again. He threw her coat over her and over her head something that smelled of dampness and mold. The doll's blanket, she thought.

She lay utterly still. They did not speak except to make sounds of urgency to one another. When the door opened, she could see a speck of light. It vanished when the door closed. She watched for the light to appear again. When it didn't, she knew that they were gone.

With her first attempt to move she almost passed out again. After that she plotted every change of position before she tried it. First she got her head out from under the blanket and studied the contents of the trailer. A table and several folding chairs. A naked unlighted bulb hung over the table. Thin, horizontal ribs of daylight streaked the ceiling, seeping through the upturned slats of the blinds. She watched for some time until a shadow moved across the ceiling. She made a noise, but from behind the gag, it wasn't much of a noise. Nor was the thump of her head on the floor.

She turned her attention to the door. Reason told her that if they had had to fasten it closed from the inside, they must have pushed it closed after them on something to make it hold when they left, a thickness of flexible material, rags, say, or folded paper. On her side, moving with care, she inched toward the door. Her hands, tightly bound, were getting numb. So were her feet. She tried to sit up and flung herself down again with the pain. Even more cautiously then, on her back, she eased close and pushed on the door with her feet. The wedge ought to have fallen but it didn't, and the pain again became more than she could handle. She rested and shepherded her strength. When she was reasonably sure of not passing out before the impact, she gathered her feet, her knees to her chest, and let them fly at the door. When it swung open, she hauled her feet back into the trailer and let the wracking pain ease off. With the fullness of light she could see her own body. Some of the knife pricks had gone in deeply. Some wounds were blood-caked, some still oozing. She tried to reach one on her breast with her tongue. Nausea. She stank all over. Sweat drenched her body, chilled and revived her. She scanned the wasteland for the vagrant with the shopping bags. Gone. She thought of trying to reach the ground. To try to hop? Even the thought was excruciating. She couldn't even handle the pain when she tried to reach the strap with which her ankles were bound. Nor could she use her numb fingers until she had pressed her wrists even more tightly together and gradually brought the pins and needles and then the feeling back into her hands. Lying on her side, she began to work her thumbs beneath the gag. She bruised her lips but managed to get one thumb into her mouth. She intended to use her teeth as a fulcrum against which to stretch the gag. And the plan was working when she discovered the consolation of having her thumb in her mouth; it gave her such comfort that she closed her eyes and for a little while was mother to herself.

The tardy watchman found her that way.

10

3
∎ ∎ ∎

Julie had ridden once before in a car with the sirens screaming—
when she'd been taken to the morgue by the police to identify a
murder victim. It drifted through her mind that if she needed identification, they would call Jeff. No.

She must have said the word aloud, for someone reassured her.
"It's going to be all right. You're safe now." She opened her eyes
and a young medic riding on the jump seat winked at her solicitously.
"They'll get the bastards."

How, she wondered, did he know there was more than one?

There were many things she wondered at as she drifted in and
out of sleep in the hours and days that followed. She wondered at
the meanings of various medical attentions. A stubborn infection set
in from the several knife wounds. The doctors were having trouble
keeping her temperature down. They'd taken to calling her Sebastian.
"How's my little Sebastian this morning?" Neither males nor saints
appealed to her. She kept silent. She wondered how Dr. Callahan
came to be sitting at her bedside one day when she opened her eyes.
How many appointments had she had to cancel to be there? She
wondered how Jeff felt, how he really felt, trying to hold her hand.
She took it away and hid it beneath the sheet. How had they first
come to know? Was it the newspapers? On television? . . . *Gossip
columnist raped*. . . . *Wife of noted newspaper columnist*. . . . She didn't want
to speak to anyone and didn't. Except to the police, who came

11

regularly to prod her for just a little more information. And any help she could give in identifying her attackers could save other women from her experience. She tried to care, to sort out why it had happened to her. Any woman would have done them, the female of any species. And there came the moment when the police therapist tried to get through to her by assuring her that her husband, an intelligent, understanding man, would not reject her because of what had happened. Julie looked at the woman, grimly amused.

"You'd be surprised," the therapist said, oozing kindness.

So would you, Julie thought, but she said nothing.

She wasn't even curious about all the flowers, from whom or from where they'd come. She did like one arrangement that arrived without any card at all, tiny golden roses. "They don't even look real," the nurse said.

Nothing much did.

When the infection healed and it was time for her to leave the hospital, she became the very model of cooperation. She intended to prove her competence; under no circumstances did she intend to return to Sixteenth Street. A friend from the Actors' Forum came and camped with her for a few days at Forty-fourth Street. The greatest healer was making living quarters out of the shop. The waves of revulsion came more rarely. She could generally turn them aside before they swamped her. Which was not so with the almost constant rage over the Jeff situation. She was sick of her own anger, but she could not escape it. She needed help. It was funny how much better she felt just admitting it. Dr. Callahan gave up a lunch hour to see her right away.

It did not seem like old times. Not at all. Except for the long silence between them before she was finally able to say, "Jeff wants a divorce."

"Let's talk about it," the doctor said, which was more than she had used to say, even to get things going. Jeff had said she would be supportive, and as usual, he was right.

Julie declined the couch. That way she was able to talk. "I don't mean he wants it because of what happened to me. I'm not laying that on him. But I keep thinking that's why it happened. I went crazy when he said it, wild, you know—out of control. The very things I didn't want to say I kept saying over and over. The only way I could stop was by getting out of the house."

"What did you say that you didn't want to say?"

"Things like 'What's going to happen to me?' Or, 'What am I going to do?' "

"Why was that such a terrible thing to say?"

"I wanted it to be me who asked for the divorce."

"Oh," the doctor said, drawing the sound out almost mockingly. Was it the truth? Julie wondered. It felt like it. "So why didn't you do it?"

"I couldn't. I was afraid to. I'm not sure what I'm saying is true, doctor. I can't remember thinking seriously of divorce until Jeff brought it out in the open. I feel I did, but that's not knowing. I'm not making sense, am I?"

"Go on."

"I panicked but I didn't want him to know it. I didn't want him to see how shaky I was, but I couldn't help myself. And that made me angry."

"With yourself?"

"Who else?"

"And you were afraid. Is that what you mean by panicked?"

Julie nodded. "All of a sudden I was nobody again. There was nothing of *me* in that living room. I remember looking for a china giraffe I'd bought in a Paris flea market, the one thing of mine, but when I found it, I put it right back on the shelf."

The doctor sat, her forefinger touching her lower lip, her dark eyes blinking as she stared at Julie while Julie recounted the length and depth of her reliance on Jeff. Then, winding up: "But I'm not going back. Even if . . . I'm not."

"All of a sudden you were nobody again." The therapist picked up on something she had said sometime before.

"Growing up with my mother's name. I never even knew my

13

father, except for his picture on the mantel. I've said this to you so many times."

"Go on."

"I think she made up all the stories about him, an Irish diplomat who up and disappeared after he got the marriage annulled. I guess he was a Catholic. And you know what that makes me as far as the church is concerned. Oh, to hell with him. To hell with him! I've been saying it all my life."

"Tut, tut, tut," the doctor chided. "You are *guessing*. You *think* she made up stories. What do you *know*?"

Julie was given pause. What did she know? As a child she had asked questions, and as a child she had liked what her mother told her, and she had believed every word, even the ones she knew were contradictory. As to the question still foremost in her mind, why the annulment? It was one question her mother answered consistently right up to the end of her life. *"Because it was what he wanted."* Her mother was great at giving men what they wanted. Julie looked at her watch.

The doctor repeated the question in that voice Julie recognized from old whenever she'd been trying to escape the couch: "What do you know?"

"I don't *know* anything."

"Not anything? No marriage license? No record of annulment? No friends of your mother's to talk to, no best man, no maid of honor at their wedding? No wedding photographs? Nothing about him on your birth certificate?"

"That was almost thirty years ago, doctor. It's a long time."

"Thank you for telling me. You amaze me: You are curious about every urchin on the street. You play detective. You dig up secret lives of celebrities and do not even know your father's name."

"I do know that," Julie said softly.

"So?"

"Thomas Francis Mooney. And I know he was born in Ireland. It's on my birth certificate."

"And your name on the birth certificate?"

14

"Julie Anne Richards."

"Your mother's maiden name, yes?"

"With a notation about my father—whereabouts unknown."

"Very curious." It was one of Dr. Callahan's rare comments. She adjusted her analyst's chair to relieve a back strain. "How do you feel about the men who attacked you?"

"I loathe them. It makes me sick to think about them."

"*Do* you think about them?"

"I can almost turn it off now, but in a way that's bad. I ought to be trying to remember things about them if I'm going to be any help to the police."

"Do you feel ashamed? Guilty?"

"I don't know about ashamed exactly. I feel dirty. As though a thousand enemas wouldn't clean me out. But guilty, no. Not this trip."

The doctor nodded understanding. "A thousand enemas will help. And getting on with your life. That is the important thing. You are not going back, so you are going forward, yes? Do you want to talk about the impending divorce?"

"I don't know what there is to talk about. The sooner the better. Did you think it would happen? I mean back when I was in therapy with you?"

The doctor almost smiled. "I am not always right," she said. "Do you wish to resume therapy?"

"No. For one thing, I can't afford it."

"Do you still have the job on the newspaper?"

"Yes."

"And there will be a divorce settlement, no? You were not married yesterday. How many years?"

"Nine. I will not take any more money from Jeff."

The therapist breathed deeply, as though she needed patience. "So you have come full circle. Independence."

Sarcasm? Julie wasn't sure. "I hope so, doctor. Maybe that way I'll get rid of the anger. I wish I understood it. It's like an obsession."

"Is it possible that you need it at the moment?"

15

Julie thought about that. She was surprised. "Possibly," she admitted.

The doctor released the brake on her chair. "Total independence is as neurotic as total dependence. Fortunately, either condition is beyond most of us. You know I am here in an emergency."

Julie thanked her.

No good-bye, no handshake, no convoy to the door: It made for a continuity of sorts, something unfinished, something that might never be finished.

4

...

If Dr. Callahan was amazed at Julie's only occasional curiosity about her father, so was Julie now that she looked at it from what might be called an adult perspective. It was as though there was a door in the house that she, as a child, had been told could not be opened. She had grown up with the feeling of truth about the unknowability of her father. There were no wedding pictures among her mother's papers, no certificate of marriage such as Julie and Jeff had received from the minister. Her mother seemed to have erased every possible image of him and filled in the vacancy when Julie asked questions with whatever came into her mind. Was the name Mooney a fabrication? No. That was on her birth certificate, not to be nullified by "whereabouts unknown." But it was totally missing from her certificate of baptism, an event that occurred eight months later in the Protestant Episcopal Church. It was a church in which to this day she felt an alien for all that she had grown up in it. The seed of Rome seemed, somehow, not to have died.

It was over two weeks since she had been in the *New York Daily* office. She did not go in regularly in the normal order of things, only to meetings and her occasional bout with the Terminal Data System when her partner was out of town. She went in that day as part of therapy—to get on with her life. With every step her dread grew stronger.

17

Tim Noble, her collaborating columnist, spotted her coming along outside the glass-enclosed editorial room and hastened to meet her. She hesitated as he came close. He stopped short. Then they rushed into each other's arms. It was hard to break away and stand face to face.

"You're looking great." Tim said.

"You too," Julie said. And he did look good to her: a homely face with a lovely smile and ears that looked as though he had been picked up by them as a child.

He tried awkwardly to keep pace with her as they reached the main aisle of the vast room. "Do you feel as good as you look?"

"I feel pretty good," she said with all the cheer she could muster.

Everybody stood up and either saluted or shook hands as she and Tim moved along to their cubicle. Such a reception wouldn't have come with an appendectomy, she thought. She willed herself off that track until she saw the bouquet of white carnations on her desk. White. With a little drop of red at their hearts. She had to stop seeing symbols even when they were obvious. The boss, Tom Hastings, came out from his office, hesitated about it, and then kissed her on the cheek.

Julie thanked him for the reward the paper had posted for information leading to the arrest and conviction . . . Five thousand dollars, recently upped to ten.

Hastings merely nodded. "It's nice to have you back on the job," he said and retreated to his office.

The others returned to their desks, the kindest thing they could have done.

"I promise I won't make jokes," Tim said.

"Oh, for God's sake, do."

"Okay. Did you ever see such a guilty bunch of dudes in your life? I'll bet there isn't a guy in the office who's laid his wife in the last two weeks."

"That's a joke?" She shuddered. She wasn't out of the trauma by any means.

Tim sank his head between his shoulders and got onto something safer. "Have you been able to read the column?"

She made an effort. "That's why I'm here. I was afraid you didn't need me anymore."

Tim grinned and reached out his hand. Involuntarily she drew away. Realizing, she grabbed his hand and squeezed it hard. "It's great you're back," he said.

She tried to sit more loosely in her chair, to feel comfortable. But it was not going to happen, not that day.

"Why don't you take off something and stay for a while?"

She shook her head. "Tim, I'm going to be wobbly for a while. Not only because of . . . the rape. There, I've said it and it feels better. I know somebody who won't say the word *cancer*. She calls it the big C."

"There are a lot of big C's—courage, confidence . . ."

"What I started to say is: Jeff and I are getting a divorce."

"Congratulations."

"Don't be frivolous about it, Tim."

"I've never been more unfrivolous in my life. I won't knock the guy, but I think it's the best thing that could happen to you."

"He's in love with another woman. God! That sounds corny."

"If you want my opinion, the only person he's in love with is himself. If he wants a divorce, make him pay for it, Julie."

"He says the same thing himself. Please don't knock him, Tim. You said you wouldn't. I'll have to defend him if you do, and I don't want to."

"What kind of shit is that? You don't have to defend anybody but yourself. Next thing, you'll be defending those buggers every man in this room would like to cut the balls off."

She had come back too soon. She wasn't ready. Or was she preparing herself never to be ready? Was she going to want to throw up at every mention of sex? She thought of Jeff and his dream of impotence and being glad about it. Not anymore he wouldn't be. "Oh, boy," she said, aware of what had just gone through her mind and how she felt about it.

"Yes?" said Tim.

"I just realized I'm not jealous of Jeff's new woman anymore."

"You've got to be jealous," Tim said in apparent contradiction

19

of himself. Then: "Otherwise you won't go after the money."

Julie smiled a little. It wasn't that she didn't like money. She just didn't want Jeff's under the circumstances.

"You won't go after it," he said. "I know you."

Julie shook her head. "I'll make out all right. . . . Is there anything in the basket I could go to work on?"

"You're sure it's okay?"

"As long as it isn't something with a heavy sex angle."

"What else is there in our business?"

Julie agreed. When she wanted to escape from the gossip business, she had to hustle a feature assignment from the Sunday-magazine editor, and she was dead sure that just now the only story she could sell Ray Duggan would be her own.

Tim brought out a folder from his middle drawer, but he didn't open it. "Why don't you give yourself a couple more days, Julie? Get around town and see people on your own so you won't be running hostile, you know?"

"Is that what I'm doing?"

"That's how it comes across to me, and that only calls attention."

She didn't know how she was going to get out of the office, how to manage the long walk to the elevator. Especially with the white carnations. But Tim got a sheet of newsprint and wrapped them, and then carried them himself as he walked her to the elevator.

She crossed Forty-second Street and made her way to the nearest church, Saint Agnes's, not far from Grand Central Station. She didn't suppose it had much of a congregation, but in bad weather a lot of people came in out of the rain or the cold. It was a raw, windy day, not a bit like summer. She sat in the front pew—a basilica-type church with its semicircular arch. A poor-man's basilica. She sat and listened to the sounds from the sacristy, someone doing the chores of God. She was making up phrases, images. Not a true believer. A sentimentalist. A seeker? A sentimentalist. She sat with the flowers in her lap waiting for the sacristan to put in an appearance out front. The fragrance wafted upward. White for the pure of heart . . . each with a drop of blood in the middle.

The sacristan emerged carrying a box, the contents of which rattled when she genuflected at the front of the altar. She was heavy and slightly lame; her shoes were badly turned over and her ankles swollen. She took the box to the rack of candles in front of the statue of the Virgin and replaced those that had burned out. Julie took the flowers to her.

"What am I going to do with them at this hour?" the woman complained. But she took them and thumped back into the sacristy for a vase. She was running hostile, to use Tim's words.

Julie felt her own trouble to be that she wasn't running at all. Leaving Saint Agnes's, she dawdled at the window of a religious bookstore. She was no great patron of bookstores. Her mother had worked in one and striven to make enough money to send Julie to Miss Page's School and then to college. She hadn't made enough money—that way. Julie dug her hands into her jacket pockets and moved on.

Her mother had worked at Books of All Nations, a shop not far from United Nations Plaza. Most of its customers were UN personnel. She remembered some pretty exotic types among her mother's friends. The store was still there, she discovered, but it was now part of a discount chain. She chose the oldest clerk on the floor and asked him if he remembered Katherine Richards, who used to work there.

"It's a name I'd like to remember, but I can't say I do." He had the soft voice and the shiny cuffs of a dignified penury.

"She worked here in the nineteen-fifties and sixties."

"Ah, that was when it was a real bookstore. I myself worked at Brentano's on Fifth Avenue at that time, and I thought that store would last forever. But nothing does. . . . Katherine Richards: I'll ask around if you want me to, but I can't think of anyone here now old enough to remember back then." His pale eyes settled on a customer a few aisles away. He made a little sound of disapproval and then said, "Excuse me a moment. If I assist him now, it may keep him out of trouble."

"Thank you," Julie called after him. A potential book thief was making tracks.

"Come and see me. I'll remember." Then, "Miss . . ."

She waited.

"It occurs to me: Why don't you go and see a man named Morgan Reynolds in our main office? He used to be the manager here. A top man in the chain now, but he might remember."

Julie murmured her thanks and fled. The name Morgan Reynolds brought on a kaleidoscope of memory: a man who smelled of licorice and pipe tobacco who was often at their house. His laugh was silent except for a wheeze every time he inhaled. His fingernails were clean and shiny. He taught her to play checkers and then one day he had brought a set of chessmen. She remembered very clearly her mother saying no to his teaching Julie chess. She could have the pieces to play with, but that was all.

Julie walked clear across town for the first time in weeks. She could smell the dust of the memory: coming home from college to find the chess pieces still lined up in opposing positions on the wide bedroom windowsill; they stood against a background of iron bars that gave an authentic feeling of dungeon, for the window overlooked the dark inside courtyard of the apartment on Ninety-first Street, where she had grown up. By then, Morgan Reynolds did not visit anymore, but she knew then and now that he had to be considered a benefactor of sorts.

5

...

Jeff had visited "the shop," as Julie called her first-floor rooms on Forty-fourth Street, only once. She said of it herself that it was an okay place to visit but she wouldn't want to live there. So when Jeff phoned to suggest that she return to Sixteenth Street while he was abroad, she was briefly tempted.

"Surely you'd be more comfortable here," he said.

Looking around at the thrift-shop assortment of necessities— dresser, a kitchen table, wall shelves, a couch, and a clothes rack— she agreed that there was no question about that.

"It's important that you have a sense of well-being just now," he went on, and then changed his approach when she was silent. "I don't want the apartment left unoccupied, and I certainly won't rent to someone I don't know. Or for that matter to anyone I do know. . . ."

So, Julie thought, his new woman wouldn't be hanging around town waiting for his return. She'd be with him. "Thank you, Jeff, but I'm getting along just fine. I have friends in the neighborhood. I like it here."

"God knows why, but however you want it, Julie. We are not the first couple to divorce, you know."

"No kidding."

"When it's convenient for you, you'll want to collect your things before I close up."

"Tomorrow," Julie said instantly. "Okay?"

"I shall leave some bank forms on the kitchen table. They need your signature. I'm putting a sum of money in an account in your name."

She said nothing, but resolved not to sign the forms.

"I wish there were something we could say to each other," he said.

"How about good-bye?" She was choking up. "No, wait. Jeff, in all those talks you and my mother used to have, did she ever tell you anything about my father?"

"Not that I remember at the moment." He thought a bit more about it. "I'd have told you by now in any case. You've asked before."

"I'd forgotten," Julie said. "She flirted with you, didn't she?"

"I suppose you could call it that. I always thought of it as her mode of flattery. . . . I don't know whether this would apply to your father or not, but I remember her saying to me once, 'I'm such a pushover for literary types.' "

"I thought he was a diplomat type," Julie said.

"Do you want me to make inquiries with the Irish UN Mission?"

"No!"

"Sorry."

"Thank you," she added softly. "I did that myself years ago."

And so she had, having since all but blocked it out. No one there or at the Irish Consulate in New York could remember him, and at the time of Julie's conception and birth the Republic of Ireland had not yet been admitted to the United Nations.

The clack of her heels on the bare floors echoed through the apartment as she went from room to room to see that she had left nothing that was hers. The rugs had already been rolled for storage, and someone had covered the furniture with sheets she did not recognize. She gathered perhaps twenty objects from almost as many countries—sculptures, glass figurines, scarves, jewelry—all Jeff's gifts from his many journeys on faraway assignments. The only thing to do with them when she got them to Forty-fourth Street would be to hold a sidewalk sale as soon as possible. Or donate them to an Actors' Forum benefit.

Jeff had had her trunk brought down from the attic. She packed the marital souvenirs in cartons, bagged her clothes, and left the trunk till last. She knew very well what was buried at the bottom underneath her ski clothes, college gown, and gym suit: her father's picture—if it was her father—and her birth certificate, something she never wanted to look at unless she had to—when she'd gotten her passport, for example. Dr. Callahan was right: She was curious about everything except herself. Not entirely so; it was more that she was afraid of what she might find out. She removed the winter woolens, her gown and gym suit, exploding the smell of camphor. Not only was there the picture of her father in its gilt frame, but one also of her grandfather on her mother's side, whom she could just remember, a man so sick at the time, she could now understand, that when he had put out his hand to touch her, he had let it fall before he could reach her face. She could remember forcing herself not to pull away from him. He had turned his face to the wall, releasing her. Beneath his picture was one of her mother, a handsome, sensual-looking woman whom Julie did not resemble. Except in name. She took her father's photograph to the mirror over the mantel in the living room. There was a resemblance, she would swear. It was in the wide separation of the deep-set gray eyes, the long, straight nose, and the large, sad mouth. She smiled at herself, and her whole expression changed. She became, she thought, someone a stranger might want to know. If only the face alongside her image could also change, would their smiles be alike?

She went back to the trunk telling herself that she had to hurry. But that wasn't so. The movers weren't due for two hours. With neither joy nor fear, with no emotion she was aware of, she reached for the manila envelope. It contained, besides the expected birth certificate, her baptism papers and her and Jeff's marriage certificate. In the name of the Father, the Son, and the Holy Spirit. Her sponsors at baptism were Jane and Allan Burlingame. They were UN friends of her mother's, and theirs was the only large family within Julie's intimate experience. One of the girls, Janice, had gone to Miss Page's School with her. She had loved to go to their home, a very large apartment on the West Side—full of noise and boys and laughter. But the Burlingames had been recalled by their government, and the last she had heard from them was on her twenty-first birthday, when they had sent her an Indian sari and a bank draft for a hundred dollars. She made herself look at the marriage scroll. Very fancy. And it, too, called on the Father, Son, and Holy Spirit. She and Jeff hadn't promised to obey, she remembered, only to love, honor, and cherish for as long as love remained. Okay. No broken promises. Their witnesses has been Frances and Tony Alexander.

She unfolded the Certificate of Live Birth. She had been born Julie Anne Richards in Doctors' Hospital in New York City. Her mother's name was Katherine Anne Richards, her age twenty-eight. She had been born in Illinois, and at the time of Julie's birth was living at the 499 East 91st Street address. The father's name was Thomas Francis Mooney, age twenty, born in Ireland, and there was a notation: "Whereabouts unknown." The name of the informant was Allan Burlingame; relation to the infant: family friend. The certifier was George Stephen Macready, M.D.

Whereabouts unknown. There had to have been a time when his whereabouts were known. To have had a marriage annulled—if that was what really happened; and if so, why didn't a notation to that effect show on the birth certificate instead of "Whereabouts unknown"? For the marriage to have been annulled it had to have occurred in the first place. In other words, there must be a record of it somewhere. She thought back to the preliminaries of her and Jeff's marriage . . . the blood tests, the application for the marriage license three days later . . . the forms, the names of parents, Richards and Mooney. A comedy team. But not very funny.

6

∎ ∎ ∎

The Sex Crime Unit detectives, Al Beamis and Mabel Hadley, came to see her every few days. This time they were accompanied by Detective Dominic Russo, a precinct man Julie had known since her first days in the shop. She thought his inclusion was intended to put more pressure on her; the police were not satisfied that she had wrung everything out of her memory that she could. They were probably right. She had recalled that neither man wore rings, that they smelled of stale beer and sweat, and one of them of medicine and some kind of machine oil or grease. She'd smelled vomit. Her memory was strong on smells, weak on what she saw. She didn't think the taller man was more than five foot ten; they had ordinary New York accents, no racial intonation that she could detect. More, more, the detectives always wanted more. She resented the repeated questioning. If they were making progress, they were not sharing the information with her.

Detective Russo lived on the West Side only a few blocks from where he had grown up—five minutes' walk from the shop and not much farther, coming from the other direction, from the building site where the attack had occurred. He was a rarity among modern urban police, a neighborhood cop. Solid and stocky, he seated himself gingerly in one of the director's chairs at the round table in Julie's living room. The others followed suit. Russo looked with solemn eyes at the table's one ornament, the large crystal ball, no doubt remembering his early encounter with Julie at this address. His wife was a believer in the occult. "Mrs. Russo sends regards," he said.

Mrs. Russo was also a friend of Mary Ryan, another neighborhood character, so that Julie had to anticipate that old lady's imminent arrival. She'd expected her before then. Loaded with soda bread and sympathy.

It was all so goddamned neighborly.

"I don't like to wait until the bastards strike again," Detective Beamis said, getting the interrogation under way.

"Am I supposed to have been their first victim?" She tried to keep the hostility out of her voice.

"We can't be sure they've always played as a team," Beamis said.

"That's some game they're playing, sir." The hostility was out in the open.

"Detective Beamis's way of speaking," Hadley explained softly. She was a good-looking, forthright young woman. "It's not unique that two men team up that way, but most rapists are loners. What was their attitude toward one another?"

"Cooperative."

"Be a little more specific, can't you, Mrs. Hayes?" she pleaded.

But Julie's control broke. "What do you want me to do? Take my clothes off and show you the scars? I'm trying to get it out of my mind, and you're screwing it in forever!"

"I'm sorry about that," Hadley said.

"If we get them, don't you see," Beamis tried, "it can help you get rid of them, get them out of your system."

Julie drew a deep breath. "I'm sorry I blew," she said. "What was it you asked?"

"You go right ahead and blow all you want," Hadley said. "You've got the right."

Beamis resumed the questioning. "Was there anything feminine about them? Swishy?"

"No." Then: "I don't know. The one with the knife giggled

every time he dug the knife in. That's what it sounded like, a kind of falsetto giggle."

"Could the knife be a tool of a particular trade?" Russo asked.

"I don't think so. A switchblade."

"Would you recognize their voices?"

"I doubt it."

"Anything about them to make you think they might live in our neighborhood?"

This was the reason, of course, that Russo had been rung in on the interrogation. The possibility of locals made Julie even more uncomfortable. She drew a deep breath. "I'll tell you again everything I can remember about them, and I'll try, damn it, to get it all up this time."

Detective Hadley checked the small tape recorder.

She told everything she remembered and became aware of adding nuances that were not there before: "the heavy black hairs on the sodomist's fingers"; she was more sure the shorter man rolled when he walked; she wouldn't now call it a limp. "He was lighter-complexioned, freckly, with hair on his body like dry dead grass. Their skin was taut. Young. They smelled young. How about that?"

"Go on."

"I felt they knew their way around the whole building project. With that strong smell of machine grease on the hands of the taller one, I figure they could be maintenance men on all that heavy machinery. . . . Yet his hands were soft and clean . . . a disinfectant soap maybe." Her mind went dead on the subject. "What about that person in the lot with the shopping bags? Why can't you find her?"

"You're sure now it was a woman?" Julie hadn't been sure before.

"Almost sure. They had no way of knowing I was going to come along from the direction I did. I think they were trying to lure that person into the trailer and I fell into the trap."

"That could be the way it happened," Beamis said, "but the trouble is, he or she has vanished."

"Did anybody see her besides me?"

"Not recently," Beamis said. "And we've pretty well sifted the men on the project payroll. That includes the subcontractors, maintenance, and supply. Negative findings all the way."

"Does that mean you'll keep coming back to me to start over?"

"No, ma'am, it doesn't mean that," Detective Hadley said. "It means the case goes on the back burner. There's a lot of work for us out there, and we don't get to choose our assignments. We'll work on this case when we can."

She couldn't possibly know how relieved Julie felt.

"They sound like klutzes," Beamis said, running his fingers through his hair. It was a desperate kind of gesture. "So why can't we nail them? They left stuff all over the place: that doll blanket, the container with grease in it. . . . They're fucking lucky, that's all."

Julie picked up on this: "A container of grease?"

"Speaking of klutzes," Hadley said, shaking her head at her partner's gaffe.

It was Russo who explained: "They collected a small amount of grease. The lab traced it to a used drum in the dumpster." He went on hurriedly, "Let's talk about those stocking masks."

"Yeah, let's," Julie said tightly, having figured out what the grease was used for.

"Have you ever heard of lisle stockings?" Russo wanted to know. "I guess you're too young for that. My grandmother wore them. The immigrants coming over, the nuns when I was a kid, before they shortened the habits. I don't even know if they're manufactured anymore, but I thought of them from your description . . . holes for the eyes and mouth, but you didn't see any runs where they'd been cut out and the stockings stretched. Right?"

"I think that's right. And I couldn't see through the material. But you can buy panty hose like that, the cheaper the heavier."

"But it's the runs I'm thinking about. I was talking about it with my wife last night. We experimented with an old pair of hers. Zip—runs up and down. Then she called her friend Mary Ryan— you know Mrs. Ryan—and went over and got a real strong pair from her."

Everybody on stage, Julie thought. She said, "Support hose."

"They didn't support much when we cut holes in them."

"I could be wrong about the runs," Julie said, becoming wildly impatient.

"And the doll?"

"I would not recognize it if I saw it again," she snapped.

"I don't blame you for being uptight. Just the same, it's the little things that work when the big ones don't. You know that from your own experience."

"Yeah," Julie said. Rare praise from a professional for an amateur detective. Sheer cajolery.

"Remember a black street girl named May Weems?"

"Yes." May Weems had been an acquaintance of a young prostitute Julie had tried to help. "Is she still in the life?"

"She's got so many arrests, so many collars now, we call her Ring-Around."

The other detectives were amused. Julie waited. Everything he'd said so far, she felt, had been leading up to this.

"These days she's hustling down in the thirties. I talked to her—about the bag lady. I think she's seen her, but there's no way that girl is going to cooperate with the police." He paused. Then: "She might talk to you, Julie."

7

...

They wanted her to go after May Weems, Julie reasoned, and she wasn't going to do it. Russo had conveniently forgotten how he had used her to lure Weems out of hiding back then. Julie had listened to the young prostitute's life story, buying her breakfast at six in the morning, gaining her confidence. May had wanted to be the first black ice-skating star. "How about that, Friend Julie?" Russo had picked May up as soon as she stepped outside Friend Julie's shop. No, sir, Julie decided, she was not going out to look for May Weems. She was going out to look for news fit to print in a gossip column.

"You're a born psychic!" Reggie Bauer cried when she walked into the Actors' Forum. He kissed her on both cheeks. "I just left a message with your service." Reggie was slight and blond and difficult to cast, but everybody at the Forum said he was a good actor. What Julie knew of him was his natural ability to pick up a story that might make her kind of news.

"What's the message?"

"Guess who's coming to the session this morning."

"Mother Jones," Julie said. "Reggie, I'm a poor guesser."

"Richard Garvy ... Mike Bowen of 'Seventeen Orchard Terrace.' "

"I know who Richard Garvy is," Julie said. The television series

"17 Orchard Terrace" had gone off the air that spring after ten fabulous years. You could still turn on a rerun at almost any hour of the day. The main character, Mike Bowen, was the owner of a garage in a New York suburb, a volunteer fireman, small-town politician, embattled family man whose kids were sometimes proud and sometimes ashamed of him. As he was of his children. "How come the Forum? Business or pleasure?"

"Somebody said he has a play he wants to do."

"Here?"

"Oh, my pet," Reggie said. "With his ego even Broadway is too small a grave. Actually, he's a friend of our esteemed director. It could be a scouting expedition. That's such stuff as dreams are made on around here this morning. Will you stay? I'll get you coffee."

"Coffee, yes, thank you." Julie did not like to attend the acting sessions. She was a member of the Forum, acting being one of the many careers to which she had once aspired. She had surprised everyone, especially herself, by winning her audition. But she was not an actor and she would not take advantage. She loved the Forum and the friends who came there to hone their craft between and sometimes during engagements. She was comfortable there, even now, when she was comfortable practically nowhere else. The actors came and went, passing through the Green Room where she sat on the arm of a sofa, some saying, "Hi," some, "How are you?" and some who wouldn't speak if spoken to, afraid it might break their concentration. If what had happened to her was known among them, no sign of it was evident; after all, it was not as though she had been replaced in rehearsal.

The office door opened and Bradley Holmes, the artistic director of the Forum, emerged. He was a slight, handsome man in his fifties with strong academic and theater credits. He greeted Julie more warmly than was his habit and, almost out of the room, paused and turned back. "Is there anything I can do for you, Julie?"

She took advantage. "Help me get an interview with Richard Garvy."

"Not in the Forum," Holmes said sharply.

"Certainly not. He can name the place."

Holmes made a sound that lacked promise. Reggie approached with a container of coffee out front of him like the Olympic torch. "For God's sake, watch it, Bauer!" The director got out of his way.

"It won't hurt you," Reggie said. "It's only lukewarm."

When Holmes headed for the reception room, the word passed, swift as telepathy, that Richard Garvy was about to arrive. Actors converged there from all directions. Even Reggie Bauer. Julie stayed where she was and sipped her coffee. When Garvy arrived, the director brought him through the Green Room on the way to his office at the back of the building. Garvy walked with the springiness of a big man who kept in shape. Like a politician, he shook hands with those who got up close, and his very blue eyes had the same sparkle that came across on television. Julie kept her feet out of the way.

But Holmes stopped. "Here's someone who wants to meet you, Dick. Julie Hayes is one of our people who's gone over to newspapering. Very good, too—a column in the *New York Daily*."

She could not have asked for more. Garvy told her to call his secretary at the Plaza. Her name was Mary Tumulty.

One thing in favor of Richard Garvy from the outset, so far as Julie was concerned: he was staying at the Plaza. The only reason she wanted to leave New York someday was so that she could come back and stay at the Plaza. She remembered as she went up in the elevator how, on her way to or from Dr. Callahan's office, she had used to route herself so that she could stop at the Plaza to use the powder room. Days of idleness and dashed careers and playing at being in love with a husband who called her his little girl.

Garvy came out to the elevator and met her himself. It was very good for her ego, never mind why he did it.

The Plaza suite was exactly what she had expected, not a piece later than Edward VII, except Miss Tumulty's electric typewriter and its stand. Just passing through. Miss Tumulty herself belonged. She was round-faced, made up softly, and wore her hair in a braid that circled her head, a silver tiara. They had talked on the phone a couple of times. Neither was surprised at the other's appearance.

"You have such a nice voice," Miss Tumulty said, "and I knew your eyes would be as big as saucers."

"I love your name," Julie said. And she liked the pleasantness of the woman's face.

Garvy touched Julie's arm, and they went on to a small sitting room. A crystal vase on the center table was crowded with anemones, an explosion of colors.

"Oh, boy!" Julie cried.

"The simple things in life, eh? They're my wife's favorite. How the management found out ... oh, I suppose Miss Tumulty. She knows when to talk and when not to. And they don't know downstairs yet that 'Orchard Terrace' has folded for good."

"Why? Everybody wants to know."

"Oh, now, admit: *Everybody*'s a slight exaggeration."

"Very slight." She took the chair he wanted her to have. It gave her a fine view of the anemones. She got out her notebook.

Garvy drew up a side chair. "I want to see if I'm still an actor. I felt as though a block of ice was building up around me in the series—Mike Bowen being preserved for exhibit as the typical American clown of the late twentieth century. The bottom line, however, is I've got a play I'm in love with. I want to direct it as well as play the lead. You couldn't recommend a producer who'd put up with the likes of that, now, could you?"

"Go for broke," Julie said. "Produce it yourself."

"I may have to at that."

"Is it Irish?"

He cocked his head and looked at her. "How did you arrive at that deduction?"

"The lilt in your voice when you spoke of it."

"Ah, now, I come by the lilt naturally. My people on my mother's side come from Ireland. I've a grandmother still alive in Sligo. She was responsible for my having a couple of years at Trinity College, Dublin. She's ninety-two and full of charms and incantations. Look, for the space you have in your column, you don't want my life story, do you?"

"I'd like more about the play," she said.

"And that I can't give you till I've got a better hold on it than a handshake with a playwright."

One last try: "Is *he* Irish?"

Garvy scowled reproachfully and said nothing.

"My own father was Irish," Julie said, as though that was relevant. "But I never knew him." She was backing off from having pressed the question.

"He died young, did he?"

"He skipped out," Julie said. "Actually, I don't know what happened. He was gone before I was born."

"Have you ever tried to find him?"

"No, but I've been thinking about it lately."

"It would make a hell of a story, wouldn't it?"

"Shouldn't we get back to the main subject, Mr. Garvy?" She had never been as easy with a "star" before.

His eyes were almost mischievous. "Was he a handsome devil?"

Julie nodded. "I do have a picture."

Garvy leaned back and folded his arms. His white shirt was gleaming, and with him in that position the buttons were at a great strain. "When you get to Ireland, you must go to see my grandmother. She's a witch and she might just conjure for you. Now, what else do you need in your notebook there?"

"Something about Trinity. You started acting then, didn't you?"

"With the Dublin Players. For which I was paid by being allowed to attend all rehearsals." He talked for a few minutes about his two years in Ireland in the 1950s. As a student abroad he had escaped the Korean War. "Better not put that in. The Mike Bowen fans would lower the flag." Then, without a change of beat: "What was his name?"

"My father's? Thomas Francis Mooney."

"He'd be about my age, would he?"

Julie nodded.

"Is it possible he and I might have been at Trinity together?"

36

"I suppose it's possible."

"Your face seems familiar to me, and you don't have a familiar kind of face at all."

Julie met his eyes, which still had a mischievous gleam. "You're putting me on, aren't you, Mr. Garvy?"

"I wouldn't say that, the way the world's shrinking. Bring his picture around sometime and let me have a look at it." He tapped her notebook. "Do you want a mug shot of me for the column?"

"Please," Julie said.

8

...

"Oh, now, aren't you the lucky one?" Mary Ryan said, holding Garvy's picture at a distance that best accommodated her eyesight. "Isn't it remarkable how that man put his finger on the pulse of the nation?" She set the picture facing her up against the crystal ball and volunteered the opinion that it was unwise of Garvy to do a play. "Unless it's a play about Orchard Terrace. Wouldn't that be fun?" As Julie had anticipated, it wasn't long after Detective Russo's visit until Mrs. Ryan arrived with a round loaf of soda bread. She wore her summer straw hat, her gray hair straggling out in wisps beneath it. Her face was getting puffy and her pale blue eyes more watery and bloodshot. She'd been either drinking or crying, Julie thought. Suddenly she realized that the old lady had come without her constant companion, an aged dachshund.

"Where's Fritzie?"

Mrs. Ryan straightened herself up and pulled in her chin. "I had to put him to sleep a week ago Friday."

The tears flooded Julie's eyes. There was no holding them back.

"There, dear, I've cried myself dry. It's why I didn't come any sooner. But he's better off. He couldn't do this and that and he couldn't contain himself any longer."

"Sorry," Julie said and wiped away the tears.

"Don't be. I know it's me you're crying for."

"Or me maybe." She went to the dresser to get a tissue, and there stood the tin box in which she kept dog biscuits for Fritzie.

"What a terrible thing happened to you," Mrs. Ryan said while Julie's back was turned.

Julie blew her nose. "Shouldn't we go to the ASPCA and get you another dog?"

"I think not. Fritzie was fourteen years old, and fourteen years from now I'll be way over eighty. No, I just don't think so." She leaned back in the chair and took another look around the room. She had foreborne until then commenting on the new pieces of furniture and the bedding. "Something's different," she said, knowing well that the place was completely rearranged from when she had last been there.

"I'll be living here for a while," Julie said. "Jeff and I are separating."

"Isn't that interesting?" The eagerness quickened in her eyes to be carrying the news to the few friends they had in common. Mary Ryan had lived over forty years in the neighborhood. She'd worked as an usher at the Martin Beck Theater. Theater was her life, and she told over and over, like the beads of her rosary, the names of actors and producers she had known. "Still, I don't suppose you're celebrating," she added.

"No."

Mrs. Ryan waited, hoping for a confidence. "He was a very successful man, wasn't he?" she tried then.

"He still is. Mrs. Ryan, do you remember telling me about Father Doyle and his ability to trace lost relatives?" She had once told the older woman how little she knew of her own father. The priest she mentioned was an assistant at Saint Malachy's.

"Julie, he's a marvel. I could name you a half dozen broken families he's put together again. After finding the pieces, you might say."

"Would he know about annulments and where the records are kept?"

"Well, if he doesn't, you may be sure he knows where to find out. I'm so glad you're doing it." Mrs. Ryan was always a leap ahead. "It's important to know all we can about ourselves. You might turn out to be an heiress to a fortune and never have known it."

She worked hard on the apartment after Mrs. Ryan left, her anxiety syndrome. Then she wrote up the interview with Richard Garvy. It would be extraordinary, she thought, if he had known her father. Somebody had known him. Somebody had witnessed the marriage and knew the reason for the annulment. "Oh, God help me!" she said aloud—half prayer, half despair. But afterward she felt a great calmness. She chose between Father Doyle, who was easy to reach, and Morgan Reynolds, who might not be. She looked up the phone number and called the executive offices of Books Unlimited. She gave her maiden name, Julie Anne Richards.

9

...

It all seemed so ridiculously simple. One phone call and she was to have lunch the next day with Morgan Reynolds, who, unless he had become manager of the bookstore afterward, was her mother's boss at the time Julie was born. Why had she not thought of him before? No problem with that question: She hadn't wanted to. On the phone the man sounded as though he'd been waiting years to hear from her—a warm, self-assured voice. She tried to remember what he looked like, but her memory of him was confused with that of her late boss, Tony Alexander, who'd been Jeff's best man when he and Julie were married. Reynolds had been her mother's lover; she knew that now. Come on, Julie, you knew it then. When had the affair started? The earliest she could place his regular visits was when she was five. She remembered sitting in the lotus position on the coffee table with the checkerboard between them. (Her mother had been taking yoga classes and, having no place to park Julie, sometimes took her along.) Julie was still in nursery school. She tried to teach a boy named Orin Isenbox how to play checkers. The thing he did best was pile the checkers up and spill them all over the board. And Uncle Morgie thought she was ready for chess. Could she have learned it, precocious brat? Eventually she learned from Jeff, but she was never good enough to beat him, not even with a two-piece handicap.

Uncle Morgie.

* * *

41

She would have recognized him anyway, but he rose and came across the restaurant to meet her, both hands outstretched. Julie was shy, holding back, giving her hands where he would have kissed her if she'd been willing. He was big, but trim and muscular, a tennis player still, she thought, remembering one more thing about him. A blue-eyed blond, hair graying. His chin was cleft, and his cheeks dimpled when he smiled.

It was a small, quiet restaurant on the far East Side with expensive space between the tables. A half-dozen pink tea roses were at her place. The maître d' centered the vase while Reynolds held her chair. A bottle of champagne was cooling. The whole scene made her uneasy. All she wanted was information about someone else.

"I've had the fantasy this would happen someday." Reynolds settled himself opposite her. "I hope you won't mind if I say you are every bit as attractive as I expected?" The voice was velvet, deep, and the quick smile a sort of punctuation. But it made the compliment seem less sincere.

"You do know that mother died a few years ago?" Julie said, wanting to divert his too intense attention.

"I did know that, and that you were married to the columnist Geoffrey Hayes. I assumed it was *that* Geoffrey Hayes when I read Katherine's obituary notice. I thought of calling you. Perhaps I should have. But I've always felt that if you wanted to see me, you would look me up. And now you have." The flash smile again. Expensive teeth. Everything about him was expensive—his tailoring, his tan, his choice of restaurant and flowers.

She could think of nothing to say. It seemed too gauche to mention Thomas Francis Mooney at once. "I remember the chess set you brought me."

"You were beating me too often at checkers. Have you children of your own?"

She shook her head. "Jeff and I have recently decided on divorce."

"I wondered." He indicated his own wedding band. The mark of where Julie had worn hers showed faintly.

42

"And *your* family?" she groped.

"My wife finally died. I say it that way because she was ill for so long. Even while I knew your mother . . ."

Julie repressed a smile. It seemed corny even if true.

". . . And the girls are long since married. One lives in London and one in Baltimore. I haven't remarried, if that's what you're wondering."

"Actually," Julie said, "I was wondering if you knew my father."

He lifted his eyebrows, a reflex that caused his hairline to seem to shift downward. "And who was he?"

Julie was taken aback.

"That was facetious," Reynolds said. "Don't you think we should put such an earnest matter aside until we know each other better?"

"All right." She felt reproved, a little girl chastised. No, she protested to herself and turned matters around. He had no right to be facetious, superior, so smugly male. And the important thing was he seemed to have known her father.

Reynolds signaled the waiter to open the wine. While he watched the man wrap the bottle in a napkin and begin to work on the cork, Julie watched Reynolds himself, ready to shift her eyes if he caught her at it. He'd be a hard man to work for, on top of every detail. Julie had worked for someone like that. But Reynolds would also be generous. No doubt he was with her mother.

He caught her eyes. "Yes?" The eyebrows shot up again.

She put a finger to her own hairline. "I remember how you used to pretend you were wearing a wig that kept slipping down on your forehead. You'd yank it back into place."

"You weren't long catching on to that one. You gave it a yank yourself, and when it didn't come off, the game was over. You were not an ordinary child, Julie. You were much too wise for your age, and much too quiet."

"Was I?" That image pleased her. Except that she had reversed the growing process. Instead of growing up, she'd grown down. Till now.

Reynolds turned his attention to the wine. "For God's sake,

man," he said to the waiter, who was still massaging the cork with his thumbs.

Fortuitously, the cork popped.

When the waiter had poured the wine and gone off, Reynolds said, "You know, Julie Anne, this meeting isn't easy for me either."

She laughed and felt better. How knowing of him to make that admission. It changed the whole atmosphere. "Uncle Morgie," she said.

"That's right!" he exclaimed as though the memory had just come fresh.

They touched glasses and talked first about the apartment on Ninety-first Street. Neither of them knew if the building was still there. "A ridiculous rental. It would cost a fortune today," he said. Then: "Your mother had a small inheritance, which I advised her on. Did you know that?"

"I think I did," Julie said. She seemed to remember.

"It brought us a little closer than manager and clerk. By that time I thought I could take over the whole book business. Your mother bristled every time I called it a business. She was not the most practical person in the world. . . . She had a marvelous laugh, didn't she?"

Julie nodded. It was crazy sitting talking about her mother when it was her father she wanted to know about. But then she hadn't known her mother very well either, as a lot of therapy had brought up.

Reynolds lifted his glass. "To Katherine."

Julie drank with him.

"And to her daughter. She must have been pleased with your marriage to Geoffrey Hayes."

Julie nodded. And after a second: "I used to think she'd arranged it."

"That she was in love with him herself?"

"Ha!" His random leap surprised her.

"She'd have wanted to marry both of you: Am I right? A member of the wedding. She was a very romantic woman—and impulsive. But I'll say this for her, she had courage."

"Oh, yes," Julie said. "At the end of her life she said to me one day that she'd never had a holiday. She'd decided to take a trip. I didn't even know she was ill. She died three months later in some small town I'd never heard of."

"Very courageous," he murmured. "And a little selfish."

"Yeah," Julie said. She wanted now to cut away from the subject.

But Reynolds mused aloud, "How extraordinary—to go off and die alone."

Off the top of her head: "Maybe she wasn't alone. How about that?"

Reynolds said, "I think we'd better have the menu now."

"I was being facetious that time," Julie said.

"All the same."

The Dover sole had arrived that morning, flown in from England, and the white asparagus was very special. She left the ordering of lunch to him. She could not remember the last really good meal she'd had. She was not great on food, for having associated so long with a gourmet. She wondered if the new woman would do something about the pot belly into which Jeff's navel was disappearing. Certainly not. That's not what new women were about.

"Hayes has to be a good deal older than you, Julie Anne. Am I right?"

"But very young at heart."

Morgan made a noise suggestive of sympathy.

It put her off. "Actually, Jeff has an old heart, but he enjoys his women young."

Morgan signaled the waiter with a snap of his fingers to pour more wine.

Julie put the subject off as long as she could. As soon as the sole was served and she had said how good it was, she held back no longer. "Please tell me what you can about Thomas Francis Mooney. All my life mother was evasive about him. She made things up sometimes—like telling me he was an Irish diplomat. Or was he?"

Reynolds drew a deep breath. He had hoped to get through lunch, she thought, before she brought the subject up again. "An

45

exaggeration. He may have worked for an Irish diplomat."

"But did he? I could take it from there, don't you see?"

He laid his knife and fork down carefully. "Do you have a profession, Julie Anne?"

"Just Julie—Julie Hayes. I'm a gossip columnist on the *New York Daily*."

Morgan Reynolds leaned back and laughed silently, a small breathy sound only. He touched his lips with his napkin. "I'd never have guessed it, not in a million years."

She shrugged. Anyone who read the *Daily* would have known. And anyone who read any paper recently should have known: He'd missed the rape and sodomy story. It was nice to know that someone had.

"Not very diplomatic of me, but it doesn't jibe at all with my notion of you. You're much too much of a lady."

"I inherited the column—half of it—when Tony Alexander was murdered. Do you know who he was?"

"I do. I remember the murder."

"I was working for Tony at the time. Jeff started *his* career as a legman for him. They were lifelong friends."

"I see." Reynolds resumed eating. It was the kind of arrangement he could approve, she thought, Jeff's getting her the same start as his own. "Do eat your luncheon, Julie. The fish isn't half as good now as it was when it was served."

What took place then was like a charade—a pantomime, a conversation without words—a quick glance, a start as though to say something that then seemed unimportant and was abandoned, a resort to food, to the very dry white wine that came when the fish was served, the unfinished champagne taken off, the meeting of his eyes with hers, a rushed smile that pulled in the dimples. Ridiculous, a man like him having dimples. Did she like him? Not really. She distrusted the dimpled smile. And yet it was a variety of flirtation that was going on between them, each of them wanting the other's approval. Why, on his part, she wasn't sure. She wanted information, every morsel she could draw from him. She refused to admit to herself that he, too, might fabricate.

46

She ate the last of the fish and the last stalk of asparagus, the combining of which had put her in low esteem with the waiter.

She said how good the meal was and then, when Reynolds put down his silver, "Could we talk about my father, Morgan?"

"Morgan," he repeated. "Thank you. I wanted you to come to it on your own. I don't suppose you remember the last time we saw each other? The day you started at Miss Page's School?"

Another evasion. She tried to prepare herself for disappointment and yet not to alienate him. "I do remember. You drove me there." She had remembered being driven to the school that first day, but she had forgotten by whom until now. "I was ten years old, wasn't I? I didn't start with Miss Page until the sixth grade."

"It seemed wise to wait until my other daughters had graduated." He said each word carefully.

Other. The dining room did a strange little tilt before Julie's eyes and then came upright again without making a sound. Everyone in the place seemed to have fallen silent. Including herself. She felt as though she had been struck dumb. She knew his eyes to be waiting hers, but she could not meet them. She wanted to and she knew she should—to see what there might be recognizable in them. There was something terribly wrong. Such revelation ought to have come in privacy, and not so abruptly. Everything in her rebelled at the idea, and slowly the numbness receded. But she mocked herself: Now she wanted a parent of her own choosing. The mockery made her sane.

Reynolds signaled the waiter to clear the table. "Leave the wine," he said, and when the man was gone, he added a few drops to Julie's glass, already almost full, and refilled his own. "I should have waited," he said. "But how could I, considering what you want to know?"

Julie brushed aside the menu and shook her head at mention of the dessert cart.

"Later," Reynolds said, and when the man had wheeled off, he asked, "Is the idea so abhorrent to you that you can't even speak?"

If she had answered, it would have been to say yes.

He knew it. "So you'd prefer I told you a romantic tale about Thomas Francis Mooney? Was that his name? I could do that for you, I suppose."

47

"No." Julie finally spoke. "Mother told me enough of them."

"And nothing about Uncle Morgie."

"Not much."

"I thought she loved me. I thought we were very much in love," he said as though reexamining that part of his life.

Julie looked at him. Squarely now. His expression was wistful, regretful. And he wasn't a very good actor, she decided. She was sure it was an act, whatever his motive might be. But then, she wanted it to be an act.

"I was married to a woman totally dependent on me," he went on. "There were two children. Katherine and I both understood, and there was never any question of my leaving Ellen. But when you were on the way, I agonized over it—"

"Why not an abortion?" Julie interrupted.

"I am a Roman Catholic. And at that point your mother had taken instruction, although I didn't know it."

"No kidding," Julie said, again brittle.

Reynolds was offended. Or feigned it. "It would have been better if your mother had told you."

"Oh, yes." Then she forced herself onto a different tack. "I'm sorry, Morgan. I didn't mean to interrupt you."

"I did propose an arrangement. It might not have worked and it would have taken time. But your mother arrived at an arrangement of her own—marriage to an Irishman considerably younger than herself. He was one of a small army of her admirers who headquartered at the bookstore—greedy as worms and just as impecunious. I have no compunction about saying what I thought was in the marriage for him: permanent resident status in this country."

"And then an annulment?" Julie prompted.

"That did happen, I believe."

"Wasn't there a time discrepancy in there somewhere? Or was I supposed to be born prematurely?"

Reynolds seemed only then to become aware that she was angry.

"It really is distasteful to you to think I might be your father."

"Well, yes," Julie said, beyond further pretense. "I think my mother would have told me that—instead of making up the business of a 'whereabouts unknown' father."

"Your mother was a magnificent fabricator. She ought to have been a writer herself."

"Herself ?"

"Aren't you a writer?"

"Oh. I thought you meant him," Julie said, disappointed.

"He might have been. *He* might have been almost anything. Katherine thought I was jealous of him. She couldn't believe the only thing I envied him was his freedom."

"And yet ten years later you were still around to enroll me in Miss Page's School."

"It wouldn't occur to you that you might have been the reason I was still around."

Julie said nothing.

Reynolds made a gesture of vast impatience. "Since you don't want to accept my account of your origins, perhaps you'll succeed in tracking down the Irish absentee and get his version."

"I'd like to. I'd hoped today might be a beginning."

"So had I."

Julie was on her feet before he could scramble to his. She wanted to get away quickly. She laid her hand on his arm, a brief light touch. "Thank you very much, Morgan."

His quick smile turned on and held until she was gone. The dimples would stay in her mind forever.

10

...

Why in the name of God would the man claim to be her father if he wasn't? And a marriage of convenience between her mother and a young man without ties made sense of the annulment as nothing else had to date. How long did it take to get an annulment? Something Father Doyle at Saint Malachy's could answer. But before there was an annulment, there had to have been a marriage, and before that, a marriage license. She could, in her mind's eye, retrace her and Jeff's trip downtown to the Marriage License Bureau. First, the blood tests three days in advance, the physician's signature, and then the long wait in line at the Bureau for the application form. On which she had written the name Thomas Francis Mooney as her father, and his birthplace, Ireland. It now gave her the feeling of truth just to go over the scene in her mind. Very dangerous, the feeling of truth. It was a working rule of Jeff's: That's when you double-check your facts.

In the morning she took the subway downtown to Worth Street and inquired what she had to do to see her parents' marriage license. She was given a form on which to request a search and transcript of marriage. The clerk was annoyed that she had no date for the ceremony. Since Julie herself had been born in April, she said the marriage had occurred within a period eight to twelve months earlier.

She wound up having to go directly to the County Clerk's Office, and on her way she contrived a more aggressive stance: She offered her press card by way of identification, although no one asked for it, and stated as the purpose of the search her claim to an inheritance. Money, somehow, gave most things a quicker legitimacy.

"No attorney?" the assistant wanted to know.

"I thought I might pick up something for my column in the *New York Daily* if I came myself. What the City Keeps—you know, that sort of thing."

"They're state records, ma'am," the man said laconically. But he authorized the search. Before lunchtime Julie knew that her mother had married Thomas Francis Mooney a good ten months before she was born. So, she reasoned, the so-called marriage of convenience had occurred before she had been an inconvenience to any of them. It made a liar out of Morgan Reynolds. A lot of men denied paternities. He'd have done it, too, back then—in his legitimate life—no matter how chivalrous his pose today.

"I've been given to understand the marriage was annulled," Julie said to her informant. "Does that show on the record?"

"No. It would only show if the annulment dated back to the day of the ceremony."

"In other words, if they hadn't slept together," Julie said.

"That's what it comes to, yes, ma'am."

She returned to the Marriage Bureau, paid her fee, and waited for the other information to be taken from the microfilm, transcribed and certified, and passed along to the office where she waited. No question: Morgan Reynolds had lied; he had juggled the order of events to suit a purpose of his own. Again she questioned: a purpose or a whim? With genuine purpose, would he not have sought her out at her mother's death? And he could have found her, knowing that she was married to Geoffrey Hayes. A sophisticated man, Morgan Reynolds ought to know that the true dates were ascertainable if she wanted badly enough to ascertain them.

A whim, she decided, contrived in the wake of her phone call. Champagne and roses, and the romance of her mother's illicit love.

51

Oh, wow! Could he really have thought she would fall into his arms and cry, "Daddy, you've been on my mind!"

The transcript came through. She did not open it until she walked out and into City Hall Park, where, in the warm noontime sun, she found a bench to herself. She felt taut as a bowstring, her heart thumping. A party of pigeons gathered around her when she sat down. "Sorry, kids," she said, having no lunch to share with them. They waddled elsewhere, and she opened the transcript.

Katherine Anne Richards, residing at 499 East 91st Street, New York City, born July 17, 1926, in Chicago, Illinois, and Thomas Francis Mooney, residing at 584 East 54th Street, New York City, born October 10, 1934, in Wicklow, Ireland, were married on July 20, 1954, at Saint Giles's Church Rectory in New York by the Reverend Stephen Flaherty. The witnesses were Margaret Fiore and Michael Desmond. There had been no previous marriage of either bride or groom.

For a moment it seemed as though she had learned a great deal, and then it seemed very little. In the City Hall basement she found a public telephone and called Saint Giles's Rectory. The church was not far from the United Nations and not far from East Fifty-fourth Street. But to her inquiry about Father Flaherty, the soft-voiced woman said, "Father Flaherty's been in his grave for over twenty years." Julie asked if there would be a parish record of the annulment of a marriage Father Flaherty had performed. "Those records are kept in the Chancery Office," the woman said.

Julie said, "I see," and thanked her, but she felt little hope of access to the Chancery Office records.

There were a number of Fiores in the Manhattan directory, but none named Margaret. Nor was there a Michael Desmond. Margaret Fiore had to be her mother's friend, Maggie. She could not remember her very well—a plump, noisy woman. Her mother had talked a lot about her at some point, which suggested that she had either died or moved away. Julie was on her way uptown when it occurred to her that she probably knew where Maggie had moved to. She remembered a quarrel with her mother over the size of a telephone bill. She had fought back because the largest item by far on that particular phone bill was a call her mother had made to Los Angeles, and it was to her friend Maggie.

Julie got off the bus at Forty-second Street and headed for the New York Public Library. There were numerous Fiores in the Los Angeles phone books, but again, none by the name of Margaret. She could have married, of course, or remarried. Inveterate housecleaner that Julie was, she had destroyed her mother's address book long ago.

Her disappointment was heavy. Then she chided herself: She could have had a rich, successful father, Morgan Reynolds, half a column in *Who's Who*. And here she was, looking for a Heathcliff. Leaving the reference room, she passed the various indexes—the *Reader's Guide to Periodical Literature*, the *Cumulative Book Index* . . .

What prompted her to stop and search she would never know—a hunch, a prayer, a jab of hope. Beginning with the year 1950, she looked up Thomas Francis Mooney in the *Reader's Guide*. In 1955 someone of that name had published a poem in *The New Yorker* called "Where the Wild Geese Fly No More."

11

...

Julie could not hold back the tears when she read the poem. Whether or not it was good, it was Irish, and she thought it beautiful. Pride, a sunburst, warmed her through. She would brook no doubts, not of the author's relationship to her nor of the poem's merit. If it was in *The New Yorker*, it had to be good. She copied the poem—of sonnet length—into her notebook and turned in the bound magazine. While she waited near the elevators for a public telephone to become available, she began to memorize it.

She called Virginia Gibbons, whom she knew through Jeff. Ginny reviewed theater for *The New Yorker*.

"Nineteen fifty-five. Even for the magazine that's going back a long time," Ginny Gibbons said. "What do you want to know?"

"Anything and everything about Thomas Francis Mooney, who wrote the poem. He might possibly be my father."

"The title and the date it appeared?" Ginny wanted to know.

Julie told her. Then: "Want me to read it to you? It's only fourteen lines."

"Wait till I get a cigarette."

"I like it," Ginny said afterward. "I suppose you know about the Wild Geese? They were Irish mercenaries, I should think, though from what I know of the Irish, they'd have fought without being paid for it. In Napoleon's army? For the French, in any case."

"We're onto something," Julie said. "I'm sure of it."

"Let me go down the hall and talk to some of the old-timers. What else has he written?"

"I'm going to go search now," Julie said.

"I'll see if there's anything on him in our files while I'm at it," Ginny said.

Julie searched back a few years from 1955 and forward to date. She found nothing. Bleary-eyed, her enthusiasm slightly blunted, she called Virginia Gibbons back.

"Sorry, Julie. Nobody around here knows the name, and there's nothing in our files. It probably came in cold. If you want me to, I'll try bookkeeping on it, but I'm not sure where those ledgers are stored, so it may take time. I have one other suggestion. It's a long shot, but you might want to try it: In those days the Walsh and Kendall Agency represented most of the Irish writers. John Walsh's father was an Irish playwright. I didn't know him, but I knew John. We had some wonderful times trying to get his father's plays produced in this country. "If it's this hard to get Walsh produced," John would say, "what would it be like if his name was Yeats or O'Casey?"

"I don't think I've ever heard of Walsh," Julie said.

"That's the point."

"Oh." She sometimes had trouble with the *New Yorker* ellipses. "I'll try Kendall and Walsh. I'm not going to let go now that I've got this far."

"Maybe he's publishing under his name in Gaelic these days." Whether or not she was serious Julie couldn't tell. "Julie?"

"I'm still here."

"Do you know the Irish playwright Seamus McNally?"

"No."

"Well, you should. He's giving a seminar at Yale this summer. Before he goes back, I'm having a gathering at my place. I'll ask you and Jeff."

"Jeff will be in Paris," Julie said.

"Then you'll come yourself, for God's sake."

Julie went from the library to a cocktail party at the Players'

Club given by the producers of a daytime television series, "Melissa's Children," to celebrate its twenty-fifth year on the air. She picked up a couple of items for the column, enough to keep her in business, and a pretty good meal of hors d'oeuvres. She fantasized a book to be called *The Well-Dressed Beggar's Guide to Manhattan; or, How to Live on Publication Parties, Opening Nights, and Bar Mitzvahs.*

She was back at the shop writing up her column material when she picked up on a call she first debated leaving for the answering service.

"Friend Julie? This is May Weems. I sure hopes you remember me."

"I do." It was the black street girl Detective Russo called Ring-Around.

"Would you like to do me a little favor, Friend Julie? Then I does one for you like . . ."

"Like what?"

"The fuzz done busted me again, and my pimp say he won't pay no more fines. He say I don't run fast enough, but I can't run no faster."

"How much is the fine?"

"I don't know till I goes before the judge, and different judges say different. I bet they don't say more'n fifty dollars seeing it's you and knowing . . ."

Knowing, Julie thought, the key word. Knowing what May Weems might be able to contribute to the apprehension of the men who attacked Julie Hayes. "Where are you?"

"They taking me to a holding pen—like I was a pig or something, so's they can deliver me first thing tomorrow morning."

"I'll find you," Julie said. She hung up the phone and sat a moment thinking back to her last encounter with May Weems—and her pimp. He affected the bad speech of the comic Stepin Fetchit back in the days when blacks were colored people or Negroes. She wondered if May imitated him. She wasn't very bright. Only cunning and pathetic. But smart enough to have avoided saying just what she'd do for Julie to return the favor.

Detective Russo, aware of the arrest—he might even have arranged it, Julie thought—tracked May Weems to the old Fifth Precinct stationhouse in Chinatown. He put Julie in touch with the desk sergeant, and she was able to learn from him that May Weems would go before Criminal Court Judge Arbiter in the morning.

12

■ ■ ■

Misery didn't love company in that courtroom. The early arrivals
were concerned spectators, who chose to sit far apart from one
another. A few were young, but most were not. They were working
women, most of them, and most of those were black. They were
losing half a day's pay to be in court, or half their sleep if they worked
by night. They had dressed to look respectable, able to cope with the
son or daughter on whose behalf they'd come. The bailiff waited at
attention; there was activity at the lawyers' tables; the court steno-
graphers were ready. The judge was in his chambers.

Prisoners began to arrive with their arraignment officers; they
congregated at the rear of the courtroom, a scruffy mix of anger and
bravura, looking only sidewise to see if there was anyone in court
for them. Their lawyers, mostly court assigned, drifted in through a
side door chatting with one another, ignoring the clients with whom
they would in their own good time make contact.

"Friend Julie!" The woman waved.

Julie waved back. She hadn't recognized her on arrival. May
Weems presently pointed her out to a sallow young man Julie was
sure would smell of mothballs. After a few words with his client he
came to Julie, introduced himself, and offered a limp hand. He reeked
of shaving lotion. Mothballs would have been better. He sat down
beside her and asked how high she could go if he could get his client
off with a fine and suspended sentence.

"Fifty bucks," Julie said.

He groaned and shook his head as though that wasn't going to do it. Then: "Is she telling the truth about being a witness in a rape case?"

"Yes."

"Okay. I'll try, Friend Julie," he drawled.

Julie glowered at him for the familiarity. Rape, the great equalizer.

Sniveling kids and arrogant punks went with state-paid lawyers before the bench of Judge Arbiter, every one of them a mother's son. Not a father in sight. One of the few professions Julie had not at one time or another made a run for was the law. She had no regrets that morning.

May Weems was called and charged with 240-37, loitering for purposes of prostitution. Her attorney asked if he might approach the bench. The black girl waited, her only curiosity a glance Julie's way to be sure she was still there. May wore tight orange pants and yellow boots. Her black T-shirt hung limp as though she had shrunk within it. No one seemed to have dressed up for court. Tatters and naked parts that showed their scars. A lot of scars. But if she were a judge, Julie thought, she would demand clean clothes as part of the court's decorum. She heard mention of her name, and then May's lawyer beckoned her to come to the bench.

"Hi, Friend Julie." May Weems wore heavy makeup, but the eyes framed in mascara were as dead as buttons.

The judge frowned at the black girl and turned to Julie. "I understand you've tried to help this woman before." Julie was surprised that May would have mentioned it.

"If you can find a way to get her off the streets, you'll be doing society a service. And you might save her life. I'm fining the defendant twenty-five dollars ... if that's satisfactory to her. ..." He glanced at May's lawyer, making the mandated query, and with hardly a pause added: "Case dismissed."

May Weems could have found her way to the court clerk's office blindfolded. Julie got a receipt for her twenty-five dollars.

"He'd've wanted more if I was to pay," May said as they waited outside the Criminal Court building, Julie trying to flag a cab. "When you ain't got no money, that's when it costs you."

"How about the favor you're going to do for me?" Julie asked.

"I intends to. The police say this old street person, did I know them? Did I know where they goes? I ain't going to say till I finds out why. And then I only say I try and find out. . . . Julie, honey, I sure glad them wasn't black men what attacked you."

A cab pulled up and discharged a passenger. Julie pushed May Weems in ahead of her. "Tell the driver where we're going."

"Make him go up the West Side and let us out when I say when."

Julie directed the cabdriver. Then to May: "This old street person—man or woman?"

"I swear she half and half. She not right in the head either. But I knowed she must be who the fuzz was talking about. Missy Glass. She say she try to get me in where she stay sometime, but they say, 'No, thank you. We don't take no 'hoes.' "

Julie was moved to touch the girl's hand. May drew it away, reminding Julie of her own problem these days with touching. She said, "You're all right, May. You've still got pride in people, so why don't you have some in yourself?"

"I ain't people. I's a whore."

Julie said nothing more. She knew as well as Judge Arbiter how very nearly hopeless it was to preach a straight gospel to May Weems.

They were approaching Twentieth Street on Eighth Avenue when May said they could walk from there. While Julie was paying the cab fare, she saw, out of the corner of her eye, May pull down the shirt to display a naked shoulder. A reflex of the profession, for by the time Julie emerged from the cab, both shoulders were again covered. They walked along a street that if not as full of grace as it had been in the nineteenth century, wore an air of respectability. Fleetingly, Julie thought of what it might be like to restore a brownstone and furnish an apartment in it for herself.

"This here," May said.

They approached a church within sight of the abandoned elevated tracks. May explained that they were going to a refuge provided by the Saint Vincent de Paul Sisters of Charity. At a side entrance to the church basement she rang the bell and gave Julie instructions: "You be the one and ask for Missy Glass."

"How do you know she's here?"

May pulled up by a couple of inches her hammered-down look. "Sometimes I takes her home when she don't know the way."

A chubby red-cheeked nun in a blue uniform and wearing a large crucifix on her breast opened the door to them. Julie asked to see Miss Glass.

"Missy's in the back room working," the nun said and led the way. She asked Julie if she worked for the city.

"No. It's a personal matter. Missy Glass may have witnessed something that happened to me."

"Something bad," May added enthusiastically.

They walked through a curtained dormitory, a dozen cots made up uniformly, and came to a recreation room—a television set and faded garden furniture, a table with a coffee urn and magazines. Only one person was present, a gaunt, stooped creature who could indeed have been taken for man or woman. She wore men's slacks and shoes, and she was sorting what Julie presently saw to be pieces of broken glass on an old pool table.

"Visitors, Missy Glass," the nun called out with a good-news air.

The woman straightened up as far as she could, to some three-quarters of what was once her normal height. Her hair was gray and brown shag. Her smile was shy, her teeth bad, her eyes furtive.

The nun approached the table and said of a laid-out assortment of glass fragments, "Aren't these pretty?" She explained to Julie that a woman who made jewelry gave a day a week to the mission. "Missy is very good." As though praising a child.

And Missy seemed hardly able to bear the praise, turning her head away, the color rising to her slack and wrinkled cheeks. The smell of the woman reminded Julie of mushrooms.

When the nun left them, May Weems said, "This here the lady

you seen getting in the trailer. Remember, Missy Glass?"

Julie stiffened. "Please, May, don't tell her what she saw. Let her tell us. . . . Would you please, Miss Glass . . . Missy? Do you remember? It was a Sunday morning. Very quiet. Did you hear anything unusual before you saw me?"

May burst in again. "She don't hear good, but she hear something."

"Can't you be quiet, May?"

The woman looked surprised or alarmed by their exchange.

"I just trying to help. Them men don't mean her no good either, Friend Julie, but she don't know that. I's the one makes her stay here and do her glass."

Julie said, "May, do *you* know the men?"

"Seem like I ought to. I knows a lot of johns that part of town."

Missy Glass was looking at Julie surreptitiously. The large, strange eyes, which made her expression seem one of continual surprise, fled when Julie tried to hold them with her own gaze.

"Tell her how they whistle at you, Missy. Like you was a dog." May said.

The woman puckered her lips and gave a short, rather sweet repetitive whistle.

"Where were they when they whistled at you?" Julie asked.

"In the doorway." Her voice was low, barely audible.

"Before that," May coached, "they was in the car and stopped."

The woman turned to her and said, as though unsure, "Were those the same men?"

"You say to me it the same whistle."

"They wanted to know what I was looking for. Pieces of glass, I told them, pieces of pretty colored glass."

"Had you been to that same place before?" Julie asked.

"It was one of my best places."

"They say to her they got lots of nice glass they wants to show her. Right, Missy?"

So, Julie reasoned, if they were neighborhood youths, they would have seen her before and they would have scouted the trailers for one that suited their purpose.

"Lots of lovely glass." The woman articulated the words carefully. She had good speech, but there was a vagueness to the inflection, as though the words had taken shape in her mind well before she was able to voice them.

The intimate memory of that scene inside the trailer came back to Julie with shocking immediacy. Anger followed, outrage at the degradation, the inhumanity intended in the assault upon this unfortunate creature. It was an anger she had not been able to summon on her own behalf.

May Weems kept trying to prime Missy Glass. Julie said, "Please, May, let's both be quiet and let Missy tell us in her own way everything that happened that Sunday."

"But nothing happened," the woman said.

And May Weems said, "See. Tell her about the baby, Missy."

But Missy, it seemed, was still one step behind. "I explained to them that unless I could collect the glass myself, it wasn't right for me. It has to weather and refine." She took up a piece and nested it in the palm of her hand to show Julie: a deep, clear blue. The arthritic fingers were curled like question marks.

"The baby," May nudged again.

"I could hear it crying in the trailer and one of the men came out to me and asked if I knew how to take care of a baby. Babies don't like me. I said it would cry even more if it saw me, and it did keep on crying. So I moved further away—where there was hardly any glass at all."

Enter Julie Hayes, Julie thought, who knows everything about babies. "What did the men look like, Missy? Say the one who came and spoke to you about the baby." They couldn't have been wearing masks then, certainly not while one of them was driving a car.

"I didn't look. I always turn away when people I don't know speak to me."

"But what could you see without looking?" Julie persisted. "You know, like out of the corner of your eye."

"He limped as though he was lame. And his red hair hung down over one cheek."

"Red?"

"Yes . . ."

"And his eyes—what color were they?"

She shook her head. She simply had not looked until he had turned away.

"How old would you say?"

Again she shook her head, and Julie thought she would learn more questioning May Weems about what Missy had told her. But first: "Where were you, Missy, when they stopped the car and spoke to you?"

"I was working my way from the street. I had my back to them."

"When they whistled?"

She nodded.

"Did they speak from the car?"

"One of them called to me, 'Whatcha doing, honey?' I didn't answer."

"Did you see what kind of car they were driving?"

"A small car—like an egg."

A Volkswagen, Julie would say. "What color was it?"

"It wasn't any color."

"Did you see them enter the trailer?"

"They couldn't get the door open at first. That's when one of them came and asked me what I was looking for. When he went back, the door was open."

"Did you see the baby?"

Missy Glass just stared, that surprised look on her face. Then she said. "The baby stopped crying when the woman came and they helped her into the trailer."

"Yeah," Julie said and let it pass. "Did you see anybody leave the trailer, Missy?"

She shook her head. "I went away then. I thought they might be watching me. I had some very good glass I didn't want stolen from me."

Julie turned to May Weems. "When did you two get together to talk all this over?"

"When the police asks me if I knowed a street person like her. I don't know from nobody till Detective Russo says it's you they do that to. I don't owe him nothing, but I say to myself Missy got to stay with the sisters if she going to help Friend Julie. She don't always come home at night."

"I don't like walls," the woman said.

"I still say she better keep staying here in case they looking for her. They in big trouble when they mess up Friend Julie. She going to find them."

13

...

Was she? She cared more about their being found than she had before, certainly. But what did she know about them now that she hadn't known before? That the shorter one had red, longish hair, a thatch of which fell all the way down to his cheek. And she knew they were bullies as well as beasts: They had baited their trap for a woman who was aging, frail, and not right in the head.

At her desk, to cleanse her mind, she looked up at the poem "Where the Wild Geese Fly No More" and recited it aloud. She concentrated on each phrase as though the poem were a mantra. Before going about the work by which she was earning her living, she looked up the literary agency of Walsh and Kendall, as Ginny Gibbons had suggested. It was now called Kendall Associates, John Walsh having retired. At least he wasn't dead. The bookkeeping department gave her an address and phone number. She phoned, and John Walsh agreed to see her the next day.

She made her business calls—one to a Sardi's Restaurant observer who was great on who was holding hands with whom, another to an apprentice printer whose boss turned out the postdated press releases for a lot of celebrities. From another source she picked up an item about the entrepreneur who collected, processed, and merchandised as plant fertilizer the droppings of zoo animals.

She reached the precinct station house in time to see Detective Russo before he went off duty.

"I knew she'd turn up the witness," he said of May Weems in a self-congratulatory tone.

"I don't know whether the police can get more out of her than I did or not." She recounted her meeting with Missy Glass.

He picked up on the red hair immediately. "And the other one is taller and dark-complexioned by your description. That's vital information, Julie. If they chum together in the neighborhood, we ought to be able to bring them in."

"Why do you keep thinking they're in the neighborhood? They had a car."

"Could the witness describe the car? I suppose it's too much to hope for a license number."

"A lot too much. A small car that looked like an egg. I'd say a Volkswagen. But no color. Whatever that means."

"That's going to be the trouble. She's not what you'd call a reliable witness."

"There isn't one good witness between us," Julie said.

"That isn't so. You'll be a better witness than you realize once you make up your mind you want to do it. How about it?"

Julie escaped by looking around the dreary, ill-lit room. It was the old interrogation room, and they sat at one end of a long table, where someone had written "Fuck the Commissioner" in the dust. Not much happened in the precinct house since the booking of suspects had become a central operation located downtown at Number One Police Plaza. There were great empty spaces in the building. They exposed the dirty floors and walls, the dangling ceiling plaster. As though cops didn't have a depressing enough job without working out of an 1890s ruin. "Yes!" she said with emphasis. "I want to do it."

"Good girl." Russo got to his feet. "Wait till I sign out and I'll buy you a beer at McGowen's."

She doubted that McGowen's was his regular bar. It was the hangout mostly of the Irish-Americans. Julie sometimes went there with Mary Ryan. "You didn't tell me why you think they might be local men," Julie said.

"A hunch, them being around there on a Sunday morning.

They're not on the work-site payroll, as far as we know. We'll try again. If they are on the project, there can't be too many redheads besides him. How about the beer?"

"Thank you," Julie said.

Billy McGowen himself was behind the bar. He almost always was. He recognized Julie and gave the detective a nod of tentative recognition. There wasn't much warmth in the keen blue eyes.

"Shall I introduce you?" Julie said. McGowen was mid-bar, drawing the beer. Several regulars were at the other end, watching the television above Julie's and Russo's heads.

"He'll soon get to know me," Russo said.

And sure enough, returning, McGowen said, "Here you are, Detective." He stood for a moment, his hands spread on the bar, as though waiting for what would come next.

Julie said, "I thought maybe Mrs. Ryan would be here."

McGowen straightened up and took a cloth to where the sweating glasses had ringed the bar. "She hasn't been in since she lost that unfortunate mutt of hers."

There was talk then about the advantages and disadvantages of getting another dog when you were Mrs. Ryan's age. "The thing is, you don't get a puppy," the detective said.

McGowen said, "You want to know what size it'll be when it grows up."

"And you want it trained."

"That's the main thing," McGowen said. "You'll never train a dog if you can't be quick with it. And she's an old lady."

Russo laid a five-dollar bill on the bar. McGowen motioned it away, but the detective let it lie there. When the barman left them to check his other customers, Russo indicated the picture centered over the back-bar mirror and asked Julie, "Who's that?"

By now she knew well, having asked the question herself sometime before. "Bobby Sands. He was an IRA hunger striker who died in prison."

Russo sighed heavily. Julie didn't want any more of her beer, but she didn't say so. McGowen came back to pick up the conversation where they'd left off. "I'd take up a collection and buy her a real pedigreed frankfurter if I thought it was the right thing to do."

"Mutts are better dogs," Russo said. "McGowen, have you seen a couple of young guys around here lately that might be looking for trouble? One is medium tall and dark—not a black man—and he's got a lot of hair on him. The other's a redhead, shorter, and rolls like a sailor when he walks."

Julie felt uncomfortable. She watched the barkeeper's eyes turn stone cold.

"Nope, can't say I have."

A few stools down a customer looked their way. His eyes and Julie's locked just for an instant. He looked up at the television and kept watching it while he groped an inside pocket for a cigarette. Something had clicked with him, Julie thought. Something.

McGowen picked up the five-dollar bill, went to the cash register, and rang up a dollar fifty. He returned with the change and said a curt "Thank you." The message was pretty clear.

On the street, Russo proposed to walk Julie to Forty-fourth Street. "What do you think?" he asked.

"They don't like informers."

"But did he recognize the description?"

"I think so. Somebody in there did."

"I noticed. You're very popular in the neighborhood, Julie. Somebody's going to turn them in."

"Maybe."

"The question is can we hold them when it happens."

14

...

John Walsh lived in an apartment hotel on lower Fifth Avenue and explained of the chaos of papers into which he conducted Julie that since his retirement he had been working on his memoirs. He swept a pile of letters to the floor so that she might have a chair.

"Now you should know why I did that," he said, "so that you won't think I'm a madman. There is something in one of those letters I simply cannot find. I know it's there, mind you, and this will give me a fresh approach. All the same, there's advice I'd give to anyone writing his memoirs. Like Macbeth on murder: If 'twere done, 'twere best done quickly. Sit down and don't look so worried. They can't find anything in the office these days either—Kendall has too many associates."

He removed a tiger cat from an Eames chair, swung the chair around to face her, and seated himself. The cat leapt up on his lap. A slight man with a tint of gold in his eyes and in his gray hair, he was someone Julie could fall in love with, so to speak, on the instant: amiable and soft-spoken . . . nonaggressive. "So, it's a poet you're interested in, and Ginny Gibbons told you to come and see me. . . ."

It hadn't gone quite that way, but Julie let his version stand.

"It's more than she's done herself lately, you might remind her." He drew from his pocket an envelope on which he had written the information Julie had given him on the phone. "Nineteen fifty-five—it's not so long ago." He looked at her quizzically. "To me. Were you born then?"

"Oh, yes."

He put on his glasses and looked again at his notes. "Someone possibly your father. I'm not about to get your hopes up falsely, young lady, but I feel I've come on the name Mooney recently, and I can only suppose it would be in this conglomeration of hopes and miseries." He tossed a hand to encompass the roomful of papers. "I don't suppose you have a copy of the poem with you?"

"No, but I could recite it," Julie said. "Or I could write it out for you. It wouldn't take long."

He smiled. "I'd much prefer that you recite it to me." He leaned back, closed his eyes, and with one finger scratched the cat's head.

Julie was on the last stanza when he began to nod in recognition. She closed her own eyes in order not to falter with the new feeling of excitement.

"Historically inaccurate, but emotionally sound—if one can be emotionally sound." He sat up and sent the cat off on its own. "I'd have thought it was written by a Michael Desmond."

"His best friend," Julie cried. "Or at least the best man when he married my mother."

"And your mother's name?"

"Katherine Richards."

"Ah, well, now I have it. I came on the name in a letter from Michael Desmond. It was a letter of introduction of his friend, Mooney. Was he a merchant seaman?"

"I was always told he was a diplomat."

"Well, I could be wrong," John Walsh said.

"So could I."

"Now, you see, what's wrong with the poem you just said for me: He's talking about Irishmen in exile, a long way from home. But the far place he's talking about is Van Diemen's Land in Australia. And while many an Irishman was exiled to Van Diemen's in the nineteenth century, they were not Wild Geese. The Wild Geese emigrated on their own to Europe after the penal laws in the seventeen-nineties. Never mind, it's a fine piece of imagery, and poets don't necessarily make good historians. But at least they get the spirit right, wouldn't you say?"

Julie nodded.

"Well, you don't need a lecture on truth in poetry, do you? And I should tell you I did not know a Wild Goose from a clay pigeon myself when I sent the poem on. Nor did anyone at the magazine, for they went ahead and printed it."

"Ginny thinks they were soldiers in Napoleon's army."

"And some might have been. . . . But let me start with Michael Desmond and try to work my way into this logjam of a memory of mine. Michael was a press representative with the Irish observers at the United Nations before the Republic was admitted, and I think he was with the Mission for a time afterward. In any case, he was an Irish newspaperman and very keen on theater. My father, who was a playwright, sent him to me. He may well be alive still. He was younger than me, but I've not heard from him in years. He did send me some cherished clients, and among them was your father." He rested and must have enjoyed what he saw on Julie's face. "I assume you are by now convinced we are speaking of your father?"

"Oh, yes."

"I wish I could tell you I met the man. I never did. But first he sent me a letter about this biography he proposed to write. Of John Mitchel. There—how's that for a break in the logjam? Whether he ever wrote the book, I have no idea."

"If he did, it wasn't published in this country." Julie said.

"You went that route, did you? Good for you. I hadn't thought there was much of a market for it here, and I suppose I told him so, for he sent me the poem next and he suggested I read a journal John Mitchel had written in jail. It's odd how it all comes back once you get a lead into it.

"I never read the journal, but I did look up John Mitchel . . . or talked to someone. At some point in his career this Young Irelander—that's what his group was called; the IRA of their day— became editor of a Richmond, Virginia, newspaper. He was a rabid pro-slavery man. The nineteen-fifties did not seem an auspicious time to look for an American publisher for his story. But about the poem and my asking you your mother's name: If I got it published, I was to send the money to her. And I did. And there's an end, I think, to my brief association with Thomas Francis Mooney. Would he have settled out there among the koalas and the kangaroos?"

Julie smiled a little.

"What I can do for you is look up the latest address I have for Michael Desmond and maybe you can get onto him. If he's alive, that is. The trouble with my address book—it's getting to look like an obituary column."

At the shop she wrote a letter to one Michael Desmond at his last known address on Kevin Street, Dublin. Then she called Father Doyle at Saint Malachy's and asked if she could see him.

"Anytime, Julie. Anytime."

He held her hand all the way from the rectory door to the office, no great distance, but far enough for two brief, reassuring squeezes. He looked perfectly in place taking the chair behind the desk under the picture of Pope John XXIII. Julie had the more recent two at her back. She told the priest about her belated start on a search for her father and Mrs. Ryan's suggestion that she talk to him.

"So she's at it again, is she?" the priest said. "God forgive her, I sometimes think she invents miracles on my behalf in order to involve herself in other people's lives."

"You're right," Julie said. "Nevertheless."

"Nevertheless, the belief in miracles runs deep. . . . Where do we start?"

"I'd like to know why the marriage was annulled. They were married at Saint Giles's Church by a priest, although my mother was a Protestant. I think the proceedings toward an annulment must have started sometime before I was born. I was baptized a Protestant and given my mother's maiden name. No mention of my father at all on the baptism certificate."

"Was it a marriage of necessity?"

73

"No, Father Doyle. I've done the arithmetic of it. And all my mother ever told me was that he had the marriage annulled and was gone before I was born. She made up lots of stories about him for me, but that was always the beginning."

"I've never heard of the church making it that simple. If it was a marriage at all. Have you talked with anyone at Saint Giles's?"

"I talked with the housekeeper on the phone."

"Ah, now, that's like talking with Mary Ryan."

Julie laughed. "But the priest who married them has since died, Father Doyle."

"Even so. Your mother would have had to take a certain amount of instruction. . . ."

"She did!" Julie remembered that information from Morgan Reynolds.

"The priest who married them might or might not have been the one to give her instruction, but at very least, that instructor would have been called as a witness before the diocese marriage tribunal."

"What are the chances of my seeing those records?" she asked.

"About equal to seeing a Kremlin confidential."

"I figured that," Julie said. "Could you tell me the grounds for annulment?"

The priest drew a deep breath. "Assuming the marriage was valid in the first place—and obviously it was—you'd have to look for deception or fraud—one party's not being free to marry or not being baptized—and that coming out only afterward. Then there are a lot of nasty possibilities: alcoholism, homosexuality, sexual perversion. You don't have to put yourself through this sort of quiz, do you, Julie? There are reasons and ramifications that wouldn't turn up in mere words even if you got to see them for yourself."

"You're right," she said.

"And as for your father having had the marriage annulled, that's not the way it happens. Just as it takes two to make a marriage, it takes two to dissolve it. In other words, your mother was a party to the petition."

"Oh, boy," Julie said. "That's something she didn't tell me."

"Tell me all you know of the man and we'll see if I have any contribution to make at all."

So Julie summarized what she had learned of Thomas Francis Mooney.

"Do you know where he was born in Ireland?" the priest asked.

"Wicklow."

"If I were you, I'd start there. He might have gone home, you know."

15

...

Days went by, the bright, quiet days of September, when all the youngsters had new clothes and somewhere to go in them—back to school. Rose Rodriguez, Julie's upstairs neighbor, came by to ask for a donation, something she could sell in the parish booth on the day of the church bazaar. No problem: Julie still had a supply of gift items. Rose's husband had been promoted to an inspector for the Metropolitan Transit Authority, and even though his relatives had moved to a place of their own, giving Rose back the privacy she'd lost when they emigrated from Puerto Rico, Julie was pretty sure she had given up turning tricks while he was away at work. Juanita, their only child, was suddenly waist high to Julie and missing any number of front teeth.

The police, so far as she knew, had made no further progress. Neither Russo nor the rape specialists had come around in over a week. It would seem the case had gone on the back burner, despite Detective Russo's efforts. The crime-scene seal would have been removed from the trailer by now; the child whose doll was stolen would have taken another favorite; some old woman would have gotten herself another pair of heavy stockings. And though Julie felt no physical pain, the scars from the stab wounds were still visible and probably would be for the rest of her life. Whether it was to the purpose of letting go herself or of digging in, Julie was not able to say, for she swung to either extreme from one day to the next, but on a Sunday morning, mid-September, she put on sneakers, slacks, and raincoat and returned to the building site on Twelfth Avenue.

It was hard to tell if the construction site itself had changed, the ground level still boarded up. The heavy machinery had been moved. The trailers were still there. She walked past them, going on for another block on the service road, observing for the first time that across the highway at the river's edge was the police pound where cars illegally parked in mid-Manhattan were hauled and garaged until redeemed. A high wire fence separated the pound from the southbound traffic. There wasn't much going on there on a Sunday morning, most parking regulations suspended. A few cars were parked outdoors, but she saw no one. Could her assailants have parked their car there? With or without permission? Did they possibly work there? Were they cops? Was that idea too far out? Yes: A waddling duck of a cop did not make sense. She turned back and imagined them as they drove alongside Missy Glass and left the car. It seemed impossible that no one had seen and reported that encounter when the crime became known—a lone woman scavenging in an area almost a block square. They must have counted on its being that way, and so it came back again: They had to have been familiar with the territory.

Julie had not wanted ever again to meet the security officer who had found her, but time was an ameliorator. She walked back to the site and found a place where she could peer through the boards. Electric lights were visible among the scaffolding. She cupped her hands to her mouth and called out, "Is anybody in there?"

No one answered, and she walked halfway around the site until she found the work entrance. The cranes, cement mixers, and tractors were all there, twentieth-century dinosaurs. She followed a precarious walkway through the scaffolding. The place smelled of mud and wet cement. Then she caught a whiff of tobacco smoke. She stood where she was and looked around, up to the highest level and down as far as her eye could reach, then up again, and spotted a man watching her from the second-tier ramp.

He took the pipe from his mouth. "What in hell do you think you're doing in here, lady?

"Looking for you," Julie called back. "If you're the security guard."

He came down the ramp, bracing his descent with his hand on the guardrail. She was sure he was the man who had unbound her and covered her nakedness. She remembered the way he kept saying, "Oh, my God, oh, my God." She took him to be in his fifties, his hair gray beneath the cap. He paused a few feet away, shielded his eyes the better to see her, and then came on. "You know you're trespassing, madam. It's against the law and it's not safe. Now turn around and go back out the way you came in and we won't have any trouble."

"Don't you recognize me?" Julie said, trying to get him to meet her eyes.

The guard sniffed a couple of times instead of speaking. He let his hand fall idle, a kind of surrender, and looked at her directly. "I'm sorry for what happened to you," he said then. Terse, reluctant. "You shouldn't have been where you were that day either. I'm not allowed to talk to you, missus. Not to anyone except the police. So there's no use you being here, is there?"

"Why can't we talk? I'm not going to sue you, if that's what you're afraid of."

Another sniff, but he was softening, she felt. "They're afraid I'm going to sue the building contractor or the city, is that it?"

"It could be they feel that way, yes, ma'am."

"It never entered my mind. But what I can't understand—why hasn't anybody come forward who saw those men? Why can't the police find them? I can't believe that nobody saw them except me and a half-crazy old woman."

"It seems strange, don't it?"

"It couldn't have been their first time here," Julie said. "They'd seen that old woman before. She was the one they wanted—until I came along."

"Bastards," he murmured.

"A poor helpless old thing," Julie said. "Only she was smart enough to elude them. Or dumb enough. Not like me—dashing in to save a child, I thought. I don't suppose you heard what sounded like a baby crying?"

"No, ma'am, I didn't."

"Was it accidental that you came to the trailer and found me —or was it part of your rounds?"

"I don't ordinarily go that way. Strictly speaking, I'm only responsible for the structure site itself. But from where I was I could see the door to the trailer hanging open. Those south doors to the trailers don't get opened once they're set on location."

"I wonder what I'd have done if you hadn't found me," Julie said.

"I'm not sorry I looked and found you, understand. But if I hadn't been off-site, like I wasn't supposed to, I'd never have noticed at all."

"So you got in trouble, too."

He nodded, a twitch of a smile at the corners of his mouth. Then, at a sound rather like a door slamming except that there were no doors, he tensed and moved warily toward the well of the construction. The sound came again, only more remote, and he returned to Julie's side. "The wind," he said. "It's always playing tricks on me."

"Maybe we could talk somewhere later," she said, and, with a solicitude she hoped did not sound false, "I don't want to get you into more trouble now."

"I think we'd be all right in the place we call the office. I'll eat my lunch so's to make it legit. My name's Sam Togarth, by the way."

"Julie Hayes."

"I know. Matter of fact, I wanted to come and see you in the hospital, Mrs. Hayes."

"I didn't want to see anybody."

"That's what my wife said, and they wouldn't let me in anyway."

The office was where Julie, peering through a crack in the siding, had seen the lights. It consisted of nothing more than a large table to lay out plans on and a couple of folding chairs. Like those in the trailer. The wind whipped in around the boards; it smelled of the river and nipped at her ankles as well as her nose. Togarth poured two cups of coffee from his thermos, and she was grateful to share it.

"Seems like the police got a lead on one of them," the watchman said, not knowing that she'd had a hand in turning up the information. "He's got red hair and some kind of limp. I never seen him to my memory. Redheads don't come a dime a dozen. I just don't think they're on this project. The guys wouldn't cover for them, not if they done something like that."

"Could they have known where you were, Mr. Togarth? They must have known there was a guard somewhere around."

"That's a touchy question, and I'll tell you why: I was over in the Traffic Police barn. And if they knew that, if they seen me there . . . you understand?"

"I get it," Julie said.

"Weekends there ain't much doing on the streets, so sometimes there's a running poker game. The guys drift in and out. Somebody could've known I was sitting in on the game, but there was no way for them to know when I was going to pull out of it."

"They had a car. Could they have left it there?"

"I don't think so. I think they come up on the service road, turned in between the construction and the trailers, and parked up a ways. Nobody would've noticed."

Including Julie Hayes. She had come that way.

"I got a theory, but I don't think the police put much stock in it when I told them," the security man went on. "I think they might've started uptown from around Twentieth Street on the docks down there where the fags hang out. Some of these macho guys get charged up just baiting them, and then they go looking for whatever they can find. My brother-in-law works at the Maritime Union headquarters on Seventeenth Street and he says you wouldn't believe some of the things."

"That's wild," Julie said.

"I guess it is," Togarth said with a sigh.

"Hey, suppose one of them was a seaman, say the redhead with that wobbly walk of his—if he'd shipped out right afterward, nobody was going to find him, right? Does your brother-in-law work at the hiring hall, Mr. Togarth?"

"Pension and Welfare. But he's been around so long he must know someone having to do with hiring."

It was such a long shot Julie decided not to confide her inquiries to anyone unless they yielded stronger results than she could cope with. The identification of the men, even if she got them within her sights and felt reasonably sure they were the right ones, was going to be a tricky business. At ten-thirty Monday morning she walked into the mammoth National Maritime Union building, and a few minutes later Sam Togarth's brother-in-law, Maurice Lynch, took her downstairs and introduced her to Andrew Carey in the Marine Inspector's Office.

The two men had already spoken, she realized, for as soon as Togarth's relative left them, Carey said, "So you're looking for a redheaded Irishman?"

"I don't know that he's Irish," Julie said, startled.

Carey, whom some might have called red-haired himself, a broad, hearty man, sandy-complexioned and dappled with freckles, said, "I'd give odds on it. Will you go to the police with any information I give you?"

"Of course."

"No personal vendetta or anything like that?"

Julie just looked at the man.

"Well, I know you're a newspaperwoman. You could be losing patience with the police and going out to scoop them."

"Exploiting my own humiliation," Julie said tightly.

"I guess not," he said. "All right. I remembered the case when Lynch called me. I didn't know about his brother-in-law: It's the curse of a family, a gambler. I don't know which is worse, that or the booze. Drugs is worse. Anyways, the reason I made the point about going to the police is this: I've got a fellow in mind who answers the description. He got his union card only last year, having landed a job with the help of his parish priest."

"Oh, God," Julie said.

"Well, it may not be him at all, but I remember him because of the priest. The padre's done a lot of good work on the waterfront, and for his sake I hope we're on the wrong track. But you'll want the police to check this man out. He shipped out an oil tanker, *The Candy Kid*, June nineteenth from Hoboken. Bound for Bermuda."

"The date is right," Julie said.

"She's due back in her berth the day after tomorrow."

"With him aboard?"

"Unless he's jumped ship."

Julie got a message through to Detective Russo and went to see him as soon as he was available. He taped her story, nodding now and then while he listened. When he turned off the machine, he sat a moment looking at her, those big dark eyes warm with pleasure or amusement—something cheerful. "It just goes to prove there's more than one way to skin a cat," he said finally. "His name is Frank Kincaid and he lives a few blocks from here on Tenth Avenue."

"Oh," Julie said, feeling foolish. Then: "What about his partner?"

"We know where he is. Don't misunderstand, your information is every bit as good as ours. We went a different route, that's all."

"An informant?" Julie said. "A guy who was in McGowen's that day you and I were there?"

Russo gave no sign that she was right or wrong. "We'll have a tail on the sailor when he lands."

"If he hasn't jumped ship."

"He's aboard," Russo said.

"Just so I won't feel schizoid," she said, "have you talked with Andrew Carey in the Marine Inspector's Office? I mean, he wanted to be sure I'd go to the police with anything he told me."

"I will now that you've made the connection for me."

He might be putting her on, Julie thought, but she didn't care.

Another concern entirely had taken hold: Now she was wildly anxious at the prospect of confronting the men who had assaulted her.

She returned to the shop and picked up her messages from the answering service. Among them was a call from Ginny Gibbons: Her party for the Irish playwright, Seamus McNally, was the next night, nine o'clock, very informal.

16

■ ■ ■

One of the last places she wanted to go that night was to a party at
Ginny Gibbons's. But the very last place she wanted to be was home,
counting hours, waiting word of *The Candy Kid* coming in to port.
How familiar the sounds of the party were when she stepped out of
the elevator—the voices, the tinkle of glasses, the sense more than
the sound of music—and how familiar the feeling of dread, for this
was Jeff's territory, where she had always traveled lightly in his wake.
She hung her coat on the rack outside the apartment door and asked
herself again why she had come. To meet an Irishman who, by some
unlikely, remote chance, might offer another lead to "Father." It sure
as hell would be nice to have one now. She pressed the buzzer.

Ginny opened the door, a glass in hand, a cigarette in her mouth.
She removed the cigarette and turned her cheek up to Julie to be
kissed. People glanced her way and kept on talking. "So many men,"
Julie murmured. It was always so at Ginny's.

"And none of them mine," Ginny said, bearing her across the
room. Virginia Gibbons was slight and very little over five feet tall.
She was something of a giant nonetheless. She wrote simply and to
the issue, and, unless provoked to the point of insult, exercised a less
lethal bite than most New York theater critics. She scattered the
guests from around Seamus McNally and introduced Julie to him.
"She's a col-ymnist, as you call them, on the *New York Daily*, and her

84

husband is Geoffrey Hayes. Most of us read him for elevation."

McNally, a large, tousled, youthful-looking man, lunged out of the chair. He slopped beer on himself and had to set the glass down to wipe his hand on his jacket before he offered it to Julie. The hand, still wet, was hard and strong. "Your chairs are too bloody close to the ground," he said to Ginny, and then to Julie, giving her hand an extra squeeze before he released it, "I've heard a bit about you. I've even had a peek at your column." While there was no praise in what he said, there was a kind of special attention paid in the way he said it. "I'll admit I've not read your husband," he added. "I'm a little too thick to understand him."

"Don't you believe it," Ginny cautioned Julie and went off among her other guests.

"I can't read him either," Julie said.

"Ah, but you try." He spoke with a lilt that almost made it a question. "Can I get you one of these?" He indicated the dark beer. "Or would you like something more transparent?"

"Later," she said, and motioned to the guests from whom Ginny had parted him; they were on their feet, waiting for him to rejoin them. "Please, I've interrupted."

He ignored her offer to release him. "Will your husband be coming round after?"

"He's in Paris," Julie said.

"Then you must trust him."

"Utterly."

He took on a look of mock solemnity. "I'll want to think over the meaning of that. Utterly. I didn't know Americans used such words. Does it mean what it says—or more than it says?"

Julie grinned and let that be her answer.

"Mind, I'm not making a pass. I'm only exploring the ground in case I might want to later." He introduced her to the guests awaiting his return, but at the same time propelled her through and beyond them to a quieter place. "When I asked Ginny who, under the age of fifty, she was jamming me in with tonight, you were her first offering."

"What did she say about me?"

"I'd have to make it up if I told you. I wasn't paying attention until you walked into the room. Then I wished I had done."

"I know you're a playwright and Irish," Julie said. "I intended to learn something more about you before tonight, but I didn't get to do it."

"As my mother used to say of good intentions, they're fine till the pigs run through them. I'm a bucolic playwright, so be kind to me. There are not many of us left."

"All right," Julie said.

He asked himself the question for her, mockingly: "And what have you written, Mr. McNally, that I might have seen on Broadway? Well, now, there was a play you might have seen open—or you might have seen close, for it happened on one and the same night. It was called *The Comeallye*."

Julie repeated the word. "Is it a dance?"

"You might call it that. You might call it any bloody thing you want, for the word's neither Gaelic nor English, it's hillbilly Irish and means whatever you want it to mean in the way of gathering in the folk. She had another description for the dance, did my mother—a come-to-me, go-from-me."

"Very suitable for disco," Julie said.

He thought about it and, having the picture, approved. There was a little separation between his front teeth that added to the boyish appearance. Julie found it very appealing. "You belong to the disco set, I suppose?"

Julie's no was lost in the braying of the buzzer and the imminent entrance of friends boisterous with joy at seeing Seamus McNally: They swarmed across the room and battered him with hugs and thumps. Julie eased herself away and out onto the balcony, which overlooked Central Park. She had observed but one woman among the new arrivals, someone closer to Ginny's age than her own and whom she recognized from the magazine, a writer of stories of which Ginny had once remarked, "They'll never make it to television." Her highest compliment. Julie thought about McNally, or more specifically, about her own reaction to him. He had come on strong, something that made her suspicious; not so much of what he had in mind, but of whether he'd got wind of the rape and was pouring on the kindness. Ridiculous. Or better, so what if that were so? Accept! Looking over the park from the nineteenth story, you could imagine it to be a large game laid out on the floor of the city. The traffic moved at regular intervals, the cars passed in and out of tunnels. Déjà vu of a sort: The boys in her godparents' family had had an electric train with tracks and tunnels and signal lights and switches; actually it had belonged to their father, and the equipment was British, the cars divided into compartments—even into classes. Had the Burlingames known her father? she wondered. Quite probably. And she could have asked Morgan Reynolds about them and hadn't, damn him. She said it every time she thought of him. Why did she loathe him so much? Because of the deception he had tried to put over on her? Or because of the truth: that he was her mother's lover?

The sirens in the distance growing ever louder signaled the approach of fire trucks. She leaned over the railing and watched their approach and passing on Fifty-ninth Street. Cars and buses, momentarily halted, moved back into the mainstream of traffic in their wake. And somewhere near the mouth of the Hudson River a tanker called *The Candy Kid* was plowing water, moving toward its dock.

McNally came out onto the balcony and drew the glass doors closed behind him on what was becoming a noisy party. "Aren't you cold?" he wanted to know.

"Yes, but I like it."

"I'm glad of that. I won't offer my coat."

"Mr. McNally, do you know a newspaperman in Dublin by the name of Michael Desmond?"

"It's not an uncommon name. I may have seen the byline, but read him I have not. Should I have?"

"I'd like to know if he's alive, and if he really is in Dublin. And if not—where he is."

"Wouldn't it be easy for your husband to find out, being himself an international journalist?"

"Jeff and I are separated, something Ginny hasn't caught up with yet." She had thrown off the shield. Deliberately.

"Are you now?" An exaggerated Irishism. McNally grinned and rubbed his hands together.

Julie laughed and moved toward the door. "I am cold," she said.

"Here. There's room enough for both of us." He opened wide his tweed jacket.

She caught the faint smell of perspiration and didn't mind, something that made her inordinately pleased with herself. She was tempted to take him up on the offer—made in jest, of course. But she was aware of wanting very much to feel the warmth of his body. He opened the door and followed her back in to the party.

"There's no doubt about your having a drink now," he said. "Even a doctor would recommend it." He took her hand and drew her after him through the crowded room to the bar. "Cognac— unless Ginny has hid it away, and I wouldn't blame her with a mob this size."

The bartender found the bottle under the bar and somehow managed to pour it out of sight, bringing up a good inch of lovely amber in each of two plastic glasses.

"Slaint," McNally said.

"Slaint." Julie remembered the Irish-American seaman from whom she had first heard the word. And again she thought of *The Candy Kid*, and the man aboard—unless he had jumped ship—named Frank Kincaid. She hoped he had jumped.

One of the early guests who'd been with McNally when Julie arrived came up to him now and asked if he'd made up his mind.

McNally introduced Ted Freeburn and then said, "I'll go if Julie goes with us. How's that?"

"Fine," Freeburn said. He was a slender man, not much taller than Julie. She'd have guessed he was a doctor. "This Irish cowboy has never seen the real break dancing," he told her.

"I should see it before it's out of fashion," McNally said.

"It's out of fashion now," Freeburn said, "but like most things on the turn, the best is last. This kid is great—Flip Masterson."

"At the Guardian Angel?" Julie asked after a second or two, trying to place the name with the club.

"Will you come?" McNally said.

She nodded. It was the brandy. Or loneliness. Not the Guardian Angel.

On their way downtown she thought about her first visit to the Guardian Angel. That was where she had first heard of Sweets Romano, the gentleman gangster who had since become her friend, albeit a mighty troublous one. The police, especially Homicide, were likely to exploit the relationship someday, although she was not sure how. What, she often wondered, would she do then? The one thing of which she was certain in this regard: She would never again call Romano on her own behalf. While in the hospital she had received a basket of tiny golden roses without a card that she felt sure had come from him. He was completely tactful with her and, no doubt, with other straight friends, and completely ruthless with his enemies.

"Long thoughts?" McNally turned to her in the taxi. He was sitting between her and Nancy Freeburn, who was inclined to chatter. Her husband was on the jumpseat at her knees, nodding while he listened to her, or pretended to listen.

"If I could shorten them, I'd tell you," Julie said of the long thoughts.

"Sure, the night's young."

They had a drink at the bar. The small Village cabaret was crowded, patrons waiting for the one o'clock show. The only open space was a few square feet with a microphone center. The walls were painted with murals of the city's street life—pushcarts, prostitutes, an open fire hydrant gushing water on the children.

"Some poor bastard painted his heart out," McNally commented.

"A sentimental drunk," Ted Freeburn said.

Freeburn was a lawyer, Julie discovered from his wife. She stored the information for future reference. Just before one o'clock the headwaiter came and said he had a table for them.

Julie knew one of the partners in the comedy team, Rudy and

Hutch, that opened the show. Every year or so they did a return engagement at the Guardian Angel. They didn't get any better, they didn't get any worse. It was something she didn't want to say in the column, so she had said nothing, and Rudy was hurt. He had written her a sad little note to the newspaper, which Julie ignored, thinking to give him mention soon. This year's routine was built around Hutch's "talking violin." It orchestrated Rudy's antics. Rudy asked the audience to choose a subject. Somebody suggested "Mother." "What's wrong with 'Father'? Why does he always have to play second fiddle?" He asked it of the violin, and Julie thought about how often the word *father* fell about her these days. The fiddle in response to Rudy's question gave a deep, bored belch. McNally's laugh caught the comic's attention, and when he looked around to see where it had come from, he spotted Julie.

He came to the table carrying the mike with him and made a great fuss over "New York's favorite New Wave gossip columnist . . ." "New waves, old wrinkles. . . . Sorry, Julie. It's so nice of you to come. . . ." Laced with sarcasm. Then, just when he was about to leave, he turned back. "Do you know who was here a few nights ago, Julie? Sitting right where you are now?"

"I can guess," she said, and she could from his nasty air of snide confidentiality.

"With the cutest little French chanteuse, Mimi Monet. Just closed at the Saint Regis, I understand. Ooo, la-la."

It seemed a very long time until they brought on the break dancer.

The taxi waited for him while McNally stood by watching Julie turn the keys in two locks. The street was solemnly quiet and desolate under the glare of streetlights so dense they could almost make day of night. From the time they had dropped the Freeburns at their Gramercy Park apartment, she had debated with herself and reached no decision. Now the words seemed simply to spring out on her: "Would you like a cup of tea?"

While Julie drew water for the kettle at the bathroom sink and put it on the hotplate, McNally stood gazing at the crystal ball and

90

the collection of Yeats's poetry. "Do you think in symbols, Julie?"

"I do look for signs. I don't always believe them."

"Is there magic in the ball here?"

"Only for the believers. It belonged to a Gypsy woman. She must have believed in it."

"I'd never have thought of you in a place like this, though I suspected you might be unconventional."

"I'm not really. I hadn't expected to live here—until recently."

"Do you want to tell me about it?"

She shrugged. "You heard it yourself tonight—he fell in love with someone else . . . Mimi Monet. I wish I could laugh."

"Do you want him back?"

"Yes." She turned away. "There's beer in the fridge."

"The tea will be fine. Was tonight the first time you heard who she was?"

Julie nodded. "Life seems to be full of surprises for me these days." She turned back to him. "I'm not sure I want Jeff back. . . ."

"You just don't want him taken away from you."

"That's it." She went to the chest and got out cups and tea. "I'm sorry, all I have are tea bags."

"It'd be better if he had died," McNally said.

Julie laughed.

"Your grief wouldn't be so humiliating."

True, all too true.

The next thing she knew, while she watched a kettle that refused to boil, he was reading "Where the Wild Geese Fly No More" where she had tacked the typed copy of it on the wall above her desk. He glanced at her over his shoulder. "I'm a rude bastard, but the words *Wild Geese* caught my eye. Thomas Francis Mooney . . . I never heard of him either. Who was it you asked me about at Ginny's? I must write down the name."

"Michael Desmond. I thought Ginny might have told you about the poem and how I came to find it in the magazine."

"I love the way you all call it 'the magazine,' as though there was none other in the world."

"Is there?" Julie set out the tray—milk and sugar, cups and

91

saucers. The kettle was on the boil, as Mrs. Ryan always said.

He came to where she was bringing the tray and made her stop and hold it between them while he looked at her. "I like your eyes," he said and took the tray from her. "How did you come on the poem there?"

It was not to be told that night. The telephone shattered the quiet of which their very voices had seemed a part.

"At three in the morning?" McNally said of the phone call.

"The answering service will pick it up."

"Aren't you curious?"

She shook her head. "I used to worry that something might have happened to Jeff."

"And you don't now?"

"It wouldn't be me they'd call."

The stillness when the ringing stopped seemed more ominous. Neither of them was able to break it before the phone rang again. This time she answered.

It was Detective Russo. *The Candy Kid* had docked early. "We've picked up the two suspects for questioning. We can't hold them for long, and we've got the Glass woman in a hotel. We can't hold her either. She's a wild bird."

"What do you want me to do?"

"We'll pick you up in five minutes."

"In five minutes," Julie repeated, looking at McNally. "Okay."

The Irishman was on his feet before she hung up the phone.

"I'm sorry, Seamus. Drink your tea until they come for me. It's the police. I'm going to have to try to identify two men."

"Criminals? That's a ridiculous question, isn't it?"

Julie smiled wryly. "I'm not sure I can identify them. I probably can't. They were wearing masks."

"And their crime, may I ask? Alleged crime, is it?"

Yes, Julie decided. It might as well be told him. She would never know how the night might have gone if Russo hadn't phoned. She said the words: "Sexual assault."

He did not speak. A gesture questioned whether she had been

92

the victim and she nodded that she had. He sank back down to the chair and put his hand to his forehead, concealing his eyes.

Just saying the words had numbed everything within her. Her heart simply froze over. Even anxiety was dead. She gathered their cups and saucers onto the tray and took it to the kitchen table.

"I'll go with you if you'll have me," McNally said. " It's no time for you to be alone."

"It is, though. I couldn't stand it otherwise." She brought his coat from the clothes tree and held it for him. "You'll get a cab on Broadway, but be careful."

"Do you want to see me again?" he asked at the door.

She shook her head. It was the truth. The very thought of his maleness revolted her.

"Ring me up in Donegal if you change your mind," he said.

Russo drove her uptown in an unmarked car. Julie slouched down in the seat beside him and dug her hands deeply into her pockets.

"We've got them at Eighty-second Street. They've got special facilities up there in case we get lucky. You know where we picked them up, don't you?"

"McGowen's?"

"We nabbed them coming out. Kincaid came into town on a bus and went there straight from the terminal, seabag and all. His pal was waiting for him. Name's Jim Donahue. It wasn't five minutes until they came out. I don't think McGowen was very hospitable."

"Do you know anything more about them? Family? Oh, Christ, what I really mean is, do they have wives? Children? Where did the doll come from?"

"Don't know that. Neither of them's married, as far as we know. They've got relatives all over the place. I don't know, Julie: They claim they've got witnesses to where they were the entire morning of June eighteenth. They're a couple of lunkheads, but they've stone-walled some pretty smart cops all night. They even volunteered to stand in a lineup, and that's what we're going after now—unless their lawyer's changed their minds for them."

"I don't see what good I'm going to be," Julie said, her anxiety coming back. Which was better than feeling dead.

"You may be able to pick up on something we can use in combination."

"Their faces are going to be an awful distraction."

Russo laughed. Gallows humor. Sometimes it was the best kind. "I think the Glass lady will feel better when she knows you're there."

"She'd feel even better if it was May Weems," Julie said.

"Otherwise engaged," Russo said, meaning it to be funny.

"Yeah."

Eight men walked past on the other side of "the mirror." Julie watched with Russo and Detective Mabel Hadley. Three of the men rolled with a waddle of sorts. One of them had red hair, but to identify him by that would render useless any other testimony she might give. Another of the shorter men had dirty blond hair, which some might call red, and the head of the one she felt was Kincaid was quite bald, possibly shaved. Some joker had included a black man among the eight. Julie suggested to the detectives that he be eliminated before Missy Glass saw them. She could easily be confused. The decision was to keep him in the lineup: He had asked to be in it.

So far as Julie was concerned, the black man was the only one of the lot she could eliminate. Her assailants might have been two of several combinations. Or none of them. She felt an equal abhorrence for them all and yet a debilitating fear of implicating innocent men.

"Well?" Russo said, annoyed when she wasn't forthcoming.

"I'd say the bald-headed one is Kincaid. But I wouldn't say any of them were the men who trapped me. Not for sure I wouldn't. Is there nothing in the crime lab by which to identify them, for God's sake?"

"It takes two sets of everything to make comparisons, Julie. To get their prints and other samples we've got to arrest them, and to do that we need probable cause. Let's listen to some tapes now and see if you can recognize any of the voices. You were right about Kincaid, by the way. He shaved off his red hair while at sea."

94

Several edited recordings were played for her, different voices, all. In one of the segments the speaker responded to the question of where he worked, saying he was a part-time warehouse loader on Greene Street. "Part-time anything else?" his interrogator asked. "Yes sir. I'm learning how to be a mortician. You know, dead people?" "Where?" "My uncle owns a funeral parlor on Forty-ninth Street. Like I said before . . ." The tape was edited at that point. Julie's first thought was that the speaker was going to have to improve his speech before he'd be allowed in the parlor to deal with the bereaved. Then she realized and signaled to stop the recorder.

"I wouldn't swear to it," she said. "I couldn't. But that's the only voice that seems at all familiar. If it's his, he's the other one."

A technician marked the segment and removed the tape.

There was a consultation among the detectives, and one of them then asked Julie if she had noticed any odor on the perpetrator that she could associate with a mortuary.

"Something medicinal—putrid, stale." The whole scene flooded back with all its associable smells—grease, vomit, and all the rest. "I don't know!" she shouted. "How in God's name would I know how a mortuary smells?"

They left her alone then until a few minutes later, when Russo came back and said, "Let's get the hell out of here."

"What?" Julie said.

"The Glass woman refused even to watch the parade. She turned her back on it. They'll be out on the street before we are and they'll be a damned sight harder to bring in the next time."

17

...

Her depression was almost overwhelming. She had prepared herself to confront, and there had been no confrontation. And her meeting with McNally now seemed like an illusion. She did not even look like herself in the mirror. She spent most of the workday on the phone and came up with nothing worth the print. Every time she thought of going out, she was put off by the thought that she might meet Kincaid or Donahue on the street and know them instantly. Then what would she do? And what would they do?

She forced herself to leave the shop and do something as close to confrontation as she could come at the moment. She walked up to Forty-ninth Street and west until she was alongside the Magee Funeral Home. The firm, according to the legend on the bronze plaque, had been established in 1922. A family business. A diminishing family if Donahue, a nephew, had been taken in. Or might it have been on the plea of his parents? Or was he an abused youngster pitied by his uncle? What the hell difference did it make? He was a sodomist. Or else he was the wrong party.

There was no vehicular entrance on Forty-ninth Street. It would be around the corner on the avenue. Across the street was a school run by the Sisters of Good Hope, and adjoining the school, the convent. It took her a few seconds to remember why that might be relevant: Russo's saying where the stocking masks might have come from. They were the kind nuns used to wear before they came out of the habit. She certainly wasn't going to ring the convent doorbell and ask what kind of stockings these reverend ladies were wearing nowadays. Okay. How about this? Did one of your older sisters pass away along about June eighteenth? And was she laid out at Magee's? The idea was so macabre it cheered her up. She went around the corner and found the business entrance to the funeral home. Crowded against the brick wall near the door stood a bright green Volkswagen bug, the paint looking shiny new. Was it the car Missy Glass said looked like an egg, now painted over? Or just one more coincidence?

Julie phoned Detective Russo, ostensibly to ask if Kincaid's and Donahue's alibis had been checked out by now. He promised to call her back when he could find out, but his voice and manner suggested that he had cooled toward the case. She decided not to lay the Volkswagen speculation on him at the moment. When he called her, then maybe. But the day passed and most of the next day and he had not called back. For all she knew, Kincaid might have gone back to sea.

Old Mary Ryan stopped by the shop. "Just to see how you're getting along, dear."

Julie made her a cup of tea. Then, against her own better judgment, she asked her if she knew a young man by the name of Frank Kincaid.

"That would be *young* Frankie." Mrs. Ryan set her teacup down. "I knew him when he was no more than a whistle. I knew his mother, and I knew his grandmother before that. The father's a traveling salesman who does more traveling than selling. Now there's one of those I was telling you about, Julie: Father Doyle got hold of him and for a while he paid up every week. Then he took off again. The Kincaid girls were all pretty little things. And the way Jennie dressed them . . ." Mrs. Ryan laid her hand on Julie's. "They were like little dolls. One of them supported the whole family for a while. She got into TV commercials. You'd know her if you saw her. Or would have. I've not seen her lately. She turned pudgy the way some girls do when they get to be ten or eleven. But you asked about Frankie. He

97

wasn't a bad boy, but when he'd get into any trouble, it was always the other fellow's fault. A whiny youngster. I don't think he's very bright. I used to see him in McGowen's now and then. Nowadays he's a great show-off, with that red hair of his. He got into the maritime service awhile back, and to hear him tell it, you'd think he was commander of the fleet. What makes you ask?"

"One of the girls at the Actors' Forum asked me if I knew him," Julie lied.

"I don't think he's more than an able-bodied seaman. But I suppose he's able-bodied enough when it comes to the girls."

Julie did not ask her about Donahue.

18

...

It promised to be an opening night to remember. *Golden Slippers* already
had a million and a half dollars in the till, and Broadway hadn't seen
such a turnout of celebrities since *Cats.* At Tim's suggestion he and
Julie attended together. Their column, "Our Beat," was making its
way: first-night tickets. They were so gussied up, as Tim put it, they
were photographed several times between the taxi and the lobby.
Julie wore a silver lamé dress and an embroidered stole of Chinese
silk around her shoulders. As with the real celebrities, a little burst
of applause greeted them as they went down the aisle.

"Who do they think we are?" Tim whispered as they settled
into seats far enough to the side to reestablish their second-string
status.

"Ginger Rogers and Fred Astaire."

"Julie, be your own age."

"John Barrymore and Theda Bara."

"Oi."

Ginny Gibbons was sitting on the aisle a few rows down, her
chin in her hand, a down coat draped over the back of her seat—a
starling among birds of paradise. Her escort was Seamus McNally.
He had on the same tweed jacket, and his dark head was wildly
tousled. Julie caught at a flash of fantasy: She was running her fingers
through his hair, his head in her lap. "Oh, nice!" she said aloud.

"What?"

"I feel just fine," she said.

"I told you you would. The bad times are behind you."

She patted his hand. "We're a good team, chum."

She would not see McNally unless she went to them during intermission. Ginny never left her seat until she fled the theater as the curtain fell. And during intermission Julie had work to do.

She started with a couple of notes on what people were wearing, something she was not good at; not that it mattered much. She could say they were wearing umbrellas as long as she said they were there. She caught sight of Richard Garvy moving out of the crush at the bar. People were hailing him still by his series name, Mike Bowen, even among this elite crowd. She eased her way to him. "Have you got a commitment yet from your playwright, Mr. Garvy?" During their interview at the Plaza he had refused to talk about his Broadway plans until he was sure of the play.

"Have *you*?" he snapped back, a mischievous tilt to his eyebrows. Was he telling her that Seamus McNally was the playwright and that they had spoken of her? He was. "You're blushing, little lady." He touched her under the chin. "So I have my answer and you have yours. Come and meet Mrs. Garvy. She doesn't turn out for these things often."

"May I put it in the column that you're doing a play by Seamus McNally?"

"You may. It's called *The Far, Far Hills of Home*."

"Nice," Julie said.

"Bucolic."

Julie laughed, remembering McNally's description of himself as a bucolic playwright. Of which there were not many left.

"We're going to try to bring it in in the spring."

Mrs. Garvy was a tall, shy woman, the very antithesis of Mike Bowen's noisy television wife. Julie wondered if they had married before or after the series caught on.

"This is the young lady with whose father I may have gone to Trinity. Remember, I told you how she loved your anemones?" A perfect non sequitur.

"Wasn't Seamus talking about her?" Mrs. Garvy asked.

"The very same," Garvy said.

She gave Julie her hand. "I do hope you find your father."

Julie wrote up her items for the column that night and phoned them in in the morning. She hadn't expected Tim to be there that early, but he came on the phone before she cut off. "What do you think, Julie?"

"About what?"

"You mean nobody's called you? You don't know?"

"I'm listening," she said, irritated. She had not slept well.

"Two guys have confessed to the attack on you. It's the lead story in the *Post*."

19

...

She put on her jacket and walked to the corner deli, the nearest place she could buy a newspaper. She ought to have known, she told herself, that the silence of the police did not mean they had abandoned the case. And yet she thought of Russo's summary after the lineup fiasco: They'll be a damned sight harder to bring in the next time. Could it be two different men? She ordered an egg salad on rye and a carton of orange juice and opened the paper. Her feeling was one of dead calm as she read the story at a glance.

At four o'clock that morning two West Side men had walked into the Nineteenth Precinct station house and confessed to the June 18th sexual assault on Julie Hayes, *New York Daily* columnist. Frank Kincaid, twenty-three, and James E. Donahue, twenty-two, were to be arraigned later in the day in Criminal Court. The men cited conscience as the motive for their surrender to the police. Neither had a previous arrest record. The *Daily* had offered a five-thousand-dollar reward at the time for information leading to the arrest and conviction of the assailants, an amount subsequently doubled.

The deli clerk stretched his neck to see what she was reading. "I know those guys. One of them's old lady comes in here all the time. What gets into kids like that? I mean in this neighborhood—what'd they need it for?" Obviously he did not know he was talking to the victim. Probably didn't know there was one. "Pickle?"

102

"Please," Julie said.

"But there's something phony about it if you ask me. I don't buy that 'conscience' business. I mean three months later? Forget it." Then a new idea hit him: "Maybe they think they'll get the reward. How about that?"

"Very funny," Julie said, but it crossed her mind that Kincaid's mother could use it.

Detective Russo called her after the arraignment. The first thing he told her was that he had been the arresting officer. "I'd just finished my tour of duty, got home, and took me shoes off. The chief called me, thought I ought to have the privilege. My wife didn't think it was such a great privilege. She didn't want me to come in. You know how superstitious she is."

"I know,"

"With us living in the neighborhood. Maybe she's right. We've been talking for years of moving out to Rockland County. She's got a sister living there. Maybe this'll make it happen. I'll go out of my mind . . . frogs and crickets—and babies. She wants babies."

Julie wondered if the problem was in her own mind: People did not seem to be making sense. This kind of personal chitchat from Russo, and at a time like this? Almost casually he came back to what had to be the focus so far as she was concerned. "Anyway, we're holding them for the Grand Jury. Their bail's set at a hundred grand each. I thought you'd like to know."

"You know—I am interested," Julie said. Then: "That's a lot of money."

"I don't think they'll have any trouble getting it up. You'll be asked to testify at the hearing. Detective Hadley'll get in touch with you."

"How come they turned themselves in?" Julie asked finally.

"Seems like they had a fight. They probably got tanked up, and one of them went soft. I'll tell you the truth: I didn't think we'd ever get them up before the Grand Jury. Now I think we can get an indictment. We have a lot of stuff once the DA can start fitting the pieces together. I think we got a good chance."

Julie had hung on as long as she could. "Am I crazy, Detective Russo, or are you holding back on something?"

"I'll tell you one thing that bothers me, Julie. The lawyer representing them at the arraignment is from Joe Quinlan's office. You know who he is, don't you?"

"I've heard the name."

"He's one of the top trial lawyers in the city. Big-shot politician."

"Yes?"

"Well, Joe Quinlan is a West Side boy, all the way up from the streets and Our Lady of Good Hope High School. All right. Here's what I'm afraid of: He's too big for us, Julie. Do you understand?"

"I guess so," she said, but she didn't.

20

...

The letter from Ireland came as Julie was leaving the shop on the morning she was to testify before the Grand Jury. She read it while hanging onto a subway pole on the way downtown.

Dear Miss Hayes:

> *Your letter to my uncle, the late Michael Desmond, was received and opened by me. He died last June, may his soul rest in peace. He lived with his sisters until they died and then with my husband and me and our four children until he went into the hospital. I was his heir, though what he left most of were debts. He did leave me his notebooks and letters, and him being a newspaperman they are important. If you will let me know what information you wish, I will go through them and look for it. I remember him talking about someone named Mooney.*

> *Can you advise me if his letters are valuable? Are there people in America who would be interested in purchasing them? I am told universities over there are very keen on collecting such papers.*

> *If I can be of service to you in Dublin here, please let me know. Dear Miss Hayes, I look forward to hearing from you in the near future.*

> > *Yours faithfully,*
> > *Sally O'Rourke*

The Grand Jury before which Julie appeared that October morning was composed of seven men and five women—racial, age, and economic factors, she assumed, well sorted out. They looked to have grown experienced in their jury tenure, self-assured and compatible. The assistant district attorney who went over Julie's testimony with her was a well-groomed young man named Eric Amberg. Everything about him, his hair brushed to a crest, his moustache without a straggle, his vested pinstripe suit, everything suggested tidiness and command; he was solicitous without being warm, his eyes fending her off in case she expect too much involvement of him. When he finished rehearsing her, Julie studied the defendants where they sat at the table with their lawyers—two lawyers now. Donahue had the pallor of the mortuary about him; he was sallow and pale, with blackish hair that looked unwashed, a clump of it falling over his forehead. He kept moistening his lips. Afraid? That ought to give her some satisfaction. Kincaid wore a white turtleneck sweater and looked like a retarded choirboy. He wanted to jump up when anyone approached their table. The lawyers kept patting his arm reassuringly. He'd have been brought up scared—of his vagrant father, of the nuns, of every kid on the block bigger than himself. The smaller ones he bullied and, she wouldn't be surprised to learn, abused.

When she took the stand, the judge questioned her at length on her state of mind that morning, the circumstances under which she had accidentally strayed into an area where she would not ordinarily have gone. She was frank about the scene between her and her husband that precipitated it. She had forgone legal counsel, and too late she realized the advantage the defense would take. If Kincaid and Donahue came to trial, she would be portrayed as a frustrated, rejected wife available to almost any man on the prowl. Furthermore, the lawyers from Joe Quinlan's firm had done some hasty research; they had learned that years before, she had studied karate. Why, the question was, had she not put up a stronger defense? The DA's man, Eric Amberg, countered by asking if that was the strongest defense Quinlan's office could put up for their clients. The judge reprimanded him for violating court decorum.

He apologized. It was all so bloody civilized, Julie thought. She was thanked and dismissed by the judge as soon as she had given her testimony. She wondered why the others were there at all, since Kincaid and Donahue had confessed. She remembered the deli clerk who'd said he did not buy the pinch of conscience as their reason. She might not buy it either if she could properly evaluate the situation. She couldn't. What she was failing to understand was their motive for the crime itself. With all the whores in the neighborhood, why Missy Glass or her? Anger, aggression, the need for power? Had it nothing to do with sex? Kincaid, she thought, had more fun using the knife than his other weapon. He couldn't have managed one without the other. He probably couldn't have managed alone, either. She looked back just before she pushed open the courtroom door. Those two were wimps—weaklings—standing up there pretending penitence. Yes. Pretending, she felt sure. So what were they pretending that Sunday morning when they assaulted her?

She pushed her way through the crowded corridor, lawyers and clients hastily settling on their pleas, battered wives and beleaguered mothers silently mulling alibis to which they'd falsely swear. What about the alibis Kincaid and Donahue had claimed? Thrown out when they confessed—like an old pair of lisle stockings.

"Friend Julie . . ."

She turned back. May Weems was trying to catch up with her. Julie's first thought was, Oh, no. Not again. Then she remembered that Missy Glass was waiting to testify—or in her case it might be not to testify—before the Grand Jury. "How are you, May?" Like old friends meeting at Broadway and Forty-second Street.

"I come when Missy Glass say to me she got to come."

"Good," Julie said. Then, not knowing why it was good, she added, "Thank you."

"What I come to tell you, Miss Julie: I couldn't help it, I told my pimp about you, you paying my fine and why, me being a witness like? I had to tell him or he'd of whipped me."

"No harm," Julie said, having no notion why the girl shouldn't have told him or why the telling was at issue now. After all, the grimmer parts of the story made headlines in the straight world. "Why shouldn't you have told him?"

May shrugged. "I just wanted you to know I done it."

"You aren't here on other business, are you?"

May Weems grinned, something she rarely did, aware that her part of "the life" was reflected in the condition of her teeth. Caps and chips and a couple of vacancies. "No, ma'am. I is clean as Missy Glass."

21

...

Within the week the Grand Jury indicted Kincaid and Donahue. Their trial was set before Judge Weinstein in the spring session of State Supreme Court. The men were free on fifteen thousand dollars bail each, a sum far lower than that set following the arraignment.

Far be it from Julie to question the amount of bail. Or anything else. Her feeling of relief was enormous: She had done what she had to do and ought now to be able to get on with her life. Whatever that meant. It was crazy, she told herself, but fast upon the relief came a feeling of emptiness, a void. She was going to have to face the specifics of living without Jeff. The change in life-style wasn't going to bother her ... except that she had never had a life-style of her own until now. She counted her money and thought about Ireland. She could manage the trip and, if she then chose and was careful, a few months' residence there. Then what? She knew exactly what she was doing—warding off decisions, hoping something would come up to forestall their need, to propel her life for her.

Suppose she searched for and found her father? That his friend Michael Desmond was dead did not mean that Thomas Francis Mooney was dead. She felt distrustful of Desmond's niece. Which wasn't like Julie. Or, let's say, the old Julie. She got out Sally O'Rourke's letter and read it again. And again decided not to answer it. What she wanted to do was to read those letters and notebooks of Michael

109

Desmond's herself. The least, and possibly the most, she could accomplish by going to Ireland was to perceive a beginning to herself, whether or not she actually found the man who was her source.

Having decided to go, she began at once to pick the decision apart. She was copping out on the job, on the stability it had given her. To ask for a leave of absence would be unfair to Tim: He'd carried her for months. She resolved her dilemma by proposing to do at least a month's hard work, to set up a series of interviews, putting her quirky humor into them, reassuring the *Daily* powers of the worth of Julie Hayes, gossip columnist.

Then she opened that morning's mail.

Two of the handwritten letters were obscene, the obscenities awkward, as though the writers were unfamiliar with the words they wrote, or maybe the writing itself. A third letter, also on cheap white stationery and written in a slope that seemed vaguely familiar, read:

> To Julie Hayes
>
> You are no good for our neighborhood. Those two boys are decent, law abiding people. They wouldn't do anything like you say they did. They are being railroaded by a rich newspaper and you are its whore. Isn't that why you live here to be near the whores? God will punish you.

There was no signature and of course no return address. Simply the New York postmark on the envelope. Julie's hand was trembling. She tried to steady it and to study the handwriting, but she already knew: It reminded her of Mary Ryan's. It wasn't hers, she was sure, but it was the way people of a certain age and upbringing wrote. When she was in control of herself, she called Mrs. Ryan and asked her if she'd like to stop by the shop for a cup of tea.

"I don't think I'd better, Julie," the old woman said. "I feel like I'm coming down with something, and you never know whether it's catching."

"I don't care," Julie said. "I'll take a chance."

"I hadn't better," Mrs. Ryan said.

"Okay . . . something's catching around here, isn't it?" She heard a deep inhalation of breath, but no words followed. "I wish I knew what I'd done that was wrong," she added.

"You shouldn't have lied to me," Mrs. Ryan said. "Saying you wanted information about Frankie for a girlfriend."

"Mrs. Ryan, do you know what happened to me? Do you really understand? Those guys confessed to rape and sodomy. They admitted it."

"I don't want to discuss it, Julie."

"But you have to! You're my friend."

"I'm an old woman and I don't feel well. I've lived here most of my life and I don't have to be told who my friends are."

"Okay," Julie said and swallowed the pain in her throat. "Take care."

She sat for a few minutes, badly shaken. Then she put the phone on service, took the letters in her carryall, and went out. She walked up Eighth Avenue to Saint Malachy's.

"My dear young friend," Father Doyle said with a sad smile, "I'm not excusing these letters, but you've got to see it the way our friend does."

"Why?"

"Try to understand. These boys have no previous record with the police. They were brought up like most of the Irish Catholic youngsters in this neighborhood—a mixture of public and parochial schools. The Donahue boy lives at home and helps support his mother. Neither of them spends much on the sporting life. If there are any doubts at all, the neighborhood's going to give them the benefit of it."

"Doesn't it mean anything, Father Doyle, that they confessed? I thought confession was a big thing with you."

The priest made a sound of disapproval at her flippancy. "I heard there was coercion," he said. "Whether it was on the part of the police, I don't know. I wouldn't claim they're young men of the strongest character."

"Neither would I," Julie said. "What kind of coercion?"

"It would almost have to be physical, wouldn't it? Their being the unsophisticated sort."

"Are you saying they were threatened—or beaten up?"

"You're not to put words in my mouth, Julie. I'm not saying at all, only what I heard. But I will tell you where I heard it: Mrs. Donahue says Jim was covered from head to foot with bruises, and all he'd say was that he got into a fight with Frankie."

"Does Mrs. Donahue think they're innocent?"

"She's his mother, after all. And they *are* innocent until proven guilty. Isn't that the way the law goes?"

Julie nodded. Then, angry with herself as much as with him: "I don't get it. Why wouldn't they give that information to the Grand Jury if they were being forced into confessing a crime they didn't commit? You've got to admit, Father Doyle, it's strange."

"Strange things have happened in this city. I've been told there are people with more power outside the law than inside it. People with a moral code of their own, and some of them think they can dispense justice more surely than the courts or even the Lord God Almighty himself."

Julie was stunned. The priest could be speaking of only one person, Sweets Romano. Romano also was a product of the West Side, and he owned a large piece of it today under a variety of covers. There was no operation, legitimate or otherwise, of which he was not informed. If the police could not enforce, he could and often did: something known, but not proven. And in his own curious way, Julie knew, Romano adored her. And equally curious, he was a puritan. The priest's eyes were soft with compassion. She had to moisten her lips before she could speak. "They have good lawyers, don't they? Kincaid and Donahue, I mean."

"The best there is. We have to take care of our own, Julie."

She nodded. "I don't suppose it's relevant, Father Doyle, but I remember hearing that Mr. Romano made the donation that saved Saint Jude's Hospital from closing." A neighborhood hospital that had gone deeply into debt.

"You may have heard that, but I'm sure the gift was anonymous."

112

* * *

"I told you my wife didn't want me to come back that morning," Russo said. "She thinks she has what her and Mary Ryan call the second sight, and sometimes I think she does. I took one look at a welt on the back of Kincaid's neck and got a police physician in to examine them before we'd even take their statements. Just to protect ourselves against a brutality charge. The doctor, in the end, couldn't say positively that they had or hadn't administered the blows to one another, and they stuck to their story. Even with Quinlan's men calling the shots, they're sticking to it."

"What do *you* think, Detective Russo?"

His heavy, dark eyes grew even more solemn. "I'm paid to ask questions, not to answer them. But I'll say this: Until the time we went before the Grand Jury, we worked our asses off to make a case out of the evidence we had. Just in case they'd change their plea."

"What would they have changed it to?"

"Innocent. What else?"

Julie smiled at her own stupidity.

"But I'll be surprised if Quinlan doesn't get them off when they come to trial, no matter what evidence we have. I'll be surprised if that confession isn't thrown out at some point."

"Then why arrest them at all?"

Russo sighed deeply.

"For their own protection," Julie said, bearing down with the sarcasm.

"That's what it could amount to."

"Oh, Christ," she said.

22
...

At least one hate letter came through the mail slot every day. Hand-delivered now. Probably by a child, she thought grimly. She stayed away from the shop until late most days, hustling her sources, doing her own leg work and using her desk in the huge *New York Daily* editorial room. The company she kept in that environment was a solace. Tim took a few days in Bermuda, and she carried the column very nicely on her own.

She went to see Ray Duggan, editor of the Sunday magazine, and tried to sell him the story of the search for her father she proposed to carry over to Ireland. He watched her out of small, shrewd eyes. Duggan had a face like a walnut, a hand that shook, and a profound reverence for the journalist's craft.

"I'm not going to say yes or no," he told her. "We'll have to see where it goes. You don't have a story yet."

"I'm sure it's there," she said. "But I have to go and get it."

"We can't finance your trip, if that's what you have in mind."

"I didn't expect that." It was not so much the money she wanted, although God knows she could have used it, as that she needed the feeling of continuity, a linkage between here and there, then and now. She needed her newspaper affiliation for confidence.

"I'll give you an assignment, if that's what you want, and if you're set on going to Ireland, that might be just the place to work on it: It's a great place for crying. . . ." He paused to light a cigarette. Julie knew what was coming. "Do your own story. Bring it right up to date and then finish it after the trial. I'll give you a two-parter on it. And I'll give you some money to go on."

"Let me think about it." Something in her had changed: She had not rejected the proposal out of hand. Then: "What if they're acquitted?"

"Then you'll need a place to let go your outrage. I'm counting on something like that to draw your fire, if you want to know. I know it's in you, girl, but what good is it to either of us if you can't get it into your copy?"

"Okay, Ray. I'll do it."

When he grinned, his eyes disappeared into the wrinkles. A walnut: very hard to crack, but the meat was worth it.

She was on her way back to her desk when the city editor shouted to her. She wheeled around. The whole room fell silent. The man behind the big desk was not in the habit of shouting.

"Kincaid and Donahue have disappeared," he told her, his hand on the phone. "The team's on the way to the DA's office. I'll catch them downstairs if you want to go along."

A lot of reporters were on hand by the time the district attorney's public relations officer read a statement to inform them that Mrs. Annie Donahue of 607 West Fifty-eighth Street had reported to Midtown North that morning that her son James was missing. He had not been home for three days. Nor had he shown up at his uncle's place of business, where he was employed as an assistant mortician. Detectives from the district attorney's office had then checked on Kincaid and learned that he had not been seen during that period either. A check of the Maritime Union hiring records showed he had not attempted to ship out, something his mother had convinced herself was the case. His attorney had applied for permission for Kincaid to ship between U.S. ports while free on bail. Kincaid and Donahue were last seen when they left McGowen's Bar at closing time early Sunday morning.

The case was reviewed, but the press officer would take no questions concerning impending police action. Getting such small pickings, the *Daily* team proposed to interview the families of the two men. It was not a trip Julie was going to take.

She was on her way out of the room when she heard her name. The voice was familiar, but she could not place it until she turned to see Lieutenant David Marks of Homicide. The sight of him at that moment made her feel queasy.

They shook hands while Julie murmured that she wouldn't have expected to see him in the DA's office. He was a tall man; there was more gray in his hair than when they had last met; his eyes seemed even more broody. A romantic figure really—a cop who thought a lot about why men did evil and whether an ounce of prevention was possible, never mind a cure. She had met him during the investigation of the murder of her then boss, Tony Alexander: The chief suspect in that case had vanished, only to surface—just identifiable—in the waters off Staten Island. It was a killing attributed to Sweets Romano. But without evidence. Julie said she wouldn't have expected to see Marks, but that wasn't true. Nor was his presence accidental.

"It's a little early," Marks said, "but could I take you to lunch?"

Julie shook her head. "I'm sorry, Lieutenant."

"How about a few minutes' talk in my office, then?"

"Oh?"

He led the way to a large room with high windows giving a view of the sky and one tall building. The walls were lined with legal tomes, and several unattached file cabinets stood out of place but usable. Julie and Marks sat at a conference table. "I should have said my office-to-be."

Julie didn't say anything.

"I'm sorry for what happened to you."

"Thanks," she murmured.

"Odd, the disappearance of the suspects, isn't it?"

She nodded. Silent.

"There's something I want to say to you, right off, Julie. Not for anything in the world, not even to nail public enemy number one, would I jeopardize a rape conviction. You must believe that."

Again she nodded. She knew what she was in for. Not that she hadn't known it was bound to come, but it seemed pretty rotten luck that she'd come downtown and saved him a trip.

Marks lit a cigarette and laid the package where she could take one if she wanted it. "Can we talk frankly?"

"I don't know. It depends on what we're going to talk about."

He took a deep drag and sent the smoke upward when he exhaled. "Your patron."

"He is not my patron." She could feel herself flush.

"But you know who and what I want to talk about. I trust you. I think you've been unwise, to say the least, in your association with him, but I do trust you."

"I guess I should say thank you, but I'm not going to. Lieutenant Marks, my husband claims that if he couldn't talk—if he couldn't pledge confidentiality if necessary—to anyone, even the devil himself, he couldn't be a newspaperman. You don't have any right to censor me."

Marks studied the next blast of cigarette smoke as it shot upward. "I suppose there's a touch of the bully in every cop. I apologize if that's the way I've come across to you. I said I trust you. See those file cabinets? That's a homicide case in preparation for the Grand Jury. I'm on loan to the DA to work on it. You know how long I've wanted to."

Julie nodded.

"But you see what I mean when I say I trust you: I don't want to go deep-sea diving in cement shoes."

"I do see that," Julie said quietly, her own anxiety easing off. His had to be even greater.

"So I'm asking for your help. Am I to have it?"

She nodded. "If you ask me questions, I'll answer them as truthfully and as fully as I can."

"Fair enough. I'm not going to ask you to speculate. First question: Has Romano moved in to play God again in this case?"

"I don't know."

"Then speculate, damn it!"

They both laughed, and she knew why she liked Marks in spite of her fear of him.

"Has he been in touch with you, Julie?"

"No. And I haven't been in touch with him. I don't expect to be ever again."

Marks grunted, not entirely believing her. "Did you know he matched your newspaper's five-thousand-dollar-reward money?"

"What?"

He nodded.

"I didn't know," she said, feeling trapped again.

" 'A concerned citizen.' I've traced the bank account from which it was drawn—an old affiliate of his going straight these days, but like half the West Side, in his debt one way or another. As you know, he does nothing in his own name."

Julie was reminded: "When I was in the hospital, there were flowers I felt might have come from him."

Marks drew a legal pad near and made a note. "No card, of course. Do you remember the florist?"

"No."

"The name of the nurse or whoever brought them to you?"

Julie shook her head. Then: "Miss Gow. How about that? I didn't know I knew."

Marks put down the pencil after writing the name, drew deeply on his cigarette, and then put it out. "Let's see if we can figure out where he picked up on Kincaid and Donahue, shall we?"

"Are you sure he did?"

"We can say *if* he picked up on them if that rides easier on your conscience. At the point where he upped the reward, I don't think he could have had any lead to your assailants."

"Nobody had at that time. The first break came when the street woman described one of them as red-haired and lame. He's not lame. He rolls when he walks." Julie then told the detective about May Weems. "She came to me the day of the Grand Jury hearing to tell me she'd had to tell her pimp what I'd done for her and why. Could the pimp be Romano's connection?"

"Oh, yes. Information's a commodity you can trade up from street to penthouse. It makes for parity in Romano's marketplace."

Julie smiled a little: not exactly cop language.

"Assume that to be the connection. Now he has a description of the redhead, but no names. Next step?"

"I went to Detective Russo with the street woman's description, and after he went off duty that day, we walked over to McGowen's Bar and had a beer. Russo did a quick sketch of the two men, including some stuff I'd been able to provide and asked Billy McGowen if he knew a couple of guys around who might fit the description. That was a mistake. McGowen turned hostile."

"Why McGowen's?"

"Detective Russo had a hunch all along that the men were locals. Before this happened, I was pretty well liked at McGowen's, a sort of Saint Patrick's Day Irish. Now it's different. The whole neighborhood's turned against me. They think Kincaid and Donahue have been framed. It's crazy."

"Not quite, but let's stay on course: Was there anyone in the bar that day who might have overheard what you said to McGowen?"

"Yes. There was a man I'm sure overheard. We were looking right at each other. I don't know how to explain it, but I knew at the time he'd picked up on the description."

"So now we have a witness who could finger the suspects if they showed up there. Or bargain their names if he knew them."

"I don't see anyone at McGowen's doing that, Lieutenant Marks. If you mean going to Romano with the information. If anybody was going to inform at all, it would be to the police, with that reward money up there."

"Turn it around, Julie. Romano's goons know every man on the take in that area. They know his price and how to protect him, and what to do with him if he becomes a liability. Can you describe the man?"

Not wanting to, she couldn't at the moment. "No, sir. I don't think I can." And why didn't she want to? Sentimental reasons out of a late, late show, a John Ford movie. Instantly she said: "Blond, watery eyes, slack mouth. A wimp."

119

Marks almost smiled, and wrote. Then: "Maybe I can find out if he was the police informant and maybe I can't. But let's say he's Romano's. The night Kincaid got back in town, the police picked up him and his buddy as they left McGowen's. Right? Was the Romano informant in McGowen's at the time? I think so. The suspects were taken to Eighty-second Street, questioned, and run through a lineup for you and the street woman. Plenty of time for Romano's henchmen to get on the scent. When the suspects went free early the next morning, why didn't the goon squad turn them around then and send them back to make their confessions? No such instructions, not at that point. And those boys don't strike a match without instructions. Two days later, when the accused were again leaving McGowen's, the enforcers were waiting for them. I must find your wimp. If he's still around."

"You say 'the enforcers,' " Julie said, thinking back. "What does that mean?"

"Do you think their confessions were voluntary? That the lumps and bruises they sustained between McGowen's closing time and four A.M. were the result of a fistfight between them? An all-out, knock-down fight doesn't last more than a half hour—it lasts more like five minutes. I know, Julie. I've been in them. But, you see, these young men went home to their mothers, who didn't buy for a minute either that their sons were rapists or that they beat up on one another. I think that's how it came about that the community turned on you."

"I helped it along," Julie said, "asking my friend Mrs. Ryan about Kincaid."

Marks lit another cigarette. He took his time and then said, "I helped it along, too: With the DA's consent and their own attorney present, I tried to get them to admit they'd been assaulted and to identify their assailants."

"No way?" Julie asked.

"No way."

Then, on a sudden thought: "What did you promise them, Lieutenant?"

"Police protection at such time as they might be subpoenaed

as witnesses." He met her eyes, a steady gaze: "I did not compromise your case, Julie. I swear to it."

"You didn't get a chance to, did you?"

"That's quite true." He smiled ruefully. "Whatever happened to that wide-eyed, trusting, exuberant gal I met a couple of years ago? Beautiful eyes. They still are."

"She met with an accident early last summer. Lieutenant Marks, where are the men now?"

"That's the question, isn't it?"

"And I don't understand their hanging in with the confession. If they had reneged—and I know the police thought they might—the Grand Jury might not have indicted them at all."

"Their lawyer wanted them to live. He can ask that the case be thrown out when they come to trial—on the same grounds, confession under duress—but he could hope that by that time Romano would be—let's say, under restraint."

"Then he knew you were after Romano, and whether or not his clients knew it, Joseph Quinlan knew that Romano was more their enemy than was the State of New York. And Romano also knew it. He has lawyers just as smart as Mr. Quinlan."

"That's pretty dangerous thinking, Julie. You're justifying a killer."

"No. I'm justifying myself. I have no more answers for you, Lieutenant. To me, I'm the important victim."

Marks squashed the cigarette in the ashtray. "I've already told you where I stand on that. I agree. But if Kincaid and Donahue don't show up alive, I will use every instrument available to me to make my case. If I have to, I'll subpoena you."

She nodded and got to her feet. "Thanks for the advance notice."

Before she reached the door, he said, "I need you on my side, Julie."

She looked back. "I'm not sure whether I need you on mine or not."

23

...

Tim Noble returned from his holiday eager to take over "Our Beat."
He had come to cherish her defections, Julie thought. If she was
going to Ireland, it was time to go. She checked her passport—the
last embarkation stamp was Orly Airport, France—and did her necessary shopping. Kincaid and Donahue had not surfaced—a bleak
image considering that they might be lying weighted in waters off
Staten Island. Lying in weight. She was finding it hard to laugh. The
hate letters had ceased, which she attributed to a changed mood in
the neighborhood: People were frightened. Her Romano association
was known. Mr. Bourke, owner of a lighting shop on Eighth Avenue,
confirmed this when she went to see him. It was Kevin Bourke who
had obtained Sweets Romano's phone number for her years before
when she was looking for a missing girl. "I'm sorry I ever gave it to
you," Bourke said. "Me too," she replied. That she should feel en-
tangled in guilt was madness, but it was also her reality. She called
Dr. Callahan.

The therapist shaded her eyes to rest them while Julie recounted
events as she understood them. When she had finished, the doctor
looked at her, studied her, it seemed to Julie, and she anticipated the
old sarcasm about the patient's affinity for the low life. But what the
doctor said was, "You look peaked. You need a vacation."

Julie was so relieved she laughed.

"Are you sure it's guilt you're feeling, or are you frightened?"

Julie held back too quick an answer and thought about it. "Both. It's true, I am frightened."

"Good. I would rather deal with fear than guilt. Guilt is a cloak of too many colors. Who would not be afraid in your position? It is like having a tiger by the tail, no?"

"Yes," Julie said. "But what to do about it?"

"You hang on until somebody shoots him. I don't think you're in a position to do anything until that happens. Then you duck."

"Oh, Doctor," Julie said. Almost a sigh.

"What about the divorce?"

"It takes time—a year's absence on Jeff's part. He went to work on it right away—with his little French helpmate. She's a chanteuse. She sang at the Saint Regis. How about that?"

"Is that good? How did you find out?"

"It was a gift. I'm in the gossip business."

"And the long-lost father?"

"I'm working on it. I found a poem he wrote. It was published in *The New Yorker*."

The doctor nodded, a kind of appreciation.

"And I fell in and out of love with an Irish playwright since I was here last." She hadn't intended to say that. She did not know if it were so, but it came up and out in the environment. "I'm going to Ireland to continue the search for my father."

"And not for the Irish playwright?"

"He's probably married, with ten children."

The doctor smiled—it showed just long enough for Julie to catch it.

"That's like me, huh, to fall for somebody like that?"

"It's you who said it. What about the job?"

"I've asked for leave without pay."

"That's like you, too. Without pay. A newspaper that big couldn't afford to keep you on salary?"

"I have an assignment from the Sunday magazine to write about myself. And if I do find my father, I ought to be able to sell that story also."

"You are using yourself. Good."

"It's what I've got."

"What more do you need?" the doctor said. "Do you know why you came here today?"

"To get your approval."

A noncommittal grunt from Dr. Callahan.

Walking out onto a windy Central Park West, where the yellow leaves were swirling at her feet, Julie said the final word to herself: "You're your own censor. Go."

PART TWO

...

24

...

Julie arrived in Dublin on a crisp Friday afternoon in late October. Traveling overseas alone for the first time in her life, she heeded the advice of the Irish Tourist Board not to be in a hurry. She settled into a room in the Greer Hotel, a renovated Georgian building not far from Trinity College, and spent her first day in Ireland meandering in one direction and then another, listening and looking and getting to recognize her own reflection in the shop windows. Early Saturday afternoon, street map in hand, she set out to find Michael Desmond's niece, Sally O'Rourke. She had an address, but no phone number was listed to the name.

Grafton Street, which by then she had already come to know, was closed at the time to vehicular traffic and swarmed with children. Poppy-cheeked and noisy, they skittered among the shoppers and the street entertainers, who were hard put to hold a tune. Julie dropped a coin that was sure to be either too much or too little into the rumpled cap of a fiddler where it lay at his feet. A tough little urchin blocked her way and demanded tenpence. "You guv him twice it," he said of her contribution to the fiddler. Or at least that was what she thought he said. "He's more musical," Julie said, and pushed by him. She inquired of two very tall policemen the best way to Kevin Street. They stooped low and made her repeat where she wanted to go on Kevin Street and between them decided that the easiest way for her to get there was to walk it.

After the bustle and fashion of Grafton Street, Kevin was a forlorn mix of nineteenth-century red brick tenements and bleak modern housing of yellow bricks and glass, row on row alike.

Sally O'Rourke lived in one of the newer buildings. The entry was crowded with buggies and strollers. A shopping cart loaded with a folded wash stood near the inside door. Julie found that cheering. She pressed the O'Rourke bell and studied Irish graffiti while she waited: "Punk not ded." She had seen a party of punks the night before, so she didn't find that any great news—chains, leather jackets, scalps shaved save for a shock of green or purple hair down the middle of the skull. No one had prepared her for such a scene in Ireland. She was about to try the bell again, when a boy of twelve or so opened the vestibule door.

"It quot work," he said, apparently of the release buzzer. "What do you want, ma'am?"

She hadn't finished explaining herself to the youngster when a woman called from the landing above, "Who is it, Michael?"

Julie climbed the stairs and answered for herself on the way.

"You couldn't ring up," Mrs. O'Rourke explained for her, before she had time to do it, "us not being on the line." She was a little woman, perpetually bent forward, possibly because she was always on the run, having to be somewhere before she could get there. "It's the children," she explained. "The girls are getting to the age of exorbitance." She ran across the living room to close a door to the rest of the flat and then ran back to recommend a large upholstered chair. She snatched off the plastic cover and stuffed it into a magazine rack behind *The Illustrated News*. "You can't keep a thing in the house decent for them. And they don't care. It's not like when you and I were kids."

It shocked Julie to realize that this bent woman with her tinted hair and pale, eager eyes thought of her as a contemporary. Mrs. O'Rourke would be wiser by far in the ways of human nature than she was. Or more cunning. She could almost feel herself being played upon. The woman perched on the edge of the sofa and plucked at the apron she wore over heavy slacks and sweater. "If I'd known you were coming, I'd have prettied myself up."

126

"You know, even when I see your uncle's papers—if you let me see them—I won't be able to say whether or not they are valuable." She wanted no assumption of false promises.

The woman gave a quick little tilt to her head and flashed a smile. "Well, they'll be valuable to you, dear, won't they?" Oh, yes: wiser by far.

"As soon as Michael comes up, he'll put on the kettle for tea, and then we'll have a nice talk." She slipped off the couch and pattered, swift as a mouse, to the hall door and opened it. Michael was bringing up, step by step, the shopping cart with the laundry in it. "Leave it on the landing, Michael, and come meet the lady from New York who's here about your great-uncle's notebooks." And while she led the boy, who was taller than she, into the room by the hand, she explained, "Michael's named after his famous antecedent. Shake hands with Mrs. Hayes, Michael. Is it Mrs. or Miss? Or do you prefer Mzzz?"

"Mrs."

The busy eyes darted to and from the hand without a wedding band. The quick smile seemed to put a price on the contradictory information. "Michael, put on the kettle like a good boy. Do you think you could make us a cup of tea without scalding yourself?"

The hand he gave Julie was as soft as snow. He gave it and took it back silently, and as silently crossed the room and left them.

"He's so good, that one," his mother said. "I don't know what I'd do without him."

Julie thought of Kincaid and Donahue, whose mothers felt the same about them.

They went into the dining room for tea, a room of plain, hard chairs and a table with plastic mats over a lacy cloth. The curtains were snowy white, and a colored print of a Dutch windmill hung on the wall. The tea was strong and biting, and the soda bread Sally O'Rourke cut into chunks and served with jam was fresh and good. Michael took his cup and plate to the kitchen while his mother explained that her husband and her older son were at the football match. They went every Saturday. The girls, she said, were into rights and demonstrations and wouldn't be home till supper. Julie glanced at her watch. It was almost three.

Mrs. O'Rourke, watching her face as though she could read it, said, "It's your father you're trying to find, is it? What makes you think he's in Ireland, dear, if you don't mind my asking?"

"He was born here, so it's a starting place."

The woman pulled back. "There, now. I didn't mean to pry, but there's no mention of him after Michael himself came home from the States. He's in earlier, the one called Frank in Michael's notebooks, and the last mention, he was on his way to Australia. They were in the secondary school together, you know, both studying with the Franciscan Brothers."

"Where?"

"Right here in Dublin, the Adam and Eve parish."

Julie repeated the name, finding it strange for a religious institution. "Adam and Eve weren't saints, were they?"

The woman thought about it. "They were the first sinners. I suppose they could've turned around and been the first saints. Look at Mary Magdalene. Isn't it strange? I never thought about it." She bounced up and brushed the crumbs onto her plate. "I'll get the books for you now, and you can sit here while the light's good. There's nothing I could find in the first three that'd interest you, but I'll bring them all, and when you're done, you can tell me what you think they're worth and what I should do with them."

As though Julie had said nothing. Four notebooks came, their mottled cardboard covers ringed by a hundred teacups or bottles or glasses. Mrs. O'Rourke had been right: She found the first mention of her father in the last book. Desmond's handwriting was neat, but the pages were stained, and there was a smell that made her think of the hymnals in an old church. They'd have come up from a damp basement when she had sent the letter she addressed to Michael Desmond. She copied into her own notebook the complete entries that mentioned her father. The first was dated February 2, 1954:

Reception at the Waldorf for Andrew Kearney and
Lady Cecelia Graham-Kearney. Rumor has it he will
be assigned our perm. rep. if we make it into the

UN this round. Odds are we won't. Frozen pawns in the cold war games. I was bored sick with the black ties and skirted broomsticks when I chanced to see a fellow I recognized from Adam and Eve, Frank Mooney. Thomas Francis Mooney he signs himself, having the notion it may ingratiate him with the Americans. Named after Thomas Francis Meagher, an Irish refugee who wound up a general in the American Civil War. Not a Yank in a million ever heard of him or any other of the Young Ireland lot Mooney thinks so magnificent. He is writing a life of John Mitchel. Who's he? said I. He was exiled to Van Diemen's Land, escaped to the United States, and became a newspaper editor. Oh, said I, one of those. Mooney doesn't have much humor, but I was glad to see him all the same. I'd thought by now he might be a monk, not a roué. He is Kearney's secretary. . . .

Julie paused and thought about the last four words. So now, after all the years, she knew why her father was in New York.

I asked him if he knew shorthand and all that. No, says he, but I can dance the mambo. I take that to mean he's better connected with Lady K than with her husband. Or else he's pulling my leg. I took him round with me afterwards to the Snug, but he doesn't drink. I never trust an Irishman who doesn't drink.

Julie reread the parts she had noted. There would be other questions later, but for now she questioned in the margin: "A. K. and Lady G-K where?" She read on. There was good New York color in the journals, lovely sketches of diplomats and pompous attachés, and of actors just below star status, and the habitués of literary drinking places; a paragraph described a younger, wild John Walsh, the literary agent who had started Julie on this mission. She determined to recommend that Sally O'Rourke consult him on the disposition of the journals. A number of entries through into the summer concerned the Army-McCarthy hearings on television. The diarist noted having been instructed by Dublin that he need not report on Washington. "In other words I don't have the right slant on Joe McCarthy. I like that dry little lawyer from Boston, who a great lot of Irish Americans think is a traitor to his race." Then:

> Mooney got into a fight with one of them. We'd gone over to Chelsea, to a dockside bar, and Frank took a swing at this baboon who said he was a disgrace to Ireland. The fellow hit him back so fast it lifted him off his feet. His nose turned into a bloody spout. It was a shame we couldn't save the runoff for a blood bank. I'm beginning to rue the day I got him off the wagon. He's a lovely drinker but a terrible drunk.

Julie felt better about her father than she had after the first mention of him, even though she had thought her own dislike of alcohol might be part of her inheritance. There was more warmth to him this way, more honor. Hit it straight, Julie: It makes him seem more of a man.

> 19 June 1954
>
> Politics seem to have turned against Kearney. There's a puritanical lot in ascendancy and of course they don't like it that Lady Graham-K has not renounced her title. It has never bothered me. Not that anyone sought my opinion, but I've always thought her a lady, with a large L or a small one. In any case, the Kearneys are going home and it will be a dull mission without them. Frank is at sixes and sevens. They'll pay his fare back and try to find him a place in the glass works. But he'd rather stay a while here. I told him if he wants, he can bunk in with me and get something on paper he can show John Walsh.

Julie questioned in the margin: glass works?

23 June 1954

We had a night last night. Mooney has found a new
lot of poets and petticoats. This is too exotic a bunch
for me. They hang around a shop called Books of All
Nations. There's a queen bee, knocking them off one
by one, if I remember my nature studies. She is a
stunning-looking woman and you wonder she could
not do better than clerking in a bookstore. I'm sure
she does. I'd say the name Richards is Anglo-Irish,
and I'm reminded how a certain kind of head-high
and bedamned-to-the-world Englishwoman seems to
take hold of an Irish youth. I used to think it was
the delusion of power on the part of the Irishman.
Now I'm thinking it's an abdication of it.

Julie liked the description of her mother. She had modeled her own
carriage after her mother's. People thought it came from her attending
Miss Page's School, but it hadn't.

Several pages of the journal were devoted to upheavals in the
Irish diplomatic corps. "The politics of pygmies." Desmond also began
to take stock of his own life. He wondered if he shouldn't go home
and settle down. "It's not fair to keep her waiting any longer, and
I'm not laying by a penny much less a pound."

1 July 1954

Bedamned to him if he isn't in love and going to
marry the woman. She's years older than him, and
if I'm not mistaken, she's marrying him out of spite.
Or do I wrong her? Is it all a bold show to hide a
fearful heart? She's taking instruction, and that surely
is a kind of submission. God Almighty, what do I
know of women anyway? What does any Irishman?
I've agreed to stand up for Frank in the rectory at
Saint Giles's. Then I wash my hands of the lot. I'm
no more than three or four years older than him, but

he seems like a child. How is he going to support himself? To say nothing of her. Ah, but he won't. She won't let him. She'll give and give and give, and that's not good for a man.

21 July
The deed was quickly done at five o'clock yesterday afternoon. We cabbed down to Rory's Restaurant in the Village afterwards, where we ate shrimp and roast beef and drank Bushmill and the good dark stout of Guinness. When the bride and groom departed, the maid of honor let down her honor and folded me into her large Italian bosom. Though it hurts me to say it, I don't know her like in Ireland. Her name is Maggie Fiore and she may cause me further dalliance in America.

Quite a lot about Maggie, but not another mention of Julie's father until:

10 September
It seems Frank has run away from home, though where to and with what, God knows. It was Mrs. Mooney herself who rang me up to see if he was here by any chance. By no chance. Maggie, for so garrulous a woman, keeps close counsel. She seems not to have said a word to Kate about us. And I suppose it's just as strange that though I've seen Frank a couple of times, I've said nothing of it to him. It would have been like saying to him—Look what I got for nothing when you had to pay the price of your freedom.

Julie wrote in the margin for her own satisfaction: "Oh, men!" Morgan Reynolds had also put a high value on freedom.

18 September
A fortnight ago I promised Father Daly I'd stop seeing Maggie, but instead I've stopped seeing Father Daly.

132

A couple of nights ago she told me what's been going on up on 91st Street. In the first place, Kate's boss came home after a three-month leave to consolidate a chain of bookstores on the West Coast. The first thing he did, after a wee visit to his wife, was go round to see Kate. He and Frank tried to throw one another out. He refused to believe Kate had married in his absence, and when she offered proof, he fired her. He has since hired her back, according to Maggie. But Mooney is gone, the poor broken-hearted go-been.

Julie noted in the margin: "The untold Reynolds story."

13 November 1954

A night on the town after theatre with John Walsh. He remains the best company I've ever kept. He has heard from Mooney. In Australia and still writing his life of John Mitchel. But he sent him a poem John thought was good and sent off to *The New Yorker*. If they take it, John is to send the cheque to Katherine *Richards*. Peculiar. Could they have had the marriage annulled? I asked Father Daly, and he said it would take years and that Maggie and I would be called as witnesses. Well, they'll have to call me long distance, for I'm going home at Christmas. Maggie is bitter and I don't blame her. It was cowardly of me to tell her I'd committed myself to a girl at home. I'll be a long time forgetting what she said, "There's no shit like an Irish shit." She's right.

Desmond's journal ended the nineteenth of December without further reference to Mooney, Kate, or Maggie.

Julie returned by the way she had come. There was no outdoor life at all, it seemed, on the somber streets of the O'Rourke neighborhood, only the occasional streaking car that appeared without warning from

133

a direction she would not have expected. The lamp lights, high and graceful, had come on along the iron fence of Saint Stephen's Green. A blue mist hung low in the sky, deepening the twilight. Across the street another set of lights came on—of the high-density variety so familiar to her from home. They shone a misty glare on the bus queues of silent people. A damp chill added to her feeling of sadness. Grafton Street had been more of what she expected of Dublin, not this. And Mrs. O'Rourke and her quiet son stayed in her mind. She'd like to have seen the girls come noisily home from their demonstrations and to have heard male voices rehashing the football game. But none of them had come when it was time for her to go. She thought now of Sally O'Rourke's lament about the two maiden aunts who died within a year of each other, leaving only her mother and her to take care of Uncle Michael when he fell on hard times and was ill. "He should have written a book himself, don't you think, having a friend in the business over there?" Then a desperate afterthought: "Do you think *you* could make a book out of what's there?" Julie suggested that someday one of Mrs. O'Rourke's children might want to do it. "Ah, dear, they can hardly scratch their own names. It's the telly being on from morning till night. I'm as much to blame as they are, but I do wonder, times, what we'd do if we couldn't afford the telly. Would the kids be better off?" At the door she had raised herself as tall as she could, and Julie had stooped down to accept the brush of dry lips against her cheek.

And at that instant she had thought of Missy Glass, who also carried on her back the invisible burden of her life.

25

...

Within hours of her arrival she had made Trinity College her special place in Dublin. Now, instead of returning to the hotel to freshen up before going on to meet the *New York Daily* special correspondent—whom Jeff would still call a stringer—she turned in at the Trinity gates and passed through the busy portico into Parliament Square. Stone buildings that looked older than they were rose on all sides, enclosing the long green with its campanile and its cobbled walkways that glistened in the misty half-light. Looking up at the "rubrics," the oldest student quarters, she asked herself if her father might have stayed there. It was all wrong to try to force a fantasy: He sounded much too Catholic for Trinity, and to have gone to the Franciscans didn't seem the right preparation. As though she knew anything about the Franciscans except for their bare feet and their founding saint. Why the Franciscans? Why Australia? The biography he thought he was going to write? Or did he happen to get a job on a boat that was going there? In the portico she read the notices on a variety of bulletin boards concerning student activities. On the call board of the Trinity Players she read:

Ladies of Players

Your opportunity for fame and fortune is at hand. The Abbey Theatre is looking for well-brought-up young ladies to play French gentlewomen in a Parisian academy in *Hotel Paradiso* by Feydeau around Christmastime. The parts are small, but there is money.

She copied it into her notebook to send to Tim, but halfway through she doubted he would find it as amusing as she had: She was traveling at a different tempo. She abandoned the college grounds and searched out a pub called the Bower on Pearse Street.

The Bower was jammed, men four and five deep at the bar, with an occasional woman, and all of them, it seemed to Julie, talking at once. If the language wasn't foreign, neither was the inflection familiar. She tried to get through to the bar, but one man simply could not get out of her way. "Could I order you something, love? You're never going to make it unless you can climb over me."

"I'm sorry," Julie said. "I'm supposed to meet a man here by the name of Roy Irwin. . . ."

"Oh, he is a man for certain." Her informant called out: "Irwin, are you in the house?"

"I am," came the voice from within the crowd.

"Bad luck to you. I was hoping to be your deputy."

The crowd pressed in on itself to make way for a large, dark-bearded young man who took her by the arm. "Julie Hayes, is it? I'm glad to make your acquaintance. What will you have? A gin and tonic?"

"God forbid," she said, more Irish-sounding than she intended. "Lager, please." But then to show off: "A half-pint."

The order went up, and Irwin introduced her to the man who had hailed him. "She's a columnist with my New York newspaper, the *Daily*."

Julie thought, not for the first time since her arrival, of Seamus McNally, who pronounced the word *columnist* the same way.

When her drink came, Irwin steered her to a table given over to them by a young couple. Cheerfully. "I get the occasional pass to give out to theater or the races or a football match," he explained. "It's better than legal tender.

136

"If you're going to theater while you're here, by the way, show your press card at the box office and mention your column. They all think Broadway is only a wing-dip away. You'll ask the manager to have a drink with you during the interval and he'll invite you to supper instead—at the Baily or someplace you couldn't afford. Or I couldn't. Would you believe I'm special correspondent to six newspapers? And still can't make a living? Four on the Continent and two in the States, but none in bally Britain. And that's where, if I had a byline, I could get on in my profession." He downed half his dark brew and wiped his mouth with the back of his hand. "They're afraid I'm IRA. That's what my wife says, and she may be right."

Julie almost said, And are you? but thought better of it.

"Drink up and tell me what I can do for you. Ah—the wife said to ask you, would you like to go disco dancing with me and her tonight? You'd have your choice of a number of decent lads when we get there, whereas if I fixed you up beforehand, we'd bog down in formalities and privileges."

"I'm willing to play it by ear," she said. "Thank you."

Irwin hesitated and then asked, "Are you here on assignment or on your own?"

Something in the way he said it put her on guard. And he wasn't as young as she had first supposed. The eyes were black and keen, but there were tiny lines around them, and the hair and beard were flecked with gray. He'd resent an assignment, she decided, fearing encroachment on his preserve. "On my own." She told him of her search for Thomas Francis Mooney and of the Desmond diary she had just seen. She consulted her notebook. "It was someone named Andrew Kearney who brought my father to New York. He was connected with the Irish observers at the UN. This was in 1954."

"Before my time. But the name's familiar," Irwin said, immediately ready to help. "I'll try and look it up for you." He made a note of the name.

"Lady Cecelia Graham-Kearney—with a hyphen," Julie said.

"Ah, now, you're in the upper register of society. A great horsewoman in her day. There's a classic race named after her. I'm going to guess she's in the west—if she's alive—Galway likely. I can look that up for you, too."

"If my father had come back to Ireland with them, they were going to find a place for him in the glass works. Is that any help?"

Irwin tapped his teeth with a thumbnail while thinking. Then: "I've got it! Kearney and Sons is an export firm, and their main line is Irish crystal."

"I should have started with the phone book," Julie said.

"So you could, but you're committed now to letting me work on it over the weekend. What you should do is go up the coast to Wicklow town, since that's where your da was born. It's a two-hour run through some of the sweetest country in Ireland. You'll go to Saint Patrick's on the hill, and it wouldn't harm to arrive in time for Mass and then have the priest put you onto the clerk of records. You know you won't be the first American to be tracing her forefathers back to their Irish christening."

"I do know that," Julie said.

"But it's not as though you were wanting a coat of arms going back to Brian Boru. The office of the Register General here in Dublin has records of births, deaths, and marriages for over a hundred years. But it's humaner going the route of the parish church. You'll get on to the family quicker that way." He sat back and looked at her and almost smiled. He was not a great smiler. "It's a romantic sort of mission. Are you going to write a book about it? Americans are always writing books, it seems to me."

"I suppose it depends on how it ends."

"If you knew that, don't you wonder—would you start it at all?"

She had met, Julie thought, her first melancholic Irishman.

She had left word at the desk that she expected to be called for, but she went downstairs a few minutes early, loitering to look at the prints on the second landing. They were illustrations from Carleton's *Irish Folklore*. The crystal chandeliers were lighted and augmented by wall sconces converted from gaslight long ago. The walls were a deep crimson, the arches and balustrades white. Georgian bits had been retained.

138

When she turned in her key, the clerk said, "Ah, Mrs. Hayes, the gentleman is waiting. . . ." But there was no gentleman to be seen. "He may have gone down to the bar. I'll get the porter to run down. . . ."

"Don't bother," Julie said. "He won't be long." She assumed Irwin's wife would be waiting in a car outside. "A dark-haired man with a bushy beard?" she asked, an afterthought.

"Ah, no. A slight man, rather pale. I told him you'd be down soon, expecting him at nine. He said he'd wait there in the lounge."

"My friends may have arranged for him to meet us here," Julie said.

But when the Irwins arrived, Roy coming in for Julie, his wife staying in the car, the man had not returned to the hotel lobby, nor did the newspaperman recognize the clerk's description: "A gray-faced man of forty or so . . . slight build, thin brownish hair . . ."

Julie asked the clerk to get whatever information he could if the man returned. Outdoors, Irwin opened the front door of the car and asked his wife if she had told anyone about Julie.

"And who would I tell?"

Irwin introduced the two women. Julie climbed into the backseat. "Let's forget him," she said and sat forward. "It's great of you to take me along tonight, Mrs. Irwin."

"You must call me Eileen. I hope the crowd is not too rough for you. You never know who's following who these days. I myself don't like the punks and their music, and they turn up everywhere."

"We're going out to have a good time, for the love of God," her husband said.

"I intend to, and you will too, Julie. The Burnigans are a wonderful rock group."

When they reached the disco and Julie saw the posters, she realized the "Burnigans" clearly were the Born Agains.

The Fiddle was a converted warehouse with more light than any pub in Dublin. It kept the neckers from going too far, though there were some, Julie noted, going quite a ways. There were more bars also, and more noise, and a startling parade of younger men stationed along the wall, hanging close to the shelf provided for their drinks. They stared at all arrivals. They looked terribly young, as though they were still growing out of their clothes. Now and then they exploded into laughter and made rude comments on the new girls as they came in.

Julie sank into a cushioned wall seat and studied Eileen Irwin while the Born Agains returned from an intermission—an "interval," in local parlance. Eileen was plump and pretty, and several times a mother despite her youth. She would fill her eyes with concern every time she was spoken to. Whenever Julie said anything to her, she seemed to listen with her whole being. When Roy went to the bar to get their drinks, someone from the stag line came and asked Eileen to dance. She looked tearful at having to turn him down. "I'm that sorry but I'm promised," she said, as though he'd asked her to marry him. Julie felt like a chaperone—or a widow. A grass widow, which she was: She tried to remember where she'd heard the expression. Mrs. Ryan probably.

The walls were painted with clowns and aerialists and crudely drawn circus animals. Over the stage angelic mobiles floated as they might over a Christmas tableau, and the Born Agains themselves wore flowing sleeves and floor-length robes, which kept them in perpetual motion when the beat took over. Irwin danced with his wife. Julie was on her own. Women on the dance floor outnumbered the men, especially among the very young; girls were stomping and shaking, bobbing their heads at one another and not letting on if they gave a damn that no boy seemed to want them. The young men hung near the wall. Julie decided on a bold move. After all, she was a Yank, and a New York Yank at that. She marched over to the stag line and chose a partner at random, except that she avoided pimples. The rest of the line collapsed in noisy mirth while a flushed and wet-palmed youth stalked solemnly into the dance with her. Once on the floor he went loose-limbed and wildly rhythmic. They didn't touch again for ten minutes.

When the music stopped, Julie threw back her head and laughed. She brushed the sweat from her forehead. Her partner offered his breast-pocket handkerchief. "I'm Julie," she said.

"I'm Sean."

They shook hands, and Sean carefully refolded the handkerchief when she returned it to him and put it back in his pocket. For his own use he had a khaki-colored rag that had been freshly laundered.

"All right," she said and started back to where the Irwins were bringing stools for another couple. The place was getting more and more crowded. Sean fell in step with her. "You're American, aren't you?"

"New York."

"I've been there. I have an aunt in Poughkeepsie. Do you know where that is?"

"Sort of." She motioned with her thumb over her shoulder. "It's up thataway."

"On the Hudson River."

She nodded.

"Will you dance with me again?"

"Of course. But you'll have to ask me this time."

"They'll all ask you now, sure."

If not all, most of them did. She could not remember when she had last danced that much. "You're doing swell!" Her partners assured her: their notion of pure Americanese. Irwin, his wife locked in conversation with a friend from her convent-school days, asked Julie to dance.

As soon as they stepped onto the floor, the Born Agains shifted from rock to a waltz and toned down the amplifiers.

"I don't believe it," Julie said.

"They're a versatile lot." He danced like Jeff, Julie thought. Oh, Christ.

In the new quiet, Irwin said, "If it turns out that Lady Graham-Kearney is in the west, and I think she is, I'll be going down Sligo way on Wednesday to cover a funeral. You could go along and chip in on the petrol. I wouldn't mind even staying over if you needed more time. I've a parcel of friends in the west."

Richard Garvy's grandmother lived in Sligo, Julie remembered, and he had said on that day long weeks ago that she ought to visit her when she got to Ireland. Said half in jest, to be sure, but Garvy was about to do a play on Broadway, and one written by an Irishman. . . "Roy, do you know the playwright Seamus McNally?"

"Well, yes." Nothing more, although she waited.

"Let me see what happens in Wicklow," Julie said of his offer. "That comes first." Where her father was born.

Irwin was no longer listening to her. "I'm going to steer us round by the wall just now. There's a queer-looking older fella just joined that lot. See if you recognize him."

She saw a stranger, someone she was sure she had not seen before. His clothes looked loose on him; his jaw was square, his nose had a bump at the bridge, his coloring was gray. When he turned his back as they approached, she had to assume he was the man who had inquired after her at the hotel. "I don't think I've seen him before, Roy."

"I think I have, but I'll be damned if I know where."

As they moved away, the gray man turned to watch them again. "Shall we pack it in?" Irwin asked.

As soon as they left the floor, the band switched back to rock. Julie went on to the ladies' room. When she came out, Sean was waiting for her a polite distance from the door. The gray man was not in sight. Julie asked Sean if he had noticed him.

"I think he cut out," Sean said. "Is he a friend or foe? He asked my chum if he knew who the man with the black beard was, the one dancing with you. That's what made me think."

"And what did your chum tell him?"

"He asked around. Somebody said he worked for a newspaper—maybe from Belfast or Derry. From the north anyway."

Which was more than Julie knew of Irwin. She had noticed a difference in his accent from those with which she was becoming slightly more familiar. "How about the man who asked? Did any of you know him?"

"Wouldn't seem like. When he left, everybody gawked and shrugged—you know, 'Who's he?' "

It was after twelve when Julie got back to the hotel. A different clerk was on duty. No one had inquired after her to his knowledge.

She and Irwin had decided that the "gray man" had not gone to the bar. He'd gone outdoors and waited in a car and, after the Irwins picked her up, had followed them to the dance. There was still a question between them about its being the same man, and as soon as Julie told Irwin that the gray one had asked the boys about him, Irwin was sure it was he, not Julie, the man was interested in. "You're not just saying that, Roy?" She'd been much relieved. "You'd better believe I'm not. I'm no bleeding knight in armor."

The hotel was quiet, and the night clerk took her upstairs in the elevator, leaving the lobby unattended. Security was not a strong point with the Greer Hotel. Julie asked him to wait until she had opened her room door. The man blocked the elevator gate and went to her door with her. "You Americans are a careful sort these days. I don't wonder with what's going on in the world, but I wouldn't like to live that way myself, being fearful all the time."

"It's a bad habit," Julie said.

26

...

Julie was the only passenger to leave the bus at the first Wicklow stop. A woman boarded there, first handing up a basket with the yellow claw of a dead chicken poking out from under the lid. "It's a soft morning, by the grace of God," she said, stepping up as Julie stepped down.

The bus driver revved his motor and took off into the town. Julie waited until the lone car on the road behind him passed and then crossed over and lingered briefly in the arcade over the entrance to the Grand Hotel. She could see no sign of guests within the hotel or, for that matter, of service personnel. The softness of the day was owing to a fine mist and perhaps to the Sunday stillness everywhere except at the corner pub. She could hear the rumble of voices when she passed, but the heavy three-quarter curtains cut off any interior view she might have had. Farm trucks were among the few cars in the courtyard behind the pub, and she caught a smell familiar to her only from the bridle path in Central Park. A road sign in both English and Gaelic told her she had a half-mile walk up the hill to Saint Patrick's church. The pub voices fell away as she started up the hill, and the quiet that then prevailed seemed to isolate her. Her sleep had been troubled, and the noise of the disco pounded in her head. She had resolved long before dawn not to watch for the Gray Man, but she found herself watching for him all the same.

At an abrupt turn in the road she saw the towering neo-Gothic church high on the hill and stark against a changing sky. The air cleared as if by magic, and by the time she reached the church gates, there was not a trace of moisture on the flagstone walk. The view from the steps when she looked back was a vast panorama of tawny hills and green wooded slopes dotted with white cottages and sheep, and with silver splashes of lakes and forking rivers; at the land's edge a far-stretching gold crescent of sand bordered the dark waters of the Irish Sea. The clouds were breaking apart and casting great shadows. Within the church a thin chorus of voices tried to hold the melody of an old hymn against the tumult of the pipe organ. She had made it before the end of noon Mass.

Miss Redmond, an ample woman of fifty or thereabouts, the parish bookkeeper as well as the clerk of records, finished her accounting of the Sunday collections and took Julie into an office in the parish house. With remarkable good cheer, considering the hour and the smell of roast beef permeating the whole rectory, she got out the registry of baptisms that included the year 1934. She told Julie while paging through it of all the people who consulted her for information on this one and that one, most of them long dead and forgotten. Julie observed among the popes and prelates on the office walls an autographed picture of President John F. Kennedy.

"Ah, now here he is," the woman said, "Thomas Francis Mooney. Born October ten, christened October twenty . . ." Her voice faded out as she read ahead. Then she explained, "I was trying to remember, that's all." She read aloud the names of parents and sponsors, the officiating cleric, and the certifying officer, pausing to let Julie write them down. The mother's maiden name was Crowley. Something in the bare-bones record had given Miss Redmond pause, Julie thought. It almost had to be a name.

She asked outright: "Do you know any of these people, Miss Redmond?"

"There's a Crowley in the town, and that's it. He lives with his daughter-in-law and her child. The house is on Strand Street near the quay. You'll know it by its green shutters and a geranium in the window. There's been a lot of dying in the family, but I'm sure you'll be welcome by them that's left." She flashed Julie a smile that seemed to belie the welcome she promised on behalf of the Crowleys.

Daughter-in-law and child, Julie thought, going down the hill into the town. Another fatherless child like herself?

The old man sat down carefully beside her, his hands on his knees. She paid attention to the hands, thinking she might be able to judge his age by them or to learn whether he worked with them or with his head. They were clean and scant of hair, the backs speckled with brown; the fingers, while not stubby, were almost square at the tips. The nails fascinated her; they seemed—the whole hands seemed —familiar, and suddenly she knew why. They were aging replicas of her own. The squared fingertips, the proportion of the nails to the length of the fingers, their shapes at the crest of cuticle, even the difference in the size of their little fingernails, that of the left hand smaller, could be attributed, she felt sure, to a common lineage.

"Look," Julie said and put out her hands alongside his. She was not wearing polish; she rarely did.

He leaned forward to see better and caught on at once, looking from her hands to his and back to her own. He touched the little finger of her left hand, then looked at his and said in amazement, "What do you know about that?" To the chubby woman on her knees in front of them trying to quicken the turf fire, he said, "Emily, get up and look at this miracle of reproduction." He smiled at Julie, a smile that sent the lines scurrying between his bright gray eyes and the corners of his mouth. "We must be kin truly, wouldn't you say?"

She agreed, aware of her heartbeat and feeling ridiculously and unexpectedly happy.

"I said to myself when she opened the door to you," he went on, " 'There stands a woman I'd love to see come into the house.' "

Emily looked around at him as though surprised. Or hurt. A burst of flame caught at the turf. She turned back and fanned it vigorously. Whereupon it vanished.

"Will you let the fire be? It'll come sooner without your ministrations."

He had been very handsome once, Julie thought; he was handsome still, a fine, long nose that had kept its shape and a large, sensual mouth. A wisp of his thin gray hair hung rakishly over his forehead.

Emily's bones cracked as she got to her feet. She was less agile than her father-in-law. "What is it you're looking at?"

"Our hands, our hands," the old man said. He and Julie, side by side, held them out before her.

She looked puzzled. "What about them?"

"They're out of the same cast. Have you no eyes in your head?"

Emily looked at her own plump hands, turning them over and back. They were quite different from theirs and showed the stains of cooking and scrub work. She hid them away under her apron and said, "I'd best put on the water for tea." She was round of face as well as body, her blue eyes more wondering than intelligent—a sweet, placid face that Julie would not have thought Irish at all. Flemish, perhaps, to be painted by a van Eyck—resignation with just the trace of puzzlement at how she had become pregnant without ever having felt the presence in her of the Holy Ghost. Julie would have liked to stretch out her hand to her, but she feared the familiarity might put the woman off.

"Now who was your mother?" the old man asked Julie. "An American, of course."

"Her name was Katherine Richards."

"And Hayes: Where does that come in?"

"My married name."

His eyes darted to her bare ring finger.

"We are separated."

He made a sound that suggested he had thought as much. "My son went off and left this one to me, an act of generosity I don't think was in his calculations. We always called your father Frank, by the way. There was another Tom in the family then, my oldest son. Frank was back, you know, years ago. But only the once to my knowledge."

"Do you know where he is now?"

The old man shook his head. "It was a while before his mother died that he was here. . . ." He looked to where his daughter-in-law

147

was now building up the fire of coals in the kitchen range. "Emily, come and sit with us. We can wait our tea. You'll cook us a meal later, love." He explained to Julie, "She'll be the one to remember him. She was greatly taken."

"No, I wasn't," Emily protested. She filled the kettle from the single tap in the sink and put it on the stove and then brought a chair from the side of the table. Julie, moving to make room for her, caught sight of a child sitting at the top of the stairs that rose steeply opposite the cottage door. Her mother saw her too. "Go back to your lessons, Mary, if you want Papa-John to go over them."

"Let her come down and meet Julie."

"She won't go back up if you let her down, and she'll make a nuisance of herself, butting in." But then to the child, who was bound to have heard what went before, "Papa-John says you can come down."

But the child chose to stay upstairs. She was not in sight when Julie glanced that way again. There were two rooms downstairs, a small bedroom with a commode off it on the far side of the staircase, and one room upstairs, she presumed, with a very low ceiling. The light was good; Emily had gone from lamp to lamp turning them on when Julie came into the house.

"Isn't she contrary?" her mother said of the child.

"As a cow's hind leg. Let her be," the old man said. "It was before the mill closed that Frank was here, and that was eleven years next spring. I remember I stopped by my sister Mary's house—the child's named after her—I'd come home those days covered with flour like a wafting ghost, and the woman with him burst out laughing at me. Do you remember her name, Emily?"

Emily shook her head. "Only her face."

"She was Irish. I know that. Or was she a Brit? A fine-looking woman. They were going to marry, I think. Or were they already married? They were, sure, for Mary came over here and stayed with us, leaving them her bed and the key to the cottage. She'd let out the other rooms after all her men were gone, you see."

Julie learned that she had two uncles, one of whom was in

148

Australia and one who'd been killed on duty with the Irish Army on a United Nations mission. "My father went to Australia when he left New York," she said.

"I heard about that, but nothing I remember about you or your mother. Isn't that strange?"

"Not so strange. It was all a mistake. The marriage was annulled."

The old man thought about that for a moment. He reached over and laid his hand on hers. "You can't annul blood. The Crowley line is as strong in you as it is in me. We're workers and have the hands for it. The Mooneys lived by the sea, fisherman and sailors, all of them dreamers. And the military went a long way back with them. There were Mooneys in Napoleon's army, and some that came home with the French to be hanged like dogs in 1798."

"Wild Geese," Julie said. "My father wrote a poem about them."

"He was a great reader as a boy, I remember—as we are ourselves in this house." An exchange of glances between him and Emily puzzled Julie. It was both shy and intimate, and yet it did not exclude her. "We read a book a week from the lending library, taking turns aloud. Little Mary says it's better than the telly, but that's because she's our principal performer. Would you like a walk on the ramparts where Frank played as a lad? I'll give you the true history. The kids never got it straight, pretending to fight off an English invasion. The Brits were already there, mounting a vigil for the French in three directions and for the Irish at their backs."

Frank hadn't gotten it straight in the poem either, Julie thought, but she didn't say so.

They walked along the strand and then climbed up to the castle ruins, where three ancient cannon still pointed out to sea. The old man was nimble and sometimes took her hand more to have it in his than to help her over the rough terrain. He made up family history when he wasn't able to remember it, she thought. It didn't matter: She had grown up on lies, but with enough of the truth to have brought her to where she was now.

They stopped at a pub on Market Street near the 1798 memorial, where he introduced her as Frank Mooney's daughter. It sounded strange to her and perhaps to the old man's familiars also, for it set them sorting among the Mooneys they could remember; the one firm in their minds was the soldier killed in Palestine. And they were shy of her, the only woman in the lounge. They smelled of the farm and stayed close to the bar except when the old man called one or another of them to come over and meet his grandniece. They shuffled forward when invited and scuttled back as soon as possible.

The child, Mary, came to tell them dinner was ready, as Julie supposed she often did with her grandfather. The men scraped and nodded as the threesome was leaving. They were in awe of the old man, and they were respectful; and every one of them turned to watch their departure, nodding solemnly.

Mary was at the gawky stage, growing too fast at twelve to know what was happening to her. She resembled her grandfather more than she did her mother. In fact, Julie realized, the girl could be taken for *her* child, and she was old enough to be her mother. Mary was not shy in the way Emily was; she had spent the afternoon accumulating questions about New York.

"I've promised she'll get to the States while I'm alive," the old man said.

"Or I'll never get there, see," said Mary.

Julie did not see, but she didn't say so.

"Don't you have a grandfather?" the girl asked.

"I must have had two of them, but I can only just remember the one in Chicago."

"They're better than fathers, aren't they?"

"Tut, tut, tut," the old man said.

"Some grandfathers are better than some fathers, how's that?" Julie said.

"It will do," he said.

As soon as they entered the cottage, the old man went through the bedroom to the commode. Julie and Mary waited at the bottom of the stairs. The girl's mother was dishing up at the far end of the room. The smell of cabbage prevailed.

"Mother doesn't read with us," Mary confided in a whisper. It

150

seemed to be something she'd wanted to say—as though to set the record straight.

"Well," Julie said, a sound without meaning.

The meat was tough and there wasn't much flavor to it, and the cabbage was overcooked, something certainly the cook could not be blamed for. But everybody at the table, including Julie, complimented Emily. While she served the sweet, the old man asked Mary if she had finished her lessons.

"Almost."

"Now, Mary," her mother said, "you don't want to grow up like me, do you?"

It was a rhetorical and oft-repeated question, Julie realized, the truth in it so obvious to the listeners it had all but lost its meaning. She met the old man's eyes where he had been watching her from the instant the woman started to speak. He made a face, wry and a little sad.

Emily said, "You're too easy with her, Papa-John."

"I am what I am," he said.

Mary said, "Papa-John, may I show Julie my picture?"

"Your picture?"

She got up and whispered in his ear.

"Ah, that one."

When Mary brought the framed picture down from her attic room, he explained, "Her Aunt Mary—her great-aunt, that is, your grandmother, Julie—when she was putting her house in order—she knew she was dying—she gave away her little treasures to those she thought might want them."

Mary put the oil painting of a clown on the table, leaning it against the teapot so that Julie could see it best. "I call him Pansy," the girl said. "There was a pansy in our garden once that looked just like him."

Julie could imagine it. Perhaps the artist did too. She did not know whether or not she liked the painting, but she leaned forward and looked at the name in the corner. The painter had liked it well enough to sign her name. "Edna O'Shea," she read aloud.

"That was her name," Emily said, "Edna. Frank called her Edna."

27

...

It was a lot to hope that Edna O'Shea was a well-known painter whose works hung in the National Gallery of Ireland. But that was Julie's fantasy, and she intended to cherish it until she learned otherwise. She asked Roy Irwin when she called him Monday morning if he had ever heard of Edna O'Shea.

"Seems like. Is she a folk singer or musician?"

Julie told him of her Wicklow experience.

"I'm not up on the art scene," he said, "So, if it were me, now, I'd first go to the Registrar General, where facts are facts. If they were married in this country, it'll be registered, and it won't hurt while you're there to search the names of the dead."

"Yeah," she said.

"It's only sensible, wouldn't you say? Now here's a bit more for you: I got on to a buddy at Iveagh House—that's the Foreign Office. Kearney is dead, but my friend is ninety-nine percent sure Lady Graham-Kearney is alive and compos mentis. She'd be living at Graham Hall, which is near Ballina in County Mayo."

"How far is that from Sligo?"

"Closer than Galway, it is."

"Can you get me a phone number?"

"I can try. Ring me up again midafternoon."

* * *

152

She spent the rest of the morning among the Customs House records and left the building no better informed than she had gone in. The birth of Thomas Francis Mooney was on record, but nothing more about him. Nor could she find any record of Edna O'Shea. They would not seem to have been married in Ireland. Nor had either of them died there. It was as a kind of thank-you to the clerk who had so patiently assisted her that she lingered afterward to tour the historic building on the River Liffey. The allegory of its principal decorated facade seemed more ironic than inspired, Hibernia and Britannia holding peace and plenty in their hands.

In the National Gallery that afternoon—in the heart of Georgian Dublin—she learned that Edna O'Shea (1930–) was a British landscape artist represented in several private collections, none of which was in Ireland. So much for Great-uncle Crowley's belief that Frank Mooney had married an Irishwoman. O'Shea had most recently exhibited at the Duval Gallery in London four years before. Still, Julie thought, her name was O'Shea, which didn't sound particularly British. She was both pleased and let down, but mostly pleased. Wherever O'Shea might be now, she was alive when the *Art Directory* was published a year before. She thanked the gallery assistant who had helped her.

"A landscape artist," the young woman mused. "She might well have painted in Ireland, and you must consider there are no taxes required of artists who live here."

"Would the Duval Gallery in London give me her last address, do you think?" Julie asked.

"It's worth ringing them up, surely," the woman said.

Julie went down the magnificent circular stairway, the walls around which were hung with portraits of Ireland's great. She was turning from the painting of a young William Butler Yeats by his father when she saw the Gray Man on the floor below her. He disappeared immediately beneath the stairs. The clatter of her heels reverberated, overlapping clops, as she ran down the marble steps wanting to overtake and confront him. There would never be a better place to do it. But though she looked in all directions and persuaded a guard to look in the men's room for him, it was in vain. He had simply vanished.

She arrived back at her hotel to learn that her New York office had been trying to reach her. Operator Seventeen.

When the call came through, Tim's voice was as clear as from across the room. "How are you doing, sweetheart?"

"What's happened?"

"Hey! You're not supposed to be uptight in Ireland. That's supposed to be the most relaxed country in the Western world."

"Okay. I'm relaxed. Tell me."

"I got a call for you from Richard Garvy's secretary. The Stadlemier group put up the money. They'll go into rehearsal after Christmas. When I told her you were in Ireland, she called back with a message from Garvy: You're to go and see his grandmother. Her name is Norah Barton Garvy. She lives in Sligo, and he'll telephone her to expect you. Let me give you the address and phone number. . . ."

"Is that all, Tim?"

"What did you expect?"

"No word on Kincaid and Donahue?"

"Not yet. Their lawyer's asked for police protection for their families."

"Oh, boy," Julie said.

"The *Post* started a series today on crimes of vengeance. It mentions Kincaid and Donahue as possible victims."

"Any suggestion of who they're victims of?"

"You mean Romano? Are you kidding? With his lawyers?"

"I'm glad I'm here," Julie said. Then she thought of the Gray Man.

"How's it going?" Tim asked.

"I'm getting some good leads."

"I've got a great title for you—'Digging Up Father.' "

"Thanks. I'll be in touch soon. . . ."

"Hey, hold on. Someone tried to wheedle your Dublin address out of me on Friday. What I did, I put him onto Roy Irwin. Have you been in touch with him yet?"

"Very much so. Who was looking for me, Tim?"

"No name. What he did say, a Father Doyle had referred him."

Father Doyle? The priest didn't know she was in Dublin. He'd suggested she might start her search in Ireland, but he didn't know that she was going to do it. "Will you do me a favor? Telephone Father Doyle at Saint Malachy's Church and ask him what it's all about. I'll call you in a couple of days from wherever I am."

It was midafternoon before she reached Roy Irwin. No one had contacted him about her Dublin address, or about her at all. She told him she had seen the Gray Man at the National Gallery. "It's as though he deliberately shows himself and then disappears. I wish I knew what it means."

"I can tell you where I think I've seen him: I think he was in the Gardai, and it might have been Special Branch. I see him in my mind's eye when there were VIPs around. From the looks of him now, he might have been invalided out of service. And what he could have done was go into the security business on his own. How does that strike you?"

"Very imaginative." She didn't need that kind of guesswork.

"Think about it," Irwin said. "Now here's the number of Graham Hall. See if you can go up with me tomorrow."

"Tomorrow's only Tuesday."

"It would be better for me if we could make the Ballina stop on the way to Sligo."

On the phone to Graham Hall she identified herself as the daughter of Thomas Francis Mooney. She was invited to lunch with Lady Graham the next day.

28

...

The cool blue mist had not yet lifted when they went out from Dublin in the morning. The traffic was light once out of the town, and they were soon traveling at a good speed through farm and cattle country where at every crossroads the milk cans were waiting for a pickup. Julie observed the road signs: No Overtaking . . . Single Carriageway . . . Lay-by. A great black circular spot on a white background marked the site of a fatal accident. With Irish perversity, Roy Irwin speeded up to pass the marker, the wheels squealing on the curve. They stopped for coffee at Cloondara and to see the River Shannon where it joined the Royal Canal. Irwin pronounced the name for her in Gaelic and told her its meaning, Meadow of Two Ring-forts.

Trying to pronounce some of the place names herself, Julie was struck with a curious thought: "Is Gaelic computerized?"

"Now that's a good question. There's a bank of Gaelic words . . . sure, anything that's on the typewriter is on the computer, but you had me for a minute there. It's a fierce language, isn't it? And you know, it's spoken still in some of the islands and parts of Donegal."

Where a bucolic playwright lived.

"When I asked you if you knew Seamus McNally the other day, I was hoping you'd tell me something about him."

"Were you?"

"He has a new play that's going to be done in New York," Julie said, "*The Far, Far Hills of Home*."

"It's not a new play. It may be that to New York, but to Ireland it's an old, old play." He glanced at her and then looked back at the road. "It was put on over here last spring, and there were near riots. That sort of thing is out of the history books—Synge and O'Casey."

Julie was surprised. Didn't Richard Garvy know that? Perhaps it was rewritten, she thought, or they might even be counting on the Dublin notoriety to pique American interest. "Did you see it?"

"No, but I heard. It was withdrawn. For more work, they said. I've not heard of it since. It's about an Irish-American entrepreneur who comes back to his Donegal village and persuades the people to invest in a scheme to drill for oil. He's a con man with a great line of gab. But they do strike oil, and before the play's over, the people are destroyed by their own greed."

It would be a great part for Garvy, Julie thought. "What happens to the con man?"

"I'm not sure about that. But the nationalists took grave offense at the play. They've been onto McNally for some time, in any case. They'll turn out to shout him down wherever his plays are shown."

"Is he married?" Julie asked.

Again Irwin looked at her. "How would I know that? I've never met the man." Then, thoughtfully, as he stared at the road ahead: "Have you?"

"Yes."

"I thought as much."

It occurred to her that Roy Irwin might be expecting more of her on this journey than a share in the cost of the petrol.

They reached Ballina shortly after twelve noon without sight or mention of the Gray Man. The countryside had all changed—now a rocky terrain with small lakes, occasional roofless ruins, in some of which the sheep were in gentle habitation. A long range—the Ox Mountains—rose to the northeast and divided County Mayo from County Sligo. Swift clouds rode the winds that came off Sligo Bay. In the town they stopped at the Downhill Hotel and got directions to Graham Hall. Julie washed up and took the number of the hotel so that she could call Irwin there when she was ready to go on. She thought it fateful, when they drove through the busy market town, to find the chief monument here, as in Wicklow, was to the fallen in the 1798 Insurrection. General Humbert had landed eleven hundred Frenchmen and taken Ballina.

Roy Irwin whistled when they passed through the gates and up the long, high-hedged entrance to Graham Hall. When the Georgian mansion came into view, he stopped the car just to gaze at it. "There aren't many of them left. The Grahams must have been mighty good Brits in the old days."

"Aren't they Irish?" Julie asked.

"Anglo-Irish, whom some consider the best kind. But, mind, I never said it." He explained, as he drove on, the devastation that occurred in the wake of independence in the early 1920s. The driveway divided in the shape of a horseshoe and surrounded a formal garden, where the only bloom left was a few roses, the last of summer, fading on toward a November sleep. In the near distance was a corral where the horses crowded the fence rail. They took off at a gallop, falling in behind one another, their manes and tails flying at the approach of the car. "Oh, Lord, wouldn't I love to be astride one of them," Irwin said.

"Why don't you stay and visit the stables? I'm sure if I asked, you'd be welcome to lunch."

"Thank you, no. I'm wanting to listen to what people hereabouts are saying. This is my chance."

A maid dressed in black with a white apron and a cambric coif opened the door to Julie. She was young and freckled, country-looking. "You're from America, Miss," she said, leading the way through a large foyer from which, just inside the double doors, a magnificent curved staircase rose and divided into two at a landing and then swept on upward in perfect symmetry.

"I am," Julie said. "I'm from New York."

"Lady Graham is very partial to New Yorkers. She lived there when the late Mr. Kearney was in diplomatic service."

Lady Graham was at a desk in the sun room, a small, simple room. She turned to greet Julie. She wore jodhpurs, a white, roughish blouse, and a sweater vest of many colors. Her first words: "Would you like to ride in the hunt this afternoon? It's a trial run. No blood. I'm sure we could outfit you."

Julie explained that she had arranged to go on to Sligo after lunch.

Her hostess rose and came, her hand extended. She was a tall, handsome woman with cropped gray hair. Her features were strong, her voice commanding, her handclasp a kind of punctuation. Julie, remembering Desmond's entries about her in his journal, decided he was no great authority on women. But he had said that himself. She gave Julie a chair in front of casement windows that looked out on a golden field of stubble, where red and white cattle and black-faced sheep were grazing, and turned a rocker for herself to where she could face her guest. She sat and lit a cigarette.

"It's a beautiful house, Lady Graham," Julie tried the title on her tongue.

"It will become historic after my death. I rather enjoy thinking of tours marching through, ninety-nine percent Americans. So long as I don't have to conduct them." And abruptly, "Your name is Julie Hayes. That ought to be easy to remember. The curious thing is, the older I get, the more difficulty I have in remembering the simple names. I have no trouble at all with Fothergill or McGillicuddy."

"I don't think I would either," Julie said, beginning to feel easier.

"I take your point," she said. "Now, what's this about Thomas Francis Mooney? I didn't know he had a child."

"I'm not sure *he* knew it," Julie said.

"Ha! Isn't that like him!" She leaned forward, fanned the smoke from between them, and took a penetrating look at Julie. "There is a resemblance—oh, yes. The mouth, the bone structure. Especially the mouth. Do you pout?"

"No," Julie said. "I've got a lot of bad habits, but I don't think I pout."

"You *are* like him."

She wasn't sure it was a compliment. Lady Graham had spoken fiercely. "I'd love to find him if I can," Julie said.

159

"Where have you looked?"

"Would you like me to tell you the whole story?"

Lady Graham sniffed. "Shall we have sherry first?"

They were at dessert, Malaga grapes, a rich, dark grape that spurted juice, when Lady Graham apologized for receiving Julie in riding clothes. It was intended to save time—in case the hounds arrived before schedule. "Your father used to ride with me in Central Park."

"And danced the mambo," Julie said.

"He was much better afoot than on horseback."

"Do you know where he is, Lady Graham?"

"I listened to your story, young lady. I should like to tell mine in my fashion."

"Of course," Julie said. But what if the hounds arrived ahead of schedule?

"Am I right that your mother was the bookstore woman?"

Julie nodded.

"I assumed so from your mention of the mambo. The time coincides."

"I've read the diary of Michael Desmond. He was a friend of my father's."

"Him," Lady Graham said with distaste. "Would you believe his niece has tried to persuade me to buy those wretched diaries?"

"She's very poor," Julie said. She knew there was far more mention of the Graham-Kearneys than she had read, searching only for her father's name.

"She will not get rich at my expense. If you're going to extort, you should *do* it and not sidle up to the subject. And I can see from this distance I behaved no worse at the time—nor better—than most women of spirit when they arrive at the age of forty. If a marriage gets over that hump, it is usually safe for life. Mr. Kearney was very wise to pack me up and bring me home. It was the briefest of attachments—your father and I—but when it became known that Kearney and I were going home—attributed to politics, not scandal, by the way—your father rushed headlong into a marriage that was disastrous, I should have thought, from the first night on. But here you are. Do you mind my saying these things to you?"

"Yes, but I want to hear them."

"He was a boy, a mere boy! He looked like an acolyte. And he was quite lost. America was no more his dish of tea than it was mine."

"He doesn't look like a boy in the picture I have of him" Julie said.

"What can I answer to that? Age, like beauty, must be in the eye of the beholder." Then of dessert: "Are you finished?"

"Thank you."

"We'll take our coffee in the music room."

The music room was for the most part a collection of old instruments, lyres and harps, most of them half strung or unstrung, and ancient keyboards. They ought to be covered, she thought, or in a museum. They stood among furniture faded with dust and daylight. Lady Graham explained that in the old days, there were musical Fridays to which people came from as far away as Castlebar and Sligo. The ceilings were very high, and dark ancestral portraits hung on the smoke-gray walls. She called attention to a young, clean-shaven face. "That's my first husband, Lord Andrew Graham. Poor boy." Nothing more.

A coal fire glowed in the grate. It looked a lot warmer than the room felt. When they approached the fireplace, a red setter jumped down from a chair and stretched. Lady Graham took the vacated chair. The dog turned around and around and then settled at her feet. Julie sank into a down-cushioned sofa, kicked off her shoes, and tucked her feet beneath her.

"I like people who can stand comfort," her hostess said. "It's not an Irish trait. It was fifteen years before I saw Frank again. I thought about it after you rang up yesterday. I met him in Dublin at a benefit to raise funds for a building to house primitive Gaelic art. It seemed to me a ridiculous idea: They already have a museum in which it is well represented. And if they collect all these objects from the countryside, they'll be robbing every locale of its indigenous art, won't they? But it was another of my lost causes, and I did meet Thomas Francis Mooney again. He was with a painter and I've been trying to remember her name . . ."

"Edna O'Shea?" Julie suggested.

"So you knew. They'd been married in London a few days before. I didn't ask him what happened to the first one. I didn't want him to think I cared. Vanity, vanity. I don't think he had any more money than when I knew him and I doubt that it mattered any more to him than it did then. The artist's a strong woman. Older than him. Rather like myself, I thought. She spoke her mind and agreed with me in the business of primitive art. I've no idea whether or not she's a good artist. Someone I asked that day said she was. Nor do I have any idea whether or not she's a good wife. They were happy then, but who knows thereafter?"

"But where are they?" Julie said. "That's what I really want to know."

Lady Graham shook her head. "For all I know he may have taken her back to Australia. Did you know you have an uncle there?"

"Yes," Julie said. She was bitterly disappointed. Then it occurred to her that the family in Wicklow would have known if her father had gone back to Australia. They were in touch with his brother there. And four years ago Edna O'Shea had shown her paintings in London. "I don't think he went back to Australia."

"Perhaps not. He was always passionately involved with Ireland. He wanted to write its history. Or to rewrite it. It's a great wonder to me, the Irish attachment to our history. What is it but a series of lamentations?"

Tardily, the maid brought the coffee and explained that she had thought they were returning to the solarium.

"It's all right, Kitty. We were only now about to miss it." When the girl was gone, she said, "I wish you could arrange to stay on a few days. I'm not often taken with my American visitors."

Julie smiled. She had begun to suspect Lady Graham's perversity. The maid had volunteered that she was very partial to New Yorkers, who, after all, were Americans.

162

The older woman lit a cigarette. "You're smiling. I suppose Kitty told you I adore Americans?"

"Something like that."

"That's a myth fashioned to her own fancy. I abhor most Americans, especially those of Irish extraction given to ancestor worship. And as for those who exploit the miserable dilemma which is Northern Ireland, I consider them downright evil. The only solution there is no solution. A periodic shake-up of the status quo by demonstration and rhetoric—in which Irishmen are not lacking—would serve to correct the imbalance of power and restore amity. It is a bad marriage, Northern Protestants and Catholics, but it was made too long ago to dissolve without the deaths of both parties. Let them squabble and spit at one another the live-long day and then crawl into the bed they must share if they are to rest the night. They need one another. They suit one another. The Northern Protestant is more Irish than was de Valera, and the Northern Catholic is an alien to the papish south. Drink your coffee before it's stone cold."

Julie was both awed and amused. Lady Graham wasn't lacking in rhetoric herself. She sipped her coffee and set the cup aside.

"Now I suppose you're going to tell me you're to be in Sligo to attend the funeral of Roger Casey."

"I'm not, but the newspaperman I drove here with is going to cover a funeral there tomorrow. I'm not really up on Irish news, Lady Graham. Who is Roger Casey?"

"A very old man being exploited in death as a last survivor of the Easter Rising. He was a drummer boy—eleven years old in 1916. For years he's been supported by the IRA, all to the purpose of having him roll the dead march for their martyrs. As Kitty says, it will be a lovely funeral. I'm giving her and two of the stablemen a half day off. It's a sight to see if the IRA turn out. You should go. If they appear, they'll be wearing their berets and their masks, their eyes burning with fratricidal hatred."

No, Julie thought, no masks; she would not see that.

"And if he dares come, you'll see your Mr. Quinlan raise his fist and pledge the support of every American with a drop of red Irish blood in his veins."

It took Julie a moment to register the name. "Mr. Quinlan?" A pulse started to pound in her head.

"You must surely have heard of him. He's the head of something called the Gaelic Relief Fund, which to my mind is no more than a blind any American politician could see through if he wanted to look."

"Joseph Quinlan?" Julie said, although she knew the answer. Now she also knew why the name Quinlan had been familiar to her when he had taken on the defense of Kincaid and Donahue.

"I believe he's a lawyer over there. Over here he's a public nuisance. Worse. Far worse."

"I do know who he is," Julie said softly.

29

...

"Ships passing in the night. If you find Thomas Francis, tell him I approve his daughter."

Julie put her hand out the car window. The elder woman grasped it tightly and then let go with a little flourish as though she were releasing a bird. The hounds were baying, and Kitty came from the house with a tweed jacket, boots, and a hunting cap for Lady Graham. She, too, waved as Julie and Roy Irwin drove off.

"Well?" Irwin said finally to her silence.

"I didn't learn much about my father. He and Edna O'Shea were married in London about fifteen years ago. I did learn that. And she's a landscape painter, but I knew that already."

"In Ireland?"

"I don't know."

"You ought to be able to find that out from the London gallery."

"I hope so." She could not throw off the turmoil Quinlan's presence in Ireland had thrown her into.

"You ought to ring them up before it's too late in the day," Irwin said.

"From where?"

"We'll stop back at the hotel, and I'll help you get through the local exchange. Are you depressed, or what?"

"She was overwhelming," Julie said. "I'll come out of it in a

165

minute." She did not intend to make a confidant of Roy Irwin. She had wanted to leave the troubled part of her life at home until she sat down to write about it. Impossible. It was an unfinished story, and this, too, was part of it. And so, she had to suppose, was the Gray Man. And whoever in New York had wanted her Dublin address and used the name of Father Doyle to try to get it. That had to be significant, the reference to Father Doyle. The query had to have come from someone who knew the West Side of Manhattan. She thought back to what her partner had said on the phone about Quinlan. He hadn't mentioned the name specifically. What he said was that Kincaid and Donahue's lawyer had asked police protection for their families. Given the opportunity, she asked herself, would she speak to Quinlan in Sligo? Would she identify herself and speak to him? She knew that she would not.

"I've a grand lot of chums in Sligo," Irwin said and described a few of them, writers and musicians. Julie made herself listen. "You'll be welcome among us tonight, even if you are a Yank."

She did not commit herself.

Irwin got Duval himself on the phone for her, but the gallery owner would not give out the address of Miss O'Shea. He'd be happy to forward a letter, but it might take some time to reach her.

"Could you tell me if she's in Ireland?" Julie asked.

He hesitated. "I can only tell you it's not a place of easy access."

"That's bound to be Ireland," Irwin said as they went out to the car. "There's nothing the Brits would rather tell you than how impossible it is to communicate with the Irish."

As they drove northeast close by the foothills of the Ox Mountains, Julie watched the change in the countryside again, the round haycocks giving way to stony grazing grounds. There were great stretches of pine woods—reforestation—and here and there small patches of yellow among the prevailing green; the gorse was still in bloom. It was said, Irwin explained, that from one end of the year to the other gorse was in bloom somewhere in the British Isles.

As they approached Sligo, Irwin told her about Roger Casey, the Easter Rising survivor whose funeral he was going to report on the next day. Casey had survived rather more than Lady Graham-Kearney accounted him: He had spent a third of his life in prison. Which seemed quite a lot for a drummer boy.

They arrived in Sligo town at teatime to discover that not a hotel room or bed-and-breakfast accommodation was to be had within miles. Half the country, it seemed, had converged on the town for Roger Casey's funeral. The press headquartered at the Lupins Hotel. In the sprawl of ground-floor rooms and bars, men who had not seen one another for years were coming together, men of all walks whose speech was sprinkled with Gaelic and was much of the time whispered—not in conspiracy, but to make their points more telling. Irwin wasn't troubled by the lack of accommodations. "I've a sleeping bag in the boot if I need it." Then, in the first suggestion of humor—Julie hoped it was humor—he added, "In a dire crisis there's room in it for two. What was it called in the States—bundling? Isn't it an old American custom?"

Julie would like to have distanced herself from the celebrants of Roger Casey's funeral, but she felt a degree of reassurance in their numbers. She and Irwin arranged to meet in the lobby at six-thirty. She stored her suitcase with the porter and gave her name at the desk in the event a cancellation occurred. Then she found a phone booth in one of the public rooms. She was third in line. When she got through to the Garvy number, she was informed that Gran Garvy never came to the phone. The person who had come seemed pretty quavery herself. "What did you say your name was?"

Julie shouted. Everybody in the hotel would know her name.

"Ah, yes. You're Richard's friend. Hold on."

While she waited, she detected beneath the rumble of voices the pulsation of rock music. You heard it everywhere in Dublin and now here. It ought to have been anachronistic, but it wasn't.

The woman returned to the phone. "You're to come right along, Norah says, and will I send someone to guide you?"

"I'll find you."

When she stepped away from the phone, the man next in line said, "You'll turn right when you go out from here and then left and carry on till you come upon John Street . . ." He gave her the exact location of the house. She didn't know whether to feel safer or less assured. She had wanted very much to love Sligo, the home of her beloved poet, Yeats. And she would! To hell with Quinlan and all the crawling anxieties his name had loosed in her. There are no snakes in Ireland: How about that? She hitched her shoulder bag into place and strode across the room. The Gray Man was at a table near the door drinking tea.

Julie stopped in front of him and demanded, "Who *are* you?"

The face was pale and pinched as if with pain, even as Irwin had observed in the Dublin disco. He half-rose and then dropped back into the chair. "My name is Edward Donavan—if it concerns you."

"I'd like to know why you've been following me," Julie said.

His colorless eyes stared up at her, blinking steadily. "Madam, to the best of my knowledge I have never laid eyes on you before in my life."

She could have been mistaken, but she was sure she wasn't. She did not apologize. She shook her head and walked on. Irwin had gone off on his own by then. She stopped at the desk and inquired if there was an Edward Donavan registered. There was. So, he would have checked in before her arrival. Which proved nothing except that in this instance at least he was not literally following her.

The town was gray with the sky going overcast. The wind was prickly and smelled of the sea. She passed yet another monument to the men of 1798. It had been erected in 1898; and so, likely, she now realized, had the other monuments in Wicklow, Ballina, and wherever else the centennial of that disaster had been celebrated. Achieving a perspective on those manifestations restored a faltering self-confidence. The Old Town, of which John Street seemed the bustling center, caught her imagination. She composed of it a background for whatever she would write about Richard Garvy's grandmother. The whole street was eighteenth-century. Even the shops had the sound of another time—a chandler, a turf accountant, the greengrocer, the chemist, a drapery shop . . . a Chinese takeaway.

Norah Garvy's was one of a series of red brick houses built wall to wall. The ribs of the fan transom above the door were freshly painted white. So were the window frames. As she approached, there was a flutter at the heavy lace curtains within.

A dumpy, red-faced little woman with her white hair stacked to a peak opened the door to her. "I'm Peg," she said, "Gran Garvy's niece. We spoke on the telephone."

She had wonderful bright blue eyes and a smile that seemed perpetual. She led the way through a narrow, high-ceilinged hall, past an open door where Julie glimpsed a tile fireplace and above it, brightly illuminated with a picture light, the portrait of the Christ Child at the age of bar mitzvah. When they reached the door at the end of the hall, Peg paused. "Will I put your coat over a chair here, or do you want to keep it? Americans find it chilly this time of year."

Julie kept her coat.

"You'll have to speak up to Gran," Peg said, her hand on the doorknob. "She's going on ninety-three, you know. And you musn't stay too long. Just tell her you'll come back and see her tomorrow."

"But if I can't?"

"It won't matter."

The very old woman sat in a platform rocker at the curtained windows where the late-afternoon sun filtered through. Her feet were on a stool, her knees covered with a shawl, and another shawl was around her shoulders. She had once been tall, Julie thought. It was at the draft of air from the opening door that she turned, not at the sound. She reached for her cane at the side of the chair. Julie went forward and introduced herself, leaning toward the ear the old woman turned her way.

"It's a pity Richard couldn't come himself. He'll come to my funeral. Tell him I said that." She had dark eyes, which Julie hadn't expected, Garvy having famous blues. "He's made his mark over there, hasn't he?"

"Oh, yes."

"Did you know I put him through Trinity?" The voice was wavery but high and clear.

Julie nodded and sat in a kitchen chair Peg brought her. Gran

169

Garvy hooked her cane around one leg of the chair and tugged. Julie drew the chair closer to her.

"A waste of money on an actor. What do you do? He told us, but I've forgotten."

"I work for a New York newspaper."

"It'd be the funeral that brought you, then. Whose is it, Peg? Roger Casey." She answered herself as soon as she'd asked the question. "Little Roger Casey. Do you know how it happened he was in Dublin at the time of the Easter Rising? His mother wanted him to go to the Christian Brothers school there and sent him to her sister." The old woman paused and drew several long breaths. Julie could hear the wheeze. Gran Garvy put an arthritic hand on hers to hold her in place until she could go on with the story. Her cheeks were sunken, but she had most of her front teeth still. "The sister, unbeknownst to the boy's mother, was a Sinn Feiner. She set him to studying the flute thinking he'd learn to play all the old airs that would catch the hearts of the people. But he was slow, and she let him take to the drums: They'd wake him up at least. Are you musical?"

"I like music," Julie shouted.

"James Galway is the best thing Ireland has exported since John McCormack—long, long before your time. I can hear music, you know, with the headphones. Is it true that Richard is going back into the theater?"

"Yes—a play by Seamus McNally."

"Not *that* one!" Peg said in alarm, and to neither Julie nor the old woman.

But Gran Garvy said, "Speak up, Peg. What did you say?"

"Richard wouldn't do that to us, would he? The one about oil wells in Ireland?"

"And why not?"

"Are you forgetting what happened when they put it on here?" To Julie then, and through it all the little smile persisted: "There were demonstrations and alarms. It puts us in a bad light. He'd not take that kind of a part, I'm sure."

Julie said nothing, but she caught the old woman squinting at her, a mischievous glint in her eyes. "Speak up!"

"*The Far, Far Hills of Home*," Julie said.

"That's the one," Peg crooned. "It'll be us they'll take it out on. I'm too old myself to be listening in the night for trouble."

"Oh, God help us," Gran Garvy said. "You're enjoying yourself. If it's a good scare you want, give me your hand and I'll read you what's left in it."

The little round woman made a ball of her fist and hid it in her bosom. Gran Garvy turned her Gypsy eyes—and that's what they were, Julie thought—toward Julie. She smiled, showing every yellowing tooth in her head. "Would you like me to read your hand for you?"

"All right."

"Make us a cup of tea, Peg."

Peg frowned and darted a glance at Julie. It seemed that already she was staying too long.

"Shall I come back tomorrow, Mrs. Garvy? Wouldn't that be better?"

"It would not. It might be too late."

So Julie drew her chair up closer while the old woman put down the cane. She opened the drawer of a sewing table beside her chair and took out a magnifying glass as wide as a hand's palm. She ordered Julie to get a cushion from another chair. She positioned the cushion on her lap and Julie's hand on top of it, palm up. This, obviously, was the pleasure of her life. She took up the cane again and with it pushed aside the curtains to let in more light. The sun had gone from sight. The very old woman explained, "I rely only on natural light to show me the truth. It is the truth you're seeking?"

"Yes." Years before Julie had gone to a reader and advisor, more out of mischief than belief. She also had played at the game herself. But when the old lady crossed herself and said a silent prayer before focusing the magnifying glass on Julie's hand, Julie decided she had better pretend more serious attention than she felt. The truth was she did not want to pay serious attention. Too many things were troubling her that a seer might pick up on.

Gran Garvy was slow to speak. Her mouth grew taut, and then she drew in her cheeks, suggesting alarm. Was it an act? Julie couldn't

171

tell. At times Gran closed her eyes to rest them and then opened them and looked again. And still she did not speak.

"Will I bring the tea when it's ready?" Peg spoke to Julie from across the room. "You ask her. She can't hear me."

Julie asked loudly and clearly, "Do you want tea now, Mrs. Garvy?"

She looked up at last and put the magnifying glass back into the drawer. She folded Julie's fingers over the palm and gave the hand a brief shake with both of her own. "Yes, tea. I cannot read your palm, dear. It is beyond me."

"What does that mean?" Julie was distressed in spite of herself.

"It means I am an old woman, too old to discuss any death save my own."

"And death is here?" Julie said, thrusting out her open hand toward the woman.

"It is you that said it. I want my tea and a scone."

"There are no scones," Peg said.

But Julie did not bother to convey the message. "I had better go now." She got up. "I will tell Richard Garvy I was here when I see him."

Quick as a piston, the old woman's cane caught Julie in the midriff and propelled her down into the chair again. "Where are you going from here?"

"To meet my friend, a newspaperman."

She had to repeat it and give the old woman Roy Irwin's name. She said she had never heard of him.

"Are you going looking for Seamus?"

"I don't know yet, Mrs. Garvy. I haven't decided."

"I shouldn't if I were you."

"I'll remember your advice," Julie said, unable to keep the chill out of her voice. "Good-bye."

Peg brought the tea, two cups of a dark brew. "You'd better have this before you go," she said. "Richard would never forgive us. Would you have a drop of whisky? You mustn't take her too serious, but for all of that, she has the gift. I wouldn't give her my hand for anything in the world."

172

"I heard every word, Peg," the old woman said. "Where's the scones?"

"It's too near your supper."

"Mrs. Garvy," Julie said, "have you ever heard of a painter named Edna O'Shea?"

The old woman repeated the name. "Is it the wild shores of Donegal she paints and pilgrim sites the likes of Lough Derg?"

"Do you know where she lives?" Julie asked.

"How would I be knowing that? But you might try Greely's Bookstore on Stephen Street. Is Maisie Craig still there, do you know, Peg?"

"Oh my, yes," Peg said; a tightness at her smiling lips suggested a low opinion of Maisie Craig. And at the door when she let Julie out: "You don't need to tell Maisie we sent you, mind."

It was dark and after six when Julie reached the bookstore. A sign on the door indicated that the bookstore would be closed the next day in honor of Roger Casey. There were window posters announcing cultural events, musical, poetic, and historical. Julie could not remember having seen a bookstore as crowded. And the shelves were well stocked, books in Gaelic and French as well as in English, paperback and hardcover. She followed a sign, Art Gallery, that took her upstairs. Watercolors and prints and a few garish oils, but nothing attributed to Edna O'Shea. "Not in my time," the young clerk said when she inquired.

She went downstairs again and browsed among the books before going to the cashier's cage to ask for Maisie Craig. She had not enjoyed her visit to the Garvy house. Nor had she done a decent job for the column: She had not even asked what Richard Garvy was like in his Trinity days, and there would have been tales aplenty. She had let her anxieties intrude, the feeling of strangeness, the Gray Man. Use your fear, Jeff would have said. Sharpen your wits on it. She found the plays of Seamus McNally, but *The Far, Far Hills of Home* was not among them. She chose *To Spite the Devil* and counted out her two pounds fifty pence before going to one of the two cashier's windows. "Are you Mrs. Craig?" she asked, paying her money.

173

"Bless you, dear, I'm not. Are you with the funeral party?"

"I'm not. I'm trying to find the painter Edna O'Shea, and I was told Mrs. Craig might help me."

"And who told you that?" The woman looked over her glasses as though the better to see her. There was no challenge in her voice, but there was the suggestion of alarm.

"I went upstairs to the gallery first," Julie said.

"Ah, well, they're all new up there." Julie had said the right thing. The woman, her tawny hair straggling out of a twist at the back of her head, poked it into place with a pencil and bade Julie step aside till she took the customer waiting behind her.

"Now then," she said, getting back to Julie. "It's several years since we were her agents here in the west. I was working upstairs myself then. She came to a disagreement with Mr. Greely, shall we say, and took her things away from Sligo entirely. I can tell you where they went—a village on Donegal Bay called Ballymahon."

"You knew her, then," Julie said and made a note of the place name.

"No, dear. I was a mere clerk."

"What about her husband?" Julie asked, her heart beginning to pound.

The woman was silent for a moment, thoughtful. Then: "Are you sure she has one?"

"Yes. Or did have."

"That would be it, then, wouldn't it?"

Julie could hardly swallow the lump of disappointment in her throat. But she told herself that she had been due for an interruption. She would go on to Ballymahon in any case. She thanked the cashier and left the store without ever meeting Maisie Craig. She wondered, thinking back, what might have happened if she had said she was with the funeral party. Of which, it was to be presumed, Joseph Quinlan was a member.

She also wondered if Gran Garvy's dire intimation of death referred to her father. Would she grieve if she learned that he was dead? And what was grief? Had she grieved for her mother? No. Not

174

as she understood other people's grief. But then, her mother wouldn't have allowed it. Or—and the possibility further shook her—was she still grieving?

She reached the hotel ten minutes late for her meeting with Roy Irwin. He was not in the lobby. Nor had he left a message at the desk. But there was good news: The hotel had a room for her.

She waited the rest of the hour—until seven-thirty—for Irwin and then went upstairs for a quick wash. The room was a fair size, but the wardrobe and the huge old bed with its bolster and its backboard made it seem small. The window overlooked a courtyard two floors down. She drew the shade, unpacked necessities, washed, and went downstairs to dinner. During which she read McNally's *To Spite the Devil*. Roy Irwin did not show up. Nor did she see the Gray Man again that night.

30

...

The hotel locked its doors and drew heavy drapes across the front windows as the funeral procession approached. Julie told herself that if she was ever going to be a decent newspaperwoman, she could not run away from the action. She went out and watched from the crowded steps of a nearby church. There was a chilly wind, and the clouds tumbled into one another crossing the sky. The casket was borne by eight young men, while eight old men, honorary pallbearers, struggled to keep in step behind them. Church bells tolled, picking up on one another, all over town. A great number of priests marched, some in red, some in black, some in purple, and some in the brown robes and sandals of the Franciscans. Behind them came the flagbearers with the green, white, and orange flag of Eire in the center, flanked by a green and gold banner that featured the Irish harp and by a faded, threadbare flag of the same tricolor as the national emblem: It might have been preserved from the 1916 Rising. Then came a half dozen ominously masked marchers in their dark berets, IRA Provisionals, she assumed, and after them some twenty or so prosperous-looking men of middle age with one white-haired woman among them. They wore green sashes and an air of elitism: They had survived an earlier service to their country. Righteous, militant, arrogant. Julie made up their résumés and hated them because she was sure that one of them was Joseph Quinlan. Three drummers drummed the dead march, and the fifes sounded a dirge. People on the church steps and along the way fell in with the procession—men, women, and children, most of the men with black armbands, and some of the women shrouded in black veils. At the end came women all in black, wailing lamentations. These were such sounds as Julie had never heard, but she knew the word was *keening*. It was a little like flamenco and yet not. Ceremonial yet primitive, savage. Such vocal grief seemed too much, unreal.

A lone woman standing beside her on the steps pulled a long face and said to Julie, but loud enough to be heard around, "They do put it on, don't they?"

One of the marching mourners whipped up her veil and spat in their direction.

"And *they* want to be called travelers," the woman said scornfully. "They'll be nought but tinkers as long as I can call them."

"It's not real grief, is it?" Julie asked.

"They're paid for it. It's all part of the show and a mockery of the tradition."

Following the procession came an ambulance and two cars marked Press. Roy Irwin stepped out of one of them and ran alongside until he got his balance. He came to Julie. "Come with us. There's room in the car. I'll walk alongside."

"I don't mind walking. I'd rather."

"I'm sorry I stood you up. When I got there, they told me you had a room. You'd gone up an hour before."

"It's all right."

"Well, it has to be. There's an American here you might find interesting. Joe Quinlan. I got wind of a meeting last night and went round and got an interview with him after. An exclusive."

"Congratulations."

"Wait till you hear. You know who he is, don't you?"

She nodded.

"Walk along with me so we won't fall behind." She fell in step with him. "A craven lot pounced on me as soon as I was alone and took the tape off me. Look." He turned his head so that she could see the purple lump at his hairline.

"Do you know who they were?"

"They didn't identify themselves, but I'd say they were part of a breakaway lot of extremists—the ONI—One Nation Indivisible. Next to them the Provos are as mild as Quakers."

One nation indivisible: They'd have one foot in America, Julie thought. "Are they for Quinlan or against him?" she asked.

"They're for themselves and whoever's useful. I'll publish the interview, bedamned to them. I'm not lost without the tape. It was only that I wanted his voice saying what he had to say." As they passed through the cemetery gates, Irwin took her arm and tried to hurry her past the crowd. "I want to get up front."

She disengaged her arm, but gently. "You go on ahead. I won't be going back to Dublin with you, Roy. I'm going on to Donegal."

"Are you so?" he said as though she had betrayed him.

"I'm very grateful to you and I'll call you as soon as I get back to Dublin. Okay?"

He shook off his pique and gave her his hand. "Good luck to you, then. I hope you find the old boy." When he had strode a few feet, he turned back. "I saw the Gray Man in the hotel last night. And while I was looking round for you, didn't he link up and go off with one of the bastards who roughed me up? I've no idea what it means. But take care of yourself."

"You too."

The best care she could take would be to leave town now, to get her things from the hotel and find the earliest transportation to Donegal. But she stayed.

Tributes and reminiscences, on and on, while the cold wind plucked at the women's veils and children tried to wrap themselves in their mother's skirts. Quinlan spoke at last. He belittled the accord signed between the British prime minister and the president of the Irish Republic. "Consultation," he mocked, throwing back his mane of gray hair. He had the flamboyance of an evangelist. "What is consultation to the party without the means to implement their position? When the lamb teams up with the lion, I ask you, which comes out the goat?" He spoke for over an hour, and amazingly, only the children were restive; a mixture of politics and economics, a course in Irish revolutionary history. He gave chapter and verse of the church interference, bowing deeply to the assorted clergy present with every ironic reference. Julie suddenly wondered if Quinlan might know her father, who shared his historical interests. The thought did not thrill her. Too many things were tightening, as though she were in the embrace of an octopus. As soon as Quinlan stepped down, she turned back toward the town.

A volley of shots rang out behind her, then the bugle and the priestly voice leading the crowd in prayer. Intermittently, as the wind willed, she heard a high tenor voice singing "The Minstrel Boy." She was well into the deserted town when she heard the roar of a motor that soon struck a rhythmic acceleration; a helicopter rose from near the cemetery and soared overhead on its way, she supposed, to an airport. Was Joseph Quinlan on his way back to New York?

A porter unlocked the hotel door to let her in. She asked if someone could give her her bill.

He looked at his watch. "Within the hour, say, one o'clock."

Julie looked at hers. Three hours had been a lot of funeral. The urge to get on with her journey was very strong. Closely examined, it might reveal itself as the urge to go home. Then she stopped to think what home was like these days. She went behind the desk and took her own key from the hook. A choice of any number was available, and they all looked suspiciously alike. She went upstairs, where the carpeting was so thin and the quiet of the hallways so pronounced she could hear the little thuds of her own footfalls. She thought of the night in Dublin when she'd asked the porter to go to her room door with her. She had not seen the Gray Man at the funeral. Would he show up in Donegal? If he did, she resolved, she would go to the police.

The stillness of the hallway seemed even deeper with the rattle of her key in the lock. A waste hamper stood nearby, as did a laundry cart stacked with clean linens. The smell of the room hit her first— as though exhaust fumes from a car had floated up from the courtyard and got locked in along with something foul like a plumbing backup.

179

The maid had not been in, the bolster still lay where Julie had pushed it onto the floor during the night. The room was in near darkness, the heavy window shade and drapes drawn. The last thing she had done before leaving the room was to open them and let in the daylight. It was the first thing she did now. Next she tried to open the window. It would not budge. She turned back and saw a man stretched his full length on the bed—clothed, even with his shoes on. Stiff with shock, she edged toward the door. Within reach of it, she looked back and shouted, "You!" as though the man were merely sleeping.

The only sound was a slow drip of water in the sink. She had first thought—hoped—the darkness on the pillow was hair, the back of the man's head. But she knew: What she saw on the pillow was all that remained of the head itself, with no shape to it at all. She heard her own moan and managed to get out of the room. She stood a couple of minutes and breathed deeply. Everything of value to her was in the room, including her shoulder bag, which she had put down on a chair when she tried to open the window. As soon as she knew she wasn't going to faint, she went back.

There was no way of knowing by sight who the man was, but she felt it was the Gray Man. Why hadn't the maid discovered—or witnessed—such a noisy crime? Or had she witnessed it and fled? Or had she merely left the laundry cart where it was when it came time for the funeral and now intended to come back and resume her chores? Julie felt the nausea returning and the cold, dank sweat of fear. Nothing of hers looked to have been disturbed. Her notebooks lay on the top of her packed but open suitcase . . . the clock on the bedside table she must not forget . . . and the panty hose hung to dry on a hanger over the sink. She touched nothing—not even the hose—only snatching up her shoulder bag from the chair.

When she reached the lobby, the street doors were open wide, the guests returning. Light streamed in through the windows where the drapes had been opened. The staff were at their posts. The scene seemed even more surreal than the abandoned lobby of a few minutes before when the porter had let her in; it was as though she had run downstairs to another facet of the same nightmare.

180

31

...

Three hours later Julie and Roy Irwin were with the young Gardai sergeant in the hotel office awaiting the arrival by air of the Murder Team from Dublin. All that was known at that point was the virtual certainty that the victim was indeed Edward Donavan, their so-called Gray Man. There had been no identification on the body, and Donavan's car was gone from where it had been parked in the courtyard until at least six o'clock the night before. At that time an assistant chef, out for a quick cigarette, had seen him put his bag into the boot and go off toward the town center. Tentative identification came from the observation by the registration clerk that Donavan was missing half of the forefinger of his right hand. As was the murder victim. The desk man had registered "Edward Donavan" but had no other address than Dublin.

Roy Irwin seemed beside himself, impatient with the restraints the district Gardai put on themselves waiting for the experts. "God's teeth!" he exploded finally. "I swear to you he was a security operative, private or government. Isn't there a license board of some sort you can get onto?"

"Mr. Irwin," the sergeant said, "in the case of murder I am no more than a caretaker government until the central authorities arrive. I'm at a loss to know why they're delayed, but there's nothing I can do about that."

"I can tell you why they're delayed," Irwin ranted. "They're keeping clear until Joe Quinlan can get out of the country."

"Have you ever thought of trying out yourself for law enforcement, Mr. Irwin?" the young officer said blandly.

Both Irwin's and Julie's statements concerning their previous encounters with the Gray Man had been taken, processed, and signed. The murder scene, except for the search of the victim for identification, remained undisturbed; her panty hose, Julie assumed, still hung over the wash basin, surely dry by now. Irwin was allowed to file his story on the Roger Casey funeral. He might fume at being detained, but it was mere bombast. He was a newsman, and murder was bigger news than a natural death, even that of a hero. But to keep him otherwise occupied, the sergeant agreed to Julie's suggestion that he be allowed to drive her to Drumcliffe so that she could visit Yeats's grave. They made their way through a few restive newsmen still on hand when the murder story broke, who waited without even the solace of the bar: afternoon closing.

The poet was buried in a bleak little churchyard cemetery where the wind flattened the uncut grass and whistled through a few lonely pine trees. An ancient high cross rose among the withered bracken and weeds, and across the road was the formidable ruin of a round tower. Not a living creature in sight. Julie stood by the pebbled grave site of Yeats and his wife, George, and read aloud the epitaph he had composed for himself and ordered carved on local stone:

> Cast a cold eye
> On Life, on Death.
> Horseman, pass by.

"What does it mean?" Irwin wanted to know.

Julie shook her head. She was not going to interpret Yeats. She took a long look at the mountain, Ben Bulben, and thought it resembled a lurching beast against the sky.

On the way back to the car she thanked Irwin.

"For what?"

"Everything. For bringing me here. I feel better now. Stronger."

"You've had a hard life, haven't you?"

"No. Not really."

"Could we find a place and talk for a piece?"

"How about the Lake Isle of Innisfree?"

"Oh, God love you. You are a romantic. That'd be Lough Gill, and I'll have to have a look at my road book."

He had no sooner got out the book than a patrol car pulled up, the garda asking if he could assist. "It must wait another time," he said when he heard where they wanted to go. "You'll soon be needed back at the hotel."

Irwin turned the car around. "I'll drive slow and give you the main points of my interview with Quinlan. I want to know who snatched my tape and why. And something else now: Does it connect up with the murder of the Gray Man?"

Neither he nor Julie could find anything remarkable in the interview. "He follows the straight IRA position," Irwin summed up.

"But you said they were something else, not IRA," she reminded him.

"I said, but I couldn't prove. I'm pretty sure that lot was the ONI, and they're to the left of the Provos. Or to the right, if you see it that way. Extremists, in any case. Ah, now, wait. You may have something: They were afraid of what Quinlan *might* have said to further discredit them. There was a confrontation of some sort at the meeting. That has to be it: what he *might* have said. Don't I wish he had said it—a Roy Irwin exclusive."

As though all the world was waiting for it, Julie thought: He was like an actor who had come within tasting distance of the part of a lifetime. "How did you get to him in the first place?"

"Ah, now. Whenever I go to a strange town, I go first to the local bookshop to find out what's going on. There's a grand woman there in a shop called Greely's—you'd take to her yourself in a minute—and you'd have seen her in the funeral cortege, marching with the boys of yesterday. When I told her I was the Irish correspondent for the *New York Daily*, she set up the interview for me."

"Maisie Craig," Julie said.

"Did you meet her?"

Julie shook her head. "But I was in the bookshop." She thought about Garvy's grandmother sending her to Maisie Craig and then her niece saying she needn't say who sent her. A house divided? And the old woman's presentiment of death. Which had not taken long to follow. "So where are we with the Gray Man?" she asked. "Is there a connection?"

Irwin glanced at her and then back at the road. He took his time before saying, "Sometimes I wonder if you've been entirely honest with me, Julie. Isn't there some reason you're in Ireland besides the quest of your father? Or is the father search a ruse altogether? You wouldn't be CIA, would you?"

"You are wrong on all counts," she said.

"What about Seamus McNally? Isn't he on your agenda, you going north? That's his territory."

"Roy, I'm an entertainment columnist. Richard Garvy is going to do *The Far, Far Hills of Home* on Broadway. That puts the author on my agenda. Yes." Entirely honest . . . oh, yes.

"You don't need to bridle," Irwin said. "McNally doesn't write the kind of poetic propaganda that lot likes exported."

"I understand," Julie said. On the instant she realized that something was missing from her hotel room: She had left the copy of McNally's play alongside the clock on her bedside table. She'd been aware of the clock after she discovered the dead man. But she was sure now the book wasn't there.

When, within the hour, she was called before Inspector Superintendent Alec Fitzgerald in the private-party room the hotel had provided him, the book was the first thing that caught her eye: *To Spite the Devil* lay before him, the solitary object on the polished table.

32

...

Inspector superintendent: the top man in Irish homicide investigation. He rose from behind the table long enough to give a courtly little bow and to indicate the chair alongside the table; a stocky and hard-jawed man with a halo of rusty red hair and peaked eyebrows and very blue eyes that seemed to have needlepoints of light in them.

"Is it yours?" he said of the book on the table.

"It could be mine. I bought a copy at Greely's bookstore yesterday."

Other men of the team were coming and going in the room, soft-footed. Fitzgerald took a pen from his pocket and poked at the book until it fell apart where it had been torn into three parts. "And would this be your doing, Mrs. Hayes?"

"No, sir."

At his signal a younger detective came and with a pair of pincers gathered the book into a plastic bag. Fitzgerald bade him come back and sit in on the interrogation. After he dispatched "that desecration." He introduced Sergeant Detective Lawrence Carr to Julie. Carr was bright-eyed and ruddy-cheeked and far more given to smiling than his chief.

"Are you an actress, Mrs. Hayes?" Fitzgerald asked.

"No, sir, but I write about theater. I work for the newspaper the *New York Daily*."

"Ah-ha. And are you working for them now? What I'm asking is, are you here on assignment or on holiday?"

"I'm on my own time, Inspector Superintendent. I may do a couple of interviews for my column, but the reason I'm in Ireland is to try to find my father. I'm not sure he's here. I'm not sure he's alive even. But I came to try to find out."

She waited then with Carr's return until he had sat down at the opposite end to her of the table. Fitzgerald soon moved him. "Bring your chair to the middle, so I won't have to swivel my head like a whirligig. You were saying, Mrs. Hayes . . . are you at the beginning or near the end of the trail?"

Julie was soon telling of her visit to Sally O'Rourke and her trip to Wicklow and Ballina, making the account as brief as possible.

"Take your time," Fitzgerald said. "After all, dead is dead, isn't it? We cannot hurry the man upstairs back to life. What is your father's name, Mrs. Hayes?"

"Thomas Francis Mooney."

Did he react to the name? He was too experienced a man to show reaction, but some small change occurred, although she could not define it. "And where will you go from here in your search?" he asked.

"A place called Ballymahon in Donegal. I've learned that he was—or is—married to an artist who lives there, Edna O'Shea."

He looked at the younger detective and repeated, "An artist named Edna O'Shea."

Julie chanced his displeasure and turned her chair so that she could see both men. Carr was making a note of the name.

Fitzgerald smiled slightly at her move, a mere downward pull at the corners of his mouth. "I'd like you now to tell us in your own words, Mrs. Hayes, all you can about Edward Donavan. I understand you and your Irish colleague called him the Gray Man for your own convenience." He reached to the chair behind him for a file. It was the transcript of the preliminary questioning by the local police. Julie had been told before she entered the room that her evidence would be recorded. It was one of the quiet activities going on in the background. She described her experience of the Gray Man from his appearance and disappearance in the lobby of the Greer Hotel, to the disco dance, to the National Gallery, to this hotel in Sligo, where she had confronted him yesterday afternoon and where he had denied having ever seen her before.

"Why did you not go to the police, Mrs. Hayes?"

"I intended to if he showed up in Donegal, where I'd be going alone. There was some doubt in my mind—Roy Irwin once suggested that *he* might be the one the Gray Man was interested in."

"And it's only natural that you would want to agree with him. Go on."

Julie had the feeling of being led. The tone was of fatherly concern. Either that or he was setting a trap on the assumption that she was not telling the whole truth. "There was doubt in my mind, Inspector," she said again, "and I did challenge him when we came face to face."

"So you did. So you did." And without pause: "Can we talk for a moment about the telephone call you received from New York at your Dublin hotel? Would there be anything in that to throw light on the situation?"

A soft zinger. *Soft* was a great word with the Irish. She could understand now why the Murder Team was delayed in arrival: They had done their Dublin homework before setting out. "The call was from my partner on the *New York Daily*." She went on to explain the Garvy-McNally association and that she had come along to Sligo primarily to see Richard Garvy's grandmother.

"*The Far, Far Hills of Home*," Fitzgerald mused aloud. "I've heard of it. Haven't you, sergeant?" It was his first direct involvement of the other detective.

"I have, sir. There was a fracas in Dublin when it opened there. Stink bombs and the like. I thought myself it was very true to life."

Fitzgerald permitted himself the downward smile, and the younger detective blushed and fell silent.

Fitzgerald then said to Julie: "Did you know Donavan gave up the hotel room he had booked so that you might have it?"

"No, sir. I was told only that a room had become available. Isn't it strange he'd do that? When did he make the reservation in the first place?"

"A good question. And from where did he make it? All we know now is that he booked yesterday noon by telephone. And used credentials somewhat exaggerated to assure the booking."

"But how would he have known I was coming to Sligo?"

"When you left Dublin, it was with Irwin, and every newspaperman in Ireland was due to arrive here last night."

"Then the question I should have asked is why he gave up the room to me."

"Has it not occurred to you that there were elements of protectiveness in Donavan's attentions?"

"I have thought about it," Julie said.

"And would there be anyone from whom you would need protection while in Ireland?"

Julie felt the pressure building. She took her time. "Not to my knowledge."

"He would not have been in your employ?"

"No, sir."

"I'm sure you agree by now that whatever Mr. Donavan's mission may have been, it was on behalf of someone concerned with your activities. Or your person." A quick switch: "Would you care for a cup of tea? A biscuit? Some sort of refreshment?"

"No, thank you." Julie's mouth was dry, but if she admitted to distress at the moment, he would pick up on it, and she was not ready to confide what she had run away from in New York. Certainly not when she did not see it as relevant. But if the Gray Man had been hired to protect her, she could think of only one person who might have hired him: Sweets Romano. What she hadn't told these Homicide men was the part of her New York phone call in which Tim said someone, using Father Doyle's name, had been trying to get her Dublin address. And Tim had referred them to Roy Irwin. It occurred to her then that the Gray Man was not much of a protector. Romano would have made a better choice. She felt justified in silence.

Fitzgerald said, "I think we must face the possibility that we are dealing here with two separate chains of events that may have somehow crossed each other. It may well be that Donavan's death has nothing to do with you at all. It may derive entirely from his previous employment."

"But he was killed in my room. Why there?" Julie said.

"He may have been followed and cornered there, and as to why he was there, you must remember he had gone to some lengths to see that you had the room. Would there be anything in those notebooks of yours that might have interested him?"

Julie shrugged. "I don't think so." But after going upstairs from dinner she had entered the day's findings in her journal, accounts of her visit to Lady Graham-Kearney and to Gran Garvy, and she had noted the discovery at Greely's of where Edna O'Shea was to be found. She had also entered the possibility that her father was not in Ballymahon, but that she was resolved to go there anyway. "It didn't look as though my notebooks had been disturbed," she said then, "but you might want to dust the covers for fingerprints."

The chief of the Murder Team pursed his lips and sniffed. "I'm afraid we've already presumed right of trespass." He then spoke to Detective Sergeant Carr. "Let's have the reporter, Irwin, in now and see if we can be more specific about Donavan's movements in Sligo. Is there nothing more in from Dublin?"

"Not yet, sir."

Fitzgerald had the grace to explain to Julie: "Donavan, it seems, lived with a sister, who's away on holiday at the moment—something she could only recently afford, according to the neighbors. Isn't that interesting?"

He was talking as much to himself as to her, she thought.

When Roy Irwin joined them, Fitzgerald offered the information that Donavan, in order to obtain the hotel room, had identified himself to the management as Special Branch.

"Wasn't he invalided out of the service, sir?" Irwin asked.

The inspector superintendent looked at him sourly: He did not like to be anticipated. "Retired for whatever reason, he was taking an advantage to which he was not entitled, and a very odd one in view of the political mix that converged on this town last night. It suggests that his mission was in no way associable with politics—so far as he knew, let's say—and he came having no sense of danger to himself from the employment in which he was engaged. Did he blunder into a nest of vipers? Very curious. We shall have to see what his service record shows and who was in town. Ach! Who wasn't! I believe you've said the Provos were here, and this break-off group, the ONI. Yes, Mr. Irwin?"

"I wouldn't swear to a man on any of them. I'm not in their counsel, sir. But the Provos marched this morning. And I'd take my oath that the man Donavan left the bar with last night was one of the gang that roughed me up and lifted the tape of my interview with Joseph Quinlan. I don't think the IRA would have done that: Quinlan's their voice in America."

"Did Donavan know you saw him in the barroom?"

"I can't say, sir. I spotted him in the back mirror when I went in to look around for Mrs. Hayes. If he had eyes, he'd have seen me."

"Please describe the scene, Mr. Irwin."

"Well, the place was ninety percent men—say a hundred or more of them, and most known to each other. Great camaraderie, sir, and you could cut the smoke with a knife. I was about to leave myself and find company to my own liking when I took a last look at Donavan. And there standing next to him was the bastard who put his knee in my groin while his partners grabbed the tape out of my coat pocket. He laid an arm across Donavan's shoulders. From that distance I couldn't tell how he took to the familiarity. But he went out with the man as meek as a lamb, and them going in the opposite direction from where I stood, I had no way of seeing if he went by choice or unfriendly persuasion."

"Was there a reaction to either of them among the other men in the room?"

"Not that I observed, sir."

"Did he have a glass in his hand while he stood at the bar?"

"He did. Turned it round and round, slopping the beer about. The barman wiped the bar and topped his glass."

"And did he drink it down before leaving?"

"I don't believe he touched it, sir. I remember thinking: at near a quid a pint."

"Just so. At the moment you are one of the last persons to have paid attention to him alive, Mr. Irwin. Doubtless, we shall turn up others, but for now the question is: Where did he spend the night? The Gardai have canvassed every hotel and public house in the town, and naught admit to having seen him. He was not an inconspicuous man, was he? Where did his assailants spend the night? With him in snug captivity? Where did you spend the night, by the way?"

"In a sleeping bag on the floor of a friend's house in Old Town. The address is in your file there. Did his murderers come into the hotel after the funeral procession started? Or were they already in, waiting for the place to clear out?"

"We shall go over the bookings, room by room."

"Weren't there Special Branch men here for the occasion?"

"There were, Mr. Irwin," the detective said dryly, "but their information is not made readily available in the case of mere murder. You may assure yourself, however, we shall not overlook the possibility of their assistance."

Irwin settled his beard on his chest, a gesture of more humility than he was likely to have felt.

"Do you know, sir, how he got into my room?" Julie asked.

"Either he walked or was carried there alive."

"But I'd locked the door."

"We are a trusting people, Mrs. Hayes, and shouldn't be burdened with keys at all. The chambermaid left the ring of them on her cart and went off to the funeral. I don't know what to say about its happening in your room. We shall need to know in whose employ he was, and we shall find it out, you may be sure. There's another question to be asked under the circumstances: Is your father political?"

Julie was startled at the abruptness of the question. "I don't know that, Inspector. I don't even know that he's alive."

"But you said he was married to an artist woman?"

"I said he is—or was—married to Edna O'Shea."

"Ah, yes. So you did. And you'll be going on to look for her in Ballymahon. Is that so?"

"Yes, sir."

"I'm going to allow you to continue your journey, Mrs. Hayes, but I want you to report in with the Gardai every day or so wherever you are. It's for your own sake as well as in the interests of this investigation. Whether by their intention or otherwise, you have crossed paths with violent men—and women, I'm sorry to say— who are arrogant to the point of ridiculous: to tear that book into three pieces and leave it on the maid's rig to be sure it was found." He shook his head in disgust. "They're full of mystical symbols and empty of human compassion, and, I might add, they've been known to use the identities of people they've killed."

He thanked Julie for her cooperation and nodded a brisk dismissal. "Help her gather her things, Sergeant Carr. And you, Mr. Irwin, I want to hear more about this tape recording that brought you to their attention. Did you see any of these men at the funeral, by the way?"

"I didn't, and believe me, I was on the lookout for them."

"Engaged elsewhere," the inspector superintendent murmured.

An artist woman, Julie remembered on her way from the room. Not ever to be confused with an artist man.

33

■ ■ ■

Roy Irwin stomped his feet where he stood keeping her company in the bus queue. A fierce wind slashed at their legs. "I wonder, will I ever see you again?" he said.

"Are you always this cheerful in the morning?" she said.

He grunted. Then: "We did all this at the cemetery, didn't we, good-bye and all?"

"Roy, why don't you go? You have a long drive ahead of you."

"I will, then. Good luck and come back safe. Give us a hug, for God's sake." He smelled of bacon as his crinkly beard brushed her cheek. "I'll see what I can find out in Dublin without getting myself mugged. After all, I've five kids to think about. I've been very biblical. I've increased and multiplied." He didn't want to leave her.

"Give my love to Eileen," Julie said. That made it easier.

The road was rough, the bus noisy with the rattle of many journeys. The wind kept blowing the door half open. She soon knew why the seat next to it had been available. She was getting soaked. Sudden rain bleared the window and then ceased entirely. In the distance she saw Ben Bulben Mountain again, long and flat as though it had been sheared off, and in between were sloping fields of vivid green. Here and there were stacks of turf, some covered with bright plastic tarpaulins. Then, passing through Drumcliffe, she saw the

Round Tower and looked back to where she and Irwin had visited Yeats's grave. At the same time she had a good look at the other passengers, farm people, she thought, many wearing heavy long sweaters. As she was about to face forward again, her eyes met those of a ruddy-faced, pleasant-looking woman across the aisle and a seat back. Alongside the woman was a woven carrier, bulging with packages, the handle of an umbrella poking out. She'd had the feeling of the woman's eyes upon her since the beginning of the journey, she realized. They were friendly now, and Julie tried to avoid contact with them. Not like her. But she would have slept if she could after a night of troubled dreams and long stretches of wakefulness. A blast of wind struck the door and forced its way in.

"Come and sit here, miss," the woman called, "before you catch your death." She put the carrier at her feet.

"You're a Yank, aren't you?" she ventured when Julie tucked in beside her. "Do you know how I can always tell? You don't pull yourselves up when you get onto a bus. You *lift* yourselves." She made a grandiose gesture of uplift. "Haven't you ever noticed? Are you going to family?"

"I've always wanted to see Donegal," she answered indirectly. The woman reminded her of Mary Ryan. Any Irishwoman over sixty would, and this one, Julie soon realized, was quite distinctly herself. She would no sooner say something than she would weigh it in the balance as though questioning its truth: There was very little forestation in Donegal, ah, but there was abundant turf, and the government was planting trees. A beautiful county, the cliffs having to be seen to be believed. Oh, but the winds, perishing. There was good grazing for the sheep, but it was a hard place to grow a potato. Three or four times she interrupted herself to inquire if Julie were going to this place or that, always with a qualified recommendation.

A van drew alongside the bus, and the driver signaled with his horn. Passengers wiped the misted windows, and the cry went up among them that it was the Wolfe Tones. The van pulled ahead, and the bus driver saluted with the same *beep-beep-beep—beep-beep* as the van had greeted the bus.

194

"Have you never heard them?" Julie's companion asked. "Then you must. They're a grand group."

Julie thought of the Born Agains. "A rock group?"

"God love you, no. They're ballad singers and they tour the States as well as here. Where do you come from?"

Julie admitted to New York.

"Oh," the woman said, plainly meaning *that* place, and she cast a sly glance Julie's way as though to reweigh her in the light of this new information. "And where will you go first in Donegal, dear?"

"Where the bus stops," Julie said, irritated with the pushy curiosity. The woman ruffled her shoulders and did not try again.

The van was unloading instruments and luggage when the bus pulled in behind it curbside to the Abbey Hotel in Donegal town. Posters such as she now remembered at Greely's advertising the Wolfe Tones's tour were alongside the hotel entry: one performance only. Julie bought herself a ticket and at the same time booked into the hotel for overnight.

What decided her to stay over when she had planned to go directly on that day to Ballymahon? A fear of what she might—or might not—find there? The need to rest? Donegal town itself, a gathering place for rural people and the shops that served them? A place with the ruins of a monastery and a high castle, all settled in the hollow of a mighty hand with the roads and streams like so many tapering fingers from its center? Or might it have been the Wolfe Tones? They were named after a figure she was reminded of at every turn, the leader of the Rising of '98. And then there was the weather, given to swift and dramatic changes. The afternoon sun was gently warm on her back as she sat on the wall of the Franciscan ruins and watched a white egret where it stood for a long time in the shallows of the estuary. When it finally flew away, she walked back down into the town. She found a bookshop off the diamond—as the center marketplace was called—and in the bookshop she found a copy of *The Far, Far Hills of Home* by Seamus McNally.

* * *

195

He came suddenly and slipped into the chair opposite her where she sat at dinner and had started to speak before she recognized him. "This is the first time in my life I've ever come on anyone reading anything I wrote unless I pushed their face into it."

Her heart leaped. "Seamus!"

"It is you, isn't it? I stood at the far end of the room saying to myself, 'Is it or isn't it?' "

"It is, it is!" She could feel the color in her cheeks.

He took her hands across the table, the book popping closed, and kissed them. "Would you have found me, I wonder?"

"I would. The woman at the bookshop promised to try to get a phone number where I could reach you."

"Well, she did better than that, didn't she?"

"Oh, Seamus, I am glad to see you."

"It's shameless of you to admit it. So, will you eat up and come home with me? I'm an hour's wild drive from here."

She hesitated.

"You're booked for the concert. Is that it? You and half the county. All right, we'll stay. You should hear them once. They bring out the best and the worst in us. I'll squeeze in somewhere, and we'll go home by moonlight."

"Have you had dinner?"

"I haven't even had a bloody drink."

"Be my guest," Julie said and waved with a great sweep of her arm for a waitress.

"I was right," he said. "Shameless."

The dividers between the public rooms had been taken away and the long bar opened. People, young and old, crowded in, all of them tidily dressed. They took over the chairs in parties, and there was great coming and going, fetching of drinks, and gathering in of other friends met only on such occasions. Seamus was known, but not well known, as he put it, and better thought of as a schoolteacher than as a playwright. Now and then he'd get a clap on the back or a quick handshake, and Julie got a hand crush or two without anyone's waiting to catch her name. It occurred to her that Seamus might have a wife somewhere more popular with these acquaintances than he was.

"Seamus, are you married?" So much for Miss Page's training never to ask a personal question directly.

"Yes and no, like yourself. We're separated—waiting for the energy or the need to take the next step."

"How about children?"

"None that I know of. But I have a great dog who makes sure that all the proprieties are observed in his house."

By the time the Wolfe Tones came onstage, looking very "country," the huge, L-shaped room was jammed. The lights were high, and so were the amplifiers. The stage was a low platform, so that whenever someone in the audience could restrain himself no longer, he would run up the aisle and try to climb aboard. The singer/players seemed to love it, and the audience disciplined their own, pulling the interloper back among them. The Wolfe Tones were heavy on sentiment. Some of their songs were their own and some vintage protest, songs of exile and separation, of oppression and defiance. Malvernia: Julie tried to place the name. Seamus, watching her out of the corner of his eye, leaned near and said, "The Falkland Islands." She was vague about what had happened there, but it was to be gathered the British had made fools and bullies of themselves in the eyes of this crowd. And how they loved it when the Tones shifted to the Broadway musical *Evita*. The phrase "I kept my promise" had political overtones. Everyone chorused it, even Julie, who had no idea of its association but felt deeply sympathetic. Two unaccustomed Irish whiskies helped. Seamus laughed and took her hand in his. She could feel the calluses, something new in her experience—the hands of a worker, the head of a writer.

During the intermission, Seamus got her another whisky and himself a Guinness, and put the evening into a saner perspective. For him this was a sad sight. "Don't you see, we're wafting all this energy like a puff of smoke, and when these lads move on to Derry in the morning, we'll have naught left us but ashes in our mouths. Neither passive nor resistant, we've been crippled by the joy of suffering."

And talk, Julie thought, but she didn't say it.

"There's a line in my play you may remember: When the old man looks down where the valley's flooded and says, 'It makes you wonder what we're being punished for.' That's very Irish. I heard the words and took them home with me. Do you like what you'd read of the play before I interrupted?"

"I do. And it's a wonderful part for Richard Garvy. I stopped and visited his grandmother in Sligo."

"A wonder, isn't she?" he said, but with a lack of enthusiasm that Julie had sense enough to realize might have little to do with Gran Garvy.

She put out her hand to him. "I am loving the play, Seamus. It's very funny and sad—the way this is tonight."

"Aye, that's the point," he said and cheered up at once. "Did she read your hand for you?"

"She started to and then decided against it."

"Having seen ill omens and alarms?"

"Something like that."

"The old devil."

"She wasn't wrong. Sligo was a bad experience. I'll tell you about it, but not now." She finished the whisky and shivered. With pleasure, she supposed: It was a shock her system took with less protest every time.

After a few seconds Seamus said, "Are you the American woman"—he lowered his voice—"I read about in the *Irish Times* today?"

She nodded. It was fair to assume so.

"They tore up a copy of *To Spite the Devil*," he said.

"That wasn't the worst they did," Julie said.

"No, but it meant something to me that they did that. And I didn't know it was you, see."

"They tore the book into three parts. Do you know anything about the ONI?"

"I wouldn't say. Not where we're sitting now, I wouldn't say," he muttered.

Foolish of her. She eased away from the subject. "Did you say the Wolfe Tones go to Derry next?" Derry, she was careful, not Londonderry. "Isn't that in the north of Ireland?"

"It's in Northern Ireland. They also play in Manchester and in London."

"The same songs?"

"The same songs and the same audience, you might say: the forlornly passionate."

Julie shook her head at the sorrow of it. A girl in the next seat accidentally jostled her, then reached over and touched her hand, saying how sorry she was. Her lips were red and her eyes were bright blue diamonds. Her boyfriend, in the next seat on, leaned forward and winked at Julie. "I can't take her out but what she disgraces me. She'll step on your toes next, watch."

There was great giggling between the two. The conviviality was spreading and was meant to draw in Julie and Seamus. She was willing. As was Seamus for her sake. With the space between his front teeth, every time he smiled, he looked like a very young adult. "What do you teach, Seamus?"

"When I was teaching, I taught everything to them who'd learn and damn little to them who wouldn't. Primary school—all subjects. And them who wouldn't learn anything else I managed to make read. I've no bloody patience for stubborn ignorance—or for laziness. They go hand in hand. It's been a hundred years since doing nothing was legitimate protest in this country, and like most of our protests, it hurt ourselves more than it hurt our enemies."

Midnight approached, and the audience wanted more and more to participate. The group sang songs they could join in, and that soon led to their standing up and crossing arms with their neighbors and swaying from side to side. "Here we go," Seamus said. He tucked his and Julie's glasses under their chairs and stood up. The boys without girls were getting drunk and noisy and in need of action. Rowdy, but not punk. Soon chairs were pushed aside and glasses kicked under them while little groups of dancers formed, some clownish and awkward, some who could really dance. Now and then a girl was called up to the platform who could show what an Irish jig was about. People were sweating, their faces red, mouths wide in laughter and singing, and Julie thought there was madness in it. Seamus, grinning, hung onto her hand for as long as he could, but the surge of the dancers split them apart, and one man, then another passed Julie and others of the girls along, giving each a whirl on the way. She forgot the stiffness left over from the Born Agains' rock. She spun around as a great bouncing youth let go of her and sailed her into the arms of a red-bearded man whose hair rose out of his scalp like bristle. His laughing face collapsed at the shock of recognition: He let go of Julie, turned, and plunged into the crowd. It was Frank Kincaid.

34

...

The whole room wavered, heads and faces like images under water. Kincaid's flight seemed very funny. He seemed to be dog-paddling into the crush of people, a Chaplinesque figure. She wanted to shriek with laughter, to explode it on the room. Momentarily. Then she was in control again, and Kincaid was gone. Seamus made his way toward her. Her impulse was to turn away from him, but she waited, holding her ground against the buffeting waves of dancers.

"Are you all right, girl?"

"Yes, but I want to go now."

"I'll give you my coat and we'll walk out a bit. All you need is a breath of air."

He had offered his coat on Ginny's balcony. The same coat. She felt back to normal. But she was not, not even in what had been her heart's desire—to be close with Seamus. He now seemed as much a stranger as any man in Ireland. She had turned cold against him again as she had the night Russo called to say he was putting Kincaid and Donahue into a lineup.

In the deserted lobby she pulled McNally toward a couch and made him sit beside her. The whole building throbbed as the concert neared its climax. "Give me your phone number, Seamus, and let me call you in a couple of days."

"I thought you were coming with me."

She shook her head. "I thought so too, but we were both wrong."

"What changed you? Did you get a fright in there or what?"

Again she shook her head. She was not afraid exactly, but what she was she didn't know. Numb. Frozen. Kincaid had been afraid; he had panicked seeing her, and that needed thinking about.

She would seem to have escaped nothing coming to Ireland. And now Kincaid must feel the same way—he who was not supposed to leave the United States but had obviously managed it. Without the dire help of Romano. Suddenly she felt on the verge of knowing what it was all about—including the Gray Man. "I'll call you from Ballymahon. Very soon. I'm sorry about this turnabout, Seamus."

"If you were an ordinary girl, I'd tell you what to do with your sorrow, but you're not, and there's more you're not telling me than you've told. I know that. I'll come and fetch you if you ask, but you know, in the States, after three strikes you're out."

She managed a smile. "Thank you, Seamus. Safe home now."

In her room, the door locked, she sat on the side of the bed and removed her shoes. She was going to have to grapple with what it meant that Kincaid and, she was sure, Donahue were in Ireland. She could be sure that Quinlan knew and had probably arranged it. But why? For their own safety? Were they meant, here, to be hidden away from Romano? To be produced in time for their own trial? Or to appear as government witnesses against Romano when that time came? A bargain between Quinlan and the district attorney's office? A bargain struck by Lieutenant David Marks, who would not under any circumstances jeopardize a rape conviction? Yeah.

In the morning she tried to reach Tim at the *New York Daily*. Without success. After thinking about it for a couple of minutes she put through a call to Father Doyle at Saint Malachy's Church on New York's West Side. The priest came to the phone out of breath. "Is it true you're calling from Ireland or are you pulling my leg?"

"It's true," she said, "but it's nothing to be upset about." She explained that someone had used his name trying to get her address in Ireland.

"Now who in the world would that be? And I had no idea you

202

were in Ireland, Julie, until the man from your office called and asked if I'd referred someone to him."

"No one asked you about me?"

"No one did. Are you having any luck over there?"

"I've found family. But not my father, not yet. Father Doyle, how are the families of Kincaid and Donahue?" She had chosen the words carefully.

"I don't know how to answer that. They're waiting every day for word and praying it won't be more than they can bear."

"That's cruel," Julie said.

"Well, now, it is for them, isn't it?"

After which they had nothing more to say to each other.

The question of whether or not to report having seen Kincaid was a troublesome one. To whom, if she were to do it? And what was to be gained? What lost? The remains of her privacy certainly. That she might reveal their whereabouts, that she might even be in pursuit of them had to be the cause of Kincaid's alarm.

She reported her own whereabouts to Gardai headquarters. Nothing more.

Donegal town was serene, with a few old men sitting about the market stalls in the diamond. The only sign of the night's wild concert was a tattered poster advertising the itinerary of the Wolfe Tones.

Edna O'Shea did have a telephone, but it was a private number. "Ah, now, you'll have no trouble finding her in Ballymahon," the telephone assistant assured her. She took the noon bus.

35

...

Every turn in the road opened another primitive vista—Donegal Bay on the one side with only an occasional white dot of a cottage on the opposite shore, and before her and further inland long stretches of rocky and barren hills. The road twisted in and out of view, as did the telegraph poles that carried but a single line. She left the bus for its few minutes' halt at Killybegs and looked down on the fishing port. The fleet was out, she was told, but the trawlers laid up for repairs, the nets stretched on the quay, the long, low factory buildings, and the smell of smoke and fish proclaimed a busy village. The whitewashed houses with their slate roofs clung to the side of the hill. The shops catered to boat fitters and to tourism, with samples on display of the hand-tufted carpets for which the village was famous.

The country grew wilder beyond Killybegs. Ballymahon, which seemed to overhang the sea, was a cluster of mean shops and pubs huddled together against the wind. The bus put her and a few locals who had boarded at Killybegs down outside a sweet and tobacco shop, dropped a bundle of newspapers, and quickly sped out of sight. Julie went into the shop and asked the woman behind the counter if she could tell her how to reach Edna O'Shea.

The woman, dark and hollow-cheeked, mumbled something Julie did not understand.

"I know she has a phone," Julie said, "but it's a private number not to be given out without her permission, and how am I to get that if I can't reach her?"

"She'd have her reasons," the woman said, but went on, "It's near three miles to the Stone Ring, which is the name on the place, after the way the buildings are strung round."

"I can walk three miles," Julie said.

"She does herself often." The woman took a shawl from a hook on the wall and came around the counter. "Best leave your bag here for the time. I'm open until half past six." Outdoors the shopkeeper tightened her grip on the shawl, for the wind would have torn it from her. She directed Julie further up the hill. "You'll go up to the cross by the abbey ruins and bear left along the river. It's no more nor a footpath from there, but it's shorter by a mile nor the road."

Julie climbed the narrow street to where the village came to an abrupt end at a gate to the ruins. The wind gusted fiercely. The river became rapids alongside the ruins and rushed noisily down the hillside. Looking down, she could see boats at anchor, heaving in the heavy waters. Beyond the inlet was the Atlantic, blue and white-capped and dappled with dark patches where the clouds threw their shadows. As she went on, she could see the coast road with an occasional cottage and bits of gay color where the stacked turf was tucked around with plastic tarps. She caught an occasional whiff of smoke, so that she knew there were people nearby—over some rocky hillock. The bleating of sheep was a forlorn sound, and whenever she came near a flock, they would flee pell-mell. She dreaded the confrontation ahead. She knew in her soul that her father was not here. Or she might have dreaded it more.

She recognized the Stone Ring in the distance. A great square tower dominated it. The nearer she came, the more detail she could make out. There was a weather vane atop the tower, which proved to be a lion rampant. It quivered as though fighting the wind. A clock faced her from the tower; on closer view she saw that it lacked hands. The buildings were several, huddled close upon one another, the roofs steep and separate. An ornamental finial crowned the arch of each facade. Most of the windows were either boarded up or shuttered. Through one that wasn't she saw piles of mattresses and oddments of bedroom furniture, and daylight through a window beyond, so that she knew the building opened onto a courtyard within. The great door near the tower was high, double, and arched, of a size that would admit a bus. She looked in vain for a bell or clapper on or alongside the big doors and finally rattled the iron handles and called out a long "Hello." Her voice was as thin to her own ears as the cry of the distant gulls. She waited and called again, and yet again. When no one came, she started to walk around the ring. Then she heard the scrape of a bolt being drawn and turned back. A tall woman wearing jeans, a coarsely knit sweater, and laced boots squeezed out and pushed the door open by another foot or two.

"Miss O'Shea?" Julie ventured.

"You must know that I am." A low growl of a voice.

She determined not to be intimidated. "I'm sorry to come without notice, but there wasn't time and I could not get your phone number. My name is Julie Hayes. I'm looking for Thomas Francis Mooney."

The woman stared at her. Not hostile, but not friendly either. Her expression suggested disbelief. Once she would have been beautiful, Julie thought. She was striking now, many lines running down from a scowl and from the corners of her mouth, the mouth itself determined, not to say tough. The eyes were deep-set and dark, the brow and cheekbones prominent, the nose long and straight. Her black hair was peppered with gray and hung in two untidy braids. "Go in," she said finally, and, when Julie had entered, followed and bolted the door. The passageway was occupied by an aged but operational Ford, the tires buoying it up. Edna O'Shea led the way into a courtyard open to the sky. Old farm machinery lay about. But what caught Julie's attention were the several large blocks of stone. One piece, surrounded by scaffolding, the ground white with chips at its base, seemed to be taking the shape of a hunched figure. A fat donkey was grazing on the withered grass. It brayed raucously as they passed, and O'Shea said, "That one does all the talking around here." The woman had humor. Julie noted her shirttails where they hung beneath the sweater, daubed with paint of many colors. She had to suppose she had interrupted the artist at her work.

O'Shea opened a door off the courtyard into a large kitchen. She wiped her feet on the whitened mat before crossing the threshold. Julie did the same. The floors were flagstone and scattered with rugs woven of red, brown, and orange strands. The kitchen ceiling was low, a loft overhead, the stairs to which were the only partition between the room and a studio so full of light it had to come from the sky. An easel stood there, a bucket beside it, and on it a work in progress draped with a sheet. At one end of the kitchen was a stone fireplace. A door alongside opened into a bedroom. At the other end stood a range much like the one she had seen in the house of her Wicklow relatives. A kettle was on the boil. On the long kitchen table, along with a pitcher of milk, a sugar bowl, and a crock of butter, were rags and paint tubes, brushes, and the artist's palette where, likely, she had set it down to cross the courtyard and open the outer doors to Julie.

"I'll take your coat," O'Shea said. She hung her own sweater on a peg behind the door, and now hung Julie's coat alongside it. "You're a walker, aren't you?" It sounded like a challenge.

Julie nodded.

"So was he."

Was. "Is he dead?"

"They say he is, gone seven years the tenth of October."

"That was his birthday," Julie said.

"He'd turned forty-five that day. . . . Sit there in the rocker out of the draft." She went to the cupboard and took two mugs from their hooks. Into each she spooned a coarse-grained sugar and half-filled the mugs with boiling water. To this she added whisky from a stone bottle, the fumes sweet and pungent when she stirred the mixture. She put Julie's mug on a footstool near her chair and turned the handle toward her. Her own drink in hand, she looked down at the visitor and said, "Could you not have come sooner?"

Julie was a second or two weighing what she had said. "Then you know that he was my father?"

"I have only to look at you."

"I didn't think he was aware of my existence."

"I'm sure he was not." She made a slight gesture with the mug toward Julie before she put it to her lips.

Julie took a careful sip. The fumes cleared her head. "I had to want to come before I could. I had to find out where to come, and I had no idea what kind of welcome I'd get if I did find him."

"It would have been a willing one. And is."

"Thank you." Almost a whisper. "I have the feeling you're not surprised that I'm here."

"Oh, I am. But I expect surprises every day of my life. Not cataclysms, thank God. Most of them are little miracles of the unexpected."

Julie was reminded of Wicklow and what her great-uncle had called the miracle of reproduction, the similarity of their hands. Edna O'Shea had also been in Wicklow town and had left a clue behind. Julie was soon telling her of how her search in Ireland had begun.

"Ah, the clown," O'Shea said, hearing of the painting the child, Mary, had brought down to show Julie. "And Frank's mother, is she gone now?"

Julie wondered why it was not already known to O'Shea that the woman was dead, why communications seemed to break abruptly where her father was concerned.

"It's a gracious part of Ireland, Wicklow, but I could not live there."

"My father couldn't either, could he?"

"Where *could* he live? If I knew, I'd tell you, and if I knew for certain where he died, I'd tell you that, for it's time I believed him dead. I've put a marker in Saint Columkills and a bit of the boat that went ashore without him, but there are no mortal remains." She tilted back her head and drank most of her toddy. She blew a little steam into the air. "Drink up before it's cold."

Julie asked, "What was he like?"

O'Shea's eyes wandered about the room, resting here and there as though she had decided on something to say and then turned from it. Julie sipped her whisky. A wry, tight smile appeared on O'Shea's lips. "What do you think he was like?"

"Romantic . . . restless . . . fun . . ." Once started, Julie plunged ahead: "Fun, good-tempered, no money, didn't care, generous anyway. A lot of solitude, sheep, the sea, not much of a fighter. I'm not sure about loyalty or humor. I don't think he'd have been cruel, and if you hurt him, he'd try to hide it. Religious maybe, anyway a seeker . . ." She had avoided the woman's eyes. Now she met them. O'Shea suppressed a smile. "Oh, boy," Julie said, "I haven't let go like that since I got off the couch—and I wasn't much good at it there. You know, Freud, free association . . ."

"I do know." Julie felt the color in her face. "It was the word *seeker* that stopped you," the woman added.

"I've done a lot of seeking," Julie said. "Maybe I'm just talking about me."

"You're not far off about him. I'll tell you what I can." She got up and took their mugs to the sink. "First I must ring up the butcher before his boy goes home for the day. "We'll have a bit of steak for our dinner. Or are you a vegetarian?" Julie shook her head. "Good. A nice bit of steak. And he'll collect your luggage from Meg Riley's and bring it up when he's coming."

Julie thought about that. "You knew I was coming as soon as I left Ballymahon."

"And I knew you were a walker by the time it took you to get here."

O'Shea went to a phone at a table near the bedroom door. She stood while she spoke and then, making a second call, slowly turned her back on Julie. Julie went to the courtyard windows, restive but not wanting to venture further within the house until invited to do so. A goat was grazing not far from the donkey, a fat or pregnant goat that made her think of Picasso and of the New York museum where she had seen the sculpture.

O'Shea went from the phone to the range, shook up the fire, and added fresh turf. She said not a word. It was as though she had forgotten Julie was there. She washed her paintbrushes, still without speaking. Finally, over her shoulder: "I should have asked you long ago—why didn't you speak up? The W. C. is through the bedroom."

Julie was grateful. On suggestion, she needed the convenience, but even more than that she wanted to escape the silence. She observed as much of the bedroom as she could in passing: a wide bed covered with a quilt, with two long rows of books on the wall behind it—heavy on history and politics, some poetry and folklore. Not a title that she recognized. A crucifix hung on the wall alongside the bed, a brightly bleeding Christus. A huge wardrobe left little room to pass. She wondered if her father's clothes might still hang at one end. The bathroom was modern mail order, including the water heater, stone cold to her touch. A box of matches stood on the shelf with the clean towels, but there was no sign of a wall or floor radiator. The room was bone-chilling, and the rush of water thunderous when she flushed the commode.

When she returned to the kitchen, O'Shea was sitting at the table, her knees drawn up, her feet on the bench. She had thrown off whatever mood had come upon her. "You came north by way of Sligo town, did you?"

"Yes." And of course she should have guessed what had gone on on the telephone: Newspapers had arrived on the bus that brought her to Ballymahon with a story until then hardly noted as it came over the television or radio. Now it would take on meaning locally with the arrival of a young American woman in the village. Why it should have silenced Edna O'Shea instead of rousing her curiosity on the instant was something she might learn in time. "A lot of weird things have been happening to me," she added.

"You're fortunate that weird is the worst word you have for it."

Julie admitted that the presence of a murdered man in the bed where she had slept the night before was not the sort of thing that happened to everybody.

"Have you any notion why?"

Julie shook her head. "Was my father a political partisan? Is it all right to ask that?"

"His mother was Ireland. There's no harm in asking, and I doubt there's much in telling." She drew a deep breath. "He was very much a partisan. Now before we go on, you and I must decide by what names we're to speak to one another. Whenever you say Miss O'Shea, I expect to be charged with some breach of the law."

210

"Everybody I know calls me Julie. Even people I don't know."

"I think for you to call me mother would take more getting used to than we'll have time for. I dare say you'll be rushing on as soon as you learn all I can tell you. So you'll call me Edna."

"Edna," Julie repeated. "I have promised to visit a friend soon—Seamus McNally. He's a playwright."

"Is he now?" Said mockingly.

"Then you know him," Julie said, again chagrined at her assumption of her stepmother's lack of sophistication. But it was not that; it was the fear of seeming herself brittle, a show-off.

"Oh, yes," O'Shea said. "But then over here most of us know one another."

"When Seamus was in New York, I asked him if he knew the name Thomas Francis Mooney. He didn't."

"I think he'd have remembered the same man under another name," O'Shea said.

36
...

Julie waited for O'Shea to give her the name by which McNally might have known her father, but it was not forthcoming, and the longer she waited, the more difficult it became to ask.

The afternoon was well on when O'Shea suddenly asked her, "Where were you seven years ago this time?"

"In New York. I must have been." She reached for the cup of strong, dark tea and held it, warming her hands. "I was two years into a marriage that recently came apart."

"By your choice, I trust."

"It takes two," Julie said. She drank her tea, her third cup of the day. It was almost dark in the room, and Edna O'Shea seemed to be an old woman in the failing light. They had drawn chairs to the fireplace, and when the turf was burning well, O'Shea had hung the blackened kettle over it and had twice refilled the teapot.

She got up now and lit a lamp. "I can go through that October day minute by minute and often have. I went out at dawn, which is my habit, to watch the sun come up. It was cold and misty, and the sun once out was like a will-o'-the-wisp. I've painted it from memory many times since. It's never been like that again, and I've not got it right yet, but I can see it true. I brought a rose in with me when I came and put it with a hand-woven shirt where I set his place at the table. I made our porridge and had my own, and when the mist lifted, the sun was hard and bright, and I went out to my work. He came out to me wearing the shirt and very handsome in it—a tall man, a head taller than myself. Those same gray eyes as yours. He said he'd be going out in the boat, that it was a good day and I was not to worry if he was gone longer than usual. I never saw him again. He left by the meadow door not to disturb me. There were some in the village who saw him cast off, but if he was seen thereafter, no word of it ever came to me. His battered boat was found washed ashore clear across the bay three days later. I've heard it said that he could have beached it there himself and vanished into another life. I don't know what to say to that to this day."

"Who said it?"

O'Shea returned to her chair. "I'll try to remember if you think it's important."

Julie felt the woman was piqued though she could not imagine why, but she pursued the question because it was important: "Do *you* feel that could have happened?"

"I do. But I also believe he's dead now. I think I'd have known. He would have let me know."

"I was told he was never in touch with my mother after he left, but I'm not sure that's so. For one thing, he published a poem and had the money for it sent to her, something she never told me at all."

" 'Where the Wild Geese Fly No More,' " O'Shea said, and both of them started to recite the lines at the same time and continued until they broke up with laughter. It was a good moment between them. The older woman said, "It's a great thing to write one poem only and to live your life by it. You and I have much to say to each other. You'd better plan to stay the week."

Julie thanked her. "I'll call Seamus in a day or two." She did want to stay on a few days with the artist: She needed the rest, and the time to sort out, and maybe someone to share the sorting with. It might have been Seamus, but it wasn't. "What was the name he would have known my father by?" The question came out so easily when the time was right.

213

O'Shea hesitated. Then: "Aengus."

"Just Aengus?"

"A cover name, known far better than the name he came with. I'm not going to burden you with information you're as well off not having, and the God's truth is I don't know myself if it was by choice he left this place and foundered at the mercy of the sea. I can tell you what made him a partisan, as you call it. That I can tell you. We were crossing the North Channel by water—I'm not fond of flying except to look at the clouds up close: golden fleece in the sunlight; silver fleece by the moon. I'd had a successful exhibition in London, and right after it Frank and I were married. Now, we'd met on that same Glasgow-to-Larne boat going the other way a month before, and no sooner met than madly in love." She gave a snort and fell to gnawing her thumbnail while she stared at the fire, her eyes aglow with its reflection. "It was a time of ecstasy, and I was having my first experience of it at the age of forty-six." She rocked back and forth. "There now: It could only happen to an Irishwoman."

Julie laughed. And then thought it was not an experience to which she had been overly exposed herself.

"I was going to say what turned him to the cause: a drunken, loose-tongued Belfastman on the boat saying that all the west of Ireland was good for was raising jackasses. I think Frank would have knocked him into the sea if I hadn't been there, and he never got over it. We weren't long settled in when he took the oath. He was a born sailor and, provided with a boat, he learned the bay waters and guided many a darkened ship through them. Nobody knew the Donegal coast like he did. He went up and down learning it and at the same time gathered materials for his writing. The sadness of his life was that he was not a writer, though he never gave up trying. He could do most anything else he put his mind to. He mended the slate roofs and built me two windows to the sky. He made the frames and stretched my canvases for me. He cooked my meals and built the scaffolding around the piece we called 'The Wandering Aengus' where it sits in the courtyard today. I did not touch it from the day he left until he was gone seven years. On that day I went out and took off the tarpaulins with which I'd shrouded it. He made the sculptor's tools for me and kept them sharp. You'll see the anvil and the furnace, the bellows and his hammer and tongs—there'd been a smithy's shop in the Ring long ago. . . ."

Julie began to see a character resemblance between her father and herself. She, too, could do fairly well, and sometimes better than that, anything she put her mind to, and what had she not, at one time or another, put her mind to? Acting, art history, psychiatry, bead-making, fortune-telling . . . a gossip columnist now, of all things . . . striving to write her way out of it. Determined to write.

"He loved to sing and he could tell a good story, mind. It was only the writing he couldn't keep alive. No one was ever blessed with better company than I," the widow went on, and her tone embraced her widowhood, more and more a croon. "If there had been a war in his lifetime, he'd have been an Irish soldier in an alien army—so long as the cause served Ireland. It was always in his head, you see, the urge to do something for this divided land. And the problem had been what to do. In olden times he would have been a servant to the king."

Julie thought of the Graham-Kearneys, whom her father had served in a number of ways. "Or the king's fool," she said.

"If he's gone from me by choice," O'Shea went on, "and I think now it may well have been that way, it's a wonder he didn't go sooner." She turned in her chair to look at Julie. "The king's fool who was wiser than anyone knew but the king?"

Julie nodded. "Did he ever speak of my mother, Katherine Richards? She's dead now too."

"He loved her very much."

Julie wondered if that answer had not been on the back of her tongue waiting for the question. "Then why did he leave her?"

"Because he could not serve. She was surrounded by servitors and some more favored than himself. He felt he had nothing to give her."

"Only me," Julie said.

"I would swear on my life he did not know of you."

215

Julie got up, unable to sit quietly any longer. "I must have been a natural consequence—even if I wasn't on their agenda, wouldn't you agree?"

"Yes, but she would not have told him, don't you see?"

"I don't know what I see. It's like a house of mirrors." She touched her foot to a square of turf that had fallen away from the rest, returning it to the fire. "She was never supposed to have seen him after he left, but wouldn't he have had to return to New York at least for the annulment?"

"Things can be done by affidavit, or—not at all."

"What were the grounds?" Julie turned from the fire. "I know it gives a Catholic a second chance. Or did back then, but there had to be some pretty stinking reason for it. It isn't just handed out like Communion."

"You're angry, and I don't wonder," O'Shea said.

"I want to know," Julie said, her voice rising, "*I want to know*."

O'Shea gave an impatient toss of her head. "Do you think either one of us will ever know the truth about him? And what would we know if we did that would be better than what we know now? Isn't it enough that I recognized you for his daughter? I, too, am a teller of tales. I could weave you a heritage. For every mortal in search of who and why he was born there is a conspiracy of witnesses who may not have been there at all. A bit of the teller's dream of himself goes into every answer. There are always circumstances which are indiscernible, and the truth is in their shadow. Come and sit down and tell me: Has anyone you've asked about him had less than a good word for Frank Mooney?"

"There was one. But he was my mother's lover—before and after my father. How about that?"

"And couldn't believe he'd missed the mark himself?" O'Shea said.

Julie, when she caught on to the implication, nodded. It might well be so.

O'Shea threw back her head and laughed heartily. "It takes two women to know any man—if he's worth the knowing at all."

It was her laugh, really, that first made Julie love her.

216

* * *

For three days they talked during most of their waking hours. They packed sandwiches and a thermos of tea in a knapsack and walked the Coast Road; they followed sheep trails high among rocky crags. They took refuge in caverns through pelting showers and from them watched the racing clouds, the clearing skies. They timed themselves to the tide and trekked along the sands, fleeing the swift reach of foamy water like children defying every wave to come and get them. They talked of painters and painting, of which Julie knew more than she had thought she knew, discovery implicit in the growth of love. She learned that Edna O'Shea had been born in England of Irish parents and she learned that the Stone Ring had been provided her by an Irish benefactor to be given to the nation on her death. The ground was sacred to saints and kings, legend had it, "and you can be sure none of them ever tried to till it. It would unmake a saint to try." Legend also had it that it had been a stopover for smugglers.

In the morning light of the fourth day Edna O'Shea brought out a number of paintings and set them one by one in front of Julie, leaving those Julie especially admired tilted against a chair leg, table leg, the leg of her easel. Julie was surprised at their severity. More and more O'Shea seemed to strive for simplicity. The latest pieces were stark, bleak. She was certainly not an artist Julie would have called a landscape painter. Except that you'd say the same of Dali or O'Keeffe. Nor was there any sign of the clown the Wicklow child called Pansy.

They gossiped—if it could be called that—about Frank's family—Julie's own, she kept reminding herself—in Wicklow. There was a high rate of desertion among the men and of fidelity among the women, who loved them more than they may have deserved. Julie told O'Shea what she could of Jeff and was surprised at how uncertain she herself was of many things about him. "It's like I was afraid to know him, except to blame him in my own mind for things that didn't matter much. I was afraid to love him the way I sure as hell wanted to love somebody."

"Why afraid?"

Julie shrugged. "I was afraid it might turn him off. Too much."

217

"Or on?"

"Maybe." She avoided the eyes of the older woman. "He's got someone now who turns him on. That's for certain."

O'Shea pounced: "And you?"

The time had come to tell her stepmother what had happened to her that Sunday morning in June after Jeff had told her he wanted a divorce.

37

...

O'Shea leaned back. She had moved her chair closer while Julie spoke. "The dirty dogs!" she cried out. "And the arrogance of sanctuary in Ireland!"

"The more I think about it, the less surprised I am," Julie said. "I believe now there's a link to everything that's happened to me. I've always said nothing is accidental."

"You saw but the one of them. Are they together, do you think?"

It had not occurred to her that they might not be. "Yes. But it's just a feeling, and that's because they're jammed into one place in my mind ... like a sickness." She'd had to grope for the word and the nausea came with it. "Oh, Christ! Like being damaged for life. I'm not! *I will not be!*"

"Indeed you're not. But they *are*. They'll never escape."

Julie saw again in her mind's eye Kincaid's wild flight from her, his crash into and break through the dancing barricade. "He was more shocked even than me."

"Do you think you're in danger for having seen him?"

"I don't know, but I don't think so. I'm pretty sure I know how they got here: It's for their own safety—they're supposed to be out of Mr. Romano's reach.... Isn't it crazy? I still call him *Mr. Romano*—a gangster."

"Who loves art," O'Shea added, for Julie had told her in the course of their long conversations of her troublous friendship with the underworld figure.

"And buys it at auction or on somebody's advice—legitimate —only not under his own name."

"Most collectors go that way." She put Julie back on the track: "Kincaid and his partner—how *did* they get here?"

"I don't know exactly how, but I think their lawyer got them over and hid them away among his Irish connections. Do you know who Joe Quinlan is?"

"I do know. Is he their lawyer? Ah, now I begin to see the shape of things."

"They were supposed to be safe and anonymous here till he brought them back to New York for their trial, or maybe even to give testimony against Romano if they can identify his thugs. Isn't it ironic? I was trying to find a safe place for myself—to get away from the whole scene. That's what finally pushed me into the search for Thomas Francis Mooney."

"And not the pending divorce?"

Julie sighed. "That too. But it's all connected. I think the man who was killed in Sligo may have been hired by Romano—either to protect me or to follow me in case I was on the track of Kincaid and Donahue. What I ought to know by now is that Romano has more ways of finding things out than the FBI, and I'll bet customs people all over the world are among his best informants."

O'Shea sat back in her chair and rocked herself gently. "It would be interesting to know if the people giving those two cover—in the Donegal hills it must be—know the nature of their offense."

"They'd do it for Quinlan," Julie said.

"Almost anything," her stepmother agreed.

A sudden thought: "Would my father have known him?"

"He might have—but, more likely, Quinlan's lieutenants."

"Do you know anything, Edna, about an organization called the ONI?"

"What makes you ask that?"

"They're more radical than the IRA, I think."

"One Nation Indivisible. Do you find that so radical?"

"I meant more violent. I used to say the words in school every morning. They're from the American Pledge of Allegiance—'one nation, under God, indivisible, with liberty and justice for all.' "

Both women were quiet for a moment. It was dark outside by then, and the wind was all but silent, only a whisper. "I feel Frank to be very close tonight," O'Shea said, her voice pitched higher than normal. "It's a sorrow to me, for I've tried these seven years to draw him near. That I couldn't I took to be a sure sign that he wasn't dead at all."

A memory of the keening women at the Casey funeral flickered in and out of Julie's mind. "I don't think he's dead," she said.

O'Shea turned in her chair to look at her.

"I don't," Julie repeated.

O'Shea turned back to the fire, which had almost gone to ashes. "Oh, child," she murmured.

After a moment Julie asked, "Who was Aengus?"

"An ancient Irish god of love and poetry. Long before Christianity cooled us off."

" 'The Wandering Aengus,' " Julie said. "I should have known from Yeats's poem: 'the golden apples of the sun, the silver apples of the moon.' I must call New York in the morning and I must call Seamus."

"Will you go on looking for your father?"

"Yes."

"And will you let me know if you find him, dead or alive?"

"I will."

They were gathering the supper dishes into the sink, the kettle on to boil for coffee, when the phone rang. There had been few calls since Julie had arrived, and O'Shea put off most of them to return, herself, at another time. She answered now in her usual manner, giving her phone number. Without a word to the caller she said, "It's a Seamus McNally for Mrs. Hayes."

Julie was quicker than she would like to have been, her step-

221

mother watching, but her heart had leaped ahead. "How did you find me, Seamus?" She had not gotten to tell him about Edna O'Shea.

"I started with Garvy's gran and came to a halt with the next stop . . ."

"Greely's Bookstore," Julie said.

"Aye, and by good fortune I was able to squeeze out the information that you'd been there to inquire after Edna O'Shea. Old man Greely himself gave me the number."

"You're a wonderful detective, and I'm glad you found me," she said softly.

"Does that mean you're ready for me to come and get you?"

"I was going to call you tonight," Julie said. "Shall I ask my stepmother to give you directions?"

"Your stepmother," he repeated. Then, after a pause, "No, love, I know where I'm going. Just tell me the name of the house."

"Tell him the Stone Ring," O'Shea said. "That's all he needs to know."

When Julie had put down the phone, her stepmother said, "Your father and Ned Greely were friends. But after Frank was gone, Ned and I never got on. I'm surprised they told you where to look for me."

"Edna, what about the person who said he might have beached the boat himself and vanished? You said to remind you."

"I don't remember saying that at all." She was becoming impatient, Julie thought, perhaps for her to go, since she was going. "It was the observation of a tubercular Franciscan, who may well be dead himself by now. He came from Rossnowlagh to say Mass on the Sunday we prayed for Frank's safe return—or the peaceful repose of his soul."

"Can't you remember his name?" Julie persisted. She might not come this way again.

"A Franciscan: Brother Daniel. It might have been that."

O'Shea made coffee that neither of them any longer wanted. And conversation had become strained. Julie proposed to go up to the loft early.

O'Shea did not protest. "I'll be up and away in the morning before you leave, and if I'm not back, be sure to close the great doors so the animals won't get out. They're the devil to catch, and the bogs are treacherous."

Julie thanked her for many kindnesses, but they did not even touch. O'Shea stood resolute, her back to the fire, her hands clasped behind her. Julie reasoned that her leaving might seem a betrayal, as though she'd made a choice between O'Shea and Seamus McNally. And for her own part, she felt the pain of yet another separation.

38

...

She awoke in the morning to a silent house and knew that O'Shea must have already gone out. In the kitchen she found a fire built up in the range that would last the morning, and on the table a framed watercolor of the pale and misted sun O'Shea had described as a will-o'-the-wisp. Alongside it was an envelope marked "Julie." It contained two lined pages from a notebook. She read one with her name on it first: "I like this watercolor the best of my attempts to catch that morning's sun. Take it in memory. And you had better have the enclosed. He wrote it out for me. Go and Godspeed. Edna."

The enclosure, the paper yellowing, was the poem "Where the Wild Geese Fly No More," in her father's hand.

She listened for the sound of Seamus's car and twice went out to the great doors when there was no one there, the wind and her imagination playing tricks on her. She tried a last time to make friends with the donkey called Maud, but she would have none of Julie, the only improvement in their relationship a dubious one: Now she waited until Julie's hand was almost upon her before turning her backside and kicking out her heels. And Julie would have none of the goat, a fragrant creature. O'Shea squeezed milk from her morning and night, a rich, strong-tasting milk that made Julie slightly ill even to think about.

Seamus came while she was in the courtyard, and she was out the big doors to meet him as soon as he had parked the car. He caught her in his arms and lifted her from the ground. "This time it will take an act of God," he said.

"Sh-h-h-h." Into his ear.

"Obeisance, not a challenge," he said.

Julie led him by the hand past the stately Ford.

"Is Edna O'Shea your stepmother truly?"

"Yes."

"And your father? Why have I not heard of him?"

"He's been dead for seven years—or gone from here anyway. But Seamus, you have heard of him. Edna said you would know him under the code name Aengus."

McNally stood stock still and turned Julie around to where the sun was full in her face. "Holy Mother of God," he said. "I've been wondering since the night we met at Ginny's who you reminded me of. I met him but the once, but I am never likely to forget it. I was doing a documentary film script on piracy and patriotism—how does that strike you?"

Julie grinned and pulled him toward the kitchen door. "Edna left early this morning. We're alone here."

"Are we? It's about time." Then, soberly: "I daresay she didn't want to see me. I've moved away from my fervent days, and I don't suppose she has, once married to Aengus. He was IRA, you know, and a Provo at that, yet the gentlest man I ever met."

"Wait," Julie said. "I want to listen carefully and hear everything right."

The tea was a lot stronger than what she had given him that night on Forty-fourth Street. "I've learned," she said in response to his compliment.

"It was like a pilgrimage," he said presently. "I climbed a mountain trail and found the cave where he sometimes lived. It's all hallowed ground, the cliffs and the hills thereabout, where saints once trod, it's told, and the fairy people are still conjured by those who need

225

them. And that's what we talked about, Aengus and I. He'd been gathering the legends of Ireland's wild west. 'I'll preserve them, never fear,' he said, 'though the land's salvation might have lain in their destruction long ago.' A lovely man, half-wise, half-simple. You know, I think I did hear that he was dead. Lost at sea, was he?"

"His boat was found ashore, but not him."

"Are you satisfied?"

"No."

"And the widow?"

"She may be—after seven years' waiting."

"Do you know where she is right now?"

"I don't. We've walked miles and miles every day since I've been here, and wherever we went, she'd been there many times before."

"You're beginning to talk Irish, girl."

Julie laughed. "I'm a chameleon."

"Could we have a wee look around the place as long as we're on our own?" he asked conspiratorially. "The Stone Ring has a dark history—smuggling, and it was once a prison for men they'd call terrorists today, during the struggle with the landlords."

Julie was reluctant to poke around the several buildings she had not been shown by O'Shea herself, who merely said they were no longer in use. And she wanted to go before the woman returned, but Seamus was alive with curiosity and primed her favor with anecdotes concerning Aengus. He was supposed to have been high in forbidden councils, at one time a district IRA commandant. So it was said. The word gave Julie no great pleasure. Such bitter romance as *The Informer* or *Odd Man Out* belonged on television at home, where it seemed much more real. Then it occurred to her that Seamus might be weaving a story he thought she wanted to hear and was reminded of what O'Shea had said—that a bit of the teller's dream goes into every tale told to the seeker of origins. She asked Seamus if he had ever been associated himself with the IRA.

"I wasn't, but I had chums who tried to recruit me. If I'd been in Derry as a kid, I'd have thrown a few rocks and banged the pot

226

lids to sound the alarm, but I don't have much taste for radical personalities, however just their cause may be. There. I hope I haven't offended you." So he had not been weaving tales.

She showed him the tower room, where all her father's papers were stored much as he had left them, notebooks now molding in the cold salt air. The stove looked not to have been lit in his absence. She was slightly hurt that Seamus showed no great curiosity about her father's writing. Hypocritical: Her own curiosity had been soon reduced when she tried to read them.

A sound like that of creaking hinges stopped them in their tracks. Julie went to the stairway and called out her stepmother's name, but no answer came. As they went down to look, one side of the double door banged in the wind. Julie was sure she had closed it behind them, although she had not bolted it, thinking they would soon leave.

"Edna," she called again from the courtyard. Her stepmother might have returned to the house by the meadow door. Then from off somewhere she heard the *gee-haw* of a donkey. "Oh, my God, she's out." The goat was placidly munching near the kitchen door. But when they rushed outside the Ring to look for Maud, the only life to be seen was a donkey-drawn flat cart with two men aboard on the road to Ballymahon. The donkey brayed, and the driver laid a whip to its flanks that hurried it along. From inside the Ring came a responsive bray.

"That's Maud—there all the time," Julie said, laughing with relief, and when they went in, they found the beast on the other side of the scaffolding.

"Maud. After Maud Gonne, do you think?" Seamus ventured.

"Yeats's beloved?"

"Cathleen Ni Houlihan herself, a patriot beyond the call. But some called her all the same."

"I don't understand," Julie said.

"She was a woman of flesh as well as spirit, and that created a terrible conflict among the patriots."

When they went out from the Ring a few minutes later and

Seamus pulled hard on the great doors to be sure the latch had caught inside, Julie said, "I can't really be sure: I may have left it open."

"And you may not have done," Seamus said.

She thought about the implications of his remark while he was putting her suitcase in the hatchback of the Nissan. She walked back to the ring of huddled stone buildings she had thought long abandoned and discovered that where the great doors on the entry were secured only by a latch and a hand bolt on the inside, the locks on two of the weathered doors she now looked at more closely were comparatively new, modern certainly. And in the loose earth close by she detected the wheel marks of a cart and the imprints of a donkey's hooves.

"What do you think it means?" she asked when Seamus joined her.

"That she has a secret life interrupted with your arrival."

"Are you serious?"

"I am and I'm not. It's you that lived near a week in her house."

"What *could* it mean?" she said.

"For one thing it could mean she's storing arms that have been smuggled into the country. Drugs, I doubt, but something. Whatever it means, Julie, I have the feeling you're better off not knowing."

"She said something like that herself concerning my father. I believed everything she told me."

"And why not? That doesn't mean she had to tell you everything, does it?"

39

∎ ∎ ∎

Julie, having decided to do nothing about the presence in Ireland of Kincaid and, presumably, Donahue, saw no point in telling Seamus they were there. If she was ever to throw off the feeling of degradation they had cast upon her, it must happen during her visit with Seamus. While he drove, he reached his hand for hers now and then and held it until the next jagged curve in the road required both hands on the wheel.

"Old friends," he said, not quite what she had hoped for. Then: "And lovers to be?"

She gave his hand a squeeze.

"Ah, love," he said and drew her hand against him.

He stopped at Glencolumbkille, a village in a deep, solemn valley that gave way at its mouth to the sea. It was particularly desolate when the clouds darkened the sun. The cliffs, where barren of growth seaward, were a reddish gold, vivid in the sunlight, muted in shadow. "Even the pilgrims are done in by the weather this time of year," he said, "but one must not pass this place without bending a knee to the ancient saints. It was from here that Saint Columba went out to convert the heathen Scots. He had a hard start to a harder end."

"Are you religious, Seamus?"

"I pay respect, but I'm a little lacking in faith."

"Me too. But sometimes I wish I had it."

"Keep an open mind. You never know when it will strike."

They went as far on the pilgrim's way as the Place of the Knees, where the stone mounds marked ancient graves. Seamus made a quick and perhaps reflexive sign of the cross. They turned back, facing into the wind, and Julie thought of the slumbering Catholic in him. With a wife, divorced or undivorced, matrimony would not be his object. Nor was it hers, she told herself, although she had not felt as deeply as this for Jeff when she had married him. Or had she? It was hard to tell from this distance. Suddenly she realized that the distance between her and Jeff had grown wider of late and that there was hardly any pain at all in remembering him.

They returned to the car, and Seamus took a silver flask from the glove compartment. He unscrewed the cap and poured her its capacity of whisky. She drank it down and commented when she could get the words out that it was almost as good as orange juice.

"I'll drink my fill of that in the coming months," Seamus said and then added, "God willing."

"In New York?"

"Aye." He gave himself a capful of whisky. "Now, we can head inland for the far, far hills of home, or take a five-mile snag further on and I'll show you where Aengus and I met and talked the clock around."

Julie chose the long way, having come this far.

They drove over a one-lane road mostly through bogs and into another long valley. The black-headed sheep ran from them, and at a thatched, whitewashed cottage a man stood with a bucket in one hand and the scruff of his mongrel dog's neck in the other hand and gave a half nod when Seamus waved at him.

"Are you hungry?" Seamus asked. "We could beg bread and a cup of tea."

"I can wait."

They came to where the road forked with a trail that had once served vehicular traffic but was now chassis-high with coarse grass. A lone cottage stood nearby. They could hear a dog barking when Seamus turned onto the trail and cut the motor. They got out of the

230

car. Neither the barking dog nor its owner showed himself.

"It's a hard mile's climb," Seamus said, "The gorse will be clawing your legs, but I'm game if you are."

Julie, wearing corduroy slacks and a short down coat, had no intention of quitting. Seamus got a flashlight from the glove compartment and his anorak from the backseat of the car. He put the flask in the inside pocket and then zipped the jacket up to his throat. He squinted up toward the headland. Julie shaded her eyes and looked where he was looking.

"What do you see up top?" he asked.

A human profile in stone, she thought, with an oval-shaped projection sticking out behind. "An Indian head?"

"That's it."

"Is the cave abandoned?"

"Long since by the looks of the trail, wouldn't you say?"

About halfway up, the climb steepened and the trail circled around on itself with only a faint footpath going on. The Indian head lost its definition as they drew closer to it, mere juts of quartzite. The curlews grew more numerous: They swooped and screamed as though they might attack. Near the top the rock formation split into two humps, a few square feet of level stone between. The climbers paused and looked back. The car where they had left it looked the size of a beetle. Someone was walking around it, a man with a dog. "Let him," Seamus said. "In the old days I'd have worried there might be Provos around who'd lift it. I remember Aengus saying when I was about to go down, 'Let me know right off if they lift your car—before they convert it.' "

"Into a booby trap?" Julie said.

"Aye." And after a moment: "A terrible phrase that—as though to be innocent was foolish."

"They don't call it that anymore anyway, do they? What? An explosive device?"

"A car bomb," he said.

The wind caught them, gusting through the hollow between the shoulders of rock. They turned their backs against it and stood firm until it eased. Underfoot the mottled red and ocher stone was plateau-level, salt- and rain-washed, speckled with bird droppings and the empty mollusk shells the sea birds had dropped to crack open. With the slackening of the wind they turned and looked at the sea—sapphire blue with crinkles of whitecaps, lucid pearl at the horizon, and the sky another, lighter shade of blue, but piercingly clear. Three fishing vessels seemed to lie at anchor far, far out. Not at anchor, Seamus said: That was an illusion. Small gray and lifeless islands broke the waters near the shore, and strangely, they seemed to be moving.

There were fissures in the rock formations, and through one of them, Seamus said, they would reach the cave. He suggested that Julie wait until he found the entrance.

She was glad to stand there and try in her mind to make the place her own, as by inheritance. This was her father's refuge. She felt elated, proud to be the daughter of a man who could live by himself in rockbound isolation.

The first alarm was the screaming of birds. Almost simulta-neously the explosion staggered her, and she felt as though something had been clapped over her ears that stopped sound. For only a second or two; then she heard her own voice calling out to Seamus.

A new sound came—like that of a waterfall—and a cloud of dust rose from where Seamus had first passed from her view, searching for the cave's entrance. The sound was the falling of crumbled rock. She pushed herself, stumbling, toward the rising dust and then passed between the jagged peaks.

She found him sitting, his feet spread, his back against rock, staring, it first seemed, at the curtain of dust at the mouth of the cave. She thought then that he was dead. But closer, she saw that his eyes blinked now and then. She ran to him, unzipped the jacket, and got the whisky. She talked, murmured, chattered, trying to coax a response while she uncapped the flask. "Open your mouth, Seamus. Please. . . . Can you hear me?"

His jaw dropped like that of a ventriloquist's dummy.

"God, God, God . . ." She pulled his head back and poured the whisky into his mouth. It brought a gurgling sound from his throat and tears into his eyes.

232

"Can't you speak?"

His eyes finally sought hers. He drew a deep breath and moaned. Then he moistened his lips and said, "Oh, Jesus . . ." and after a few seconds: "What a fool I am."

"How would you have known? And you're alive. That's what matters."

A crack of a smile, not enough to show teeth. "They almost trapped a booby."

The pain was obviously bad when he tried to move, but he was soon able to speak. "I knew there was something and I almost jumped clear in time. It was a mine or some such I touched off. But look, I still have both feet and shoes on them."

"Seamus, don't make jokes about it. Tell me what to do and I'll try to do it."

"I wonder now if there's another way that goes down to the sea. There must be, and I should have known it. Could you take great care and have a look?"

Julie approached the seaward ledge of rock. At one end there was a great fissure between it and the mountainous clump of stone within which, some thirty or so yards from its sea face, was the cave. The entrance was still roiling with dust when she looked back. She lay down on the level rock and eased herself, snakelike, to where she could look downward. She caught hold of scrub growth and managed a few inches more. She could see no life below but a buoy rocked in the choppy water. She could not see the shoreline for the projections of the cliff. She knew from her walks with Edna O'Shea that there were unmapped coast roads of short distances between local points, roads often lost to the tides or storm. The wind gusted. She lowered her head and hung on. In the lull that followed she studied another ledge a few feet below and roughly parallel to where she lay. It could be man-hewn, she thought, and the more she studied it, the more clearly she saw it to be a trail, faint and narrow, that would have started this side of the fissure and likely continued layer by layer down to the sea's edge.

She squiggled back and returned to Seamus. He was on his feet, clutching at the wall, his face as pale as the seagulls' feathers. They

233

decided it was safest to try to go back the way they had come. Seamus sent her to see if the car was still where they had left it. It was. Solitary: The curious cottager and his dog were nowhere in sight.

"He'll have heard, the cotter will," Seamus said, "but he won't let on. He may or may not know what's here."

"What *is* here?"

"That's what I'd like to know myself. I think I blew up everything that was going to blow. If only I could wiggle my arse, I'd go in, but whatever's wrong is down near my backside. . . . Can you drive the car?"

"In an emergency."

"It's at hand," he said.

The flashlight lay halfway between him and the cave entrance on the very rim of the hole the blast had left. Without a word, Julie retrieved it and, finding that it worked, went around the hole, staying every step of the way on solid rock. She avoided cracks and crevices. She groped her way through the thinning dust that now hung like a theater scrim between her and the cave's entrance. Inside, the dust was more ancient and settled. The beam of her flashlight discovered walls supported by crude, knotty logs. To one side four plain wooden coffins stood roughly end to end. Whatever was or had been in them, the arrangement suggested that their tops might have been used as seats—or even beds, for there were sacks and moldering blankets stacked on one of them. A house door was stretched between four kegs and had been used as a table. Two other kegs might have served as chairs. On the table were pots and dishes, canned goods, a camp stove, and a teapot. Someone would seem to have left in a hurry, for a shriveled potato and what might have been a carrot or turnip lay, shrunken tiny as mouse food, on a plate, along with the brown bone of a chicken leg. A five-gallon milk can might have contained water, but Julie was afraid to try it, much less offer anything from it to Seamus. Coils of rope lay in a heap alongside a machine of several wheels, a handle on one, so that Julie surmised it to be a pulley device. Then she came upon three cardboard boxes standing aside, and these were new. Very little dust on them. Over the grocery labels the word *Clothes* had been scrawled with a black marker on one; on a second were the words *Tinned Goods* and on a third, repeated in several places, *Caution*. She did not wait to examine them.

Seamus was of the opinion that they must get away at once. "It won't be bloody safe to stay or to be found here. And the cotter may already have raised the alarm. I'm going down with you," he went on fiercely. "It's only pain, and you'll spit in my face if I pass out."

He pulled himself along the wall of rock by the scrub growth until they reached the open. There he shifted his hands onto Julie's shoulders, then onto one shoulder, and ordered her to put an arm around him. His grasp was hard. She bit her lip and made no sound. "One, two . . . one, two," he guided their steps in unison. "They work!" he cried out. "The bloody legs work!" Julie's own legs were shaking, and she wished she could carry him on her back. There was no way—a hundred and eighty pounds of him. She might be able to drag him if she had to, his arms around her neck. "One . . . two . . ." Her legs became steadier, and well it was: Downhill and on the overgrown path the footing was treacherous. "You're doing grand," Seamus shouted. "You've a gorgeous pair of shoulders on you and the back of an Amazon."

"Save your breath," Julie called back.

They paused every few steps. It could not be called resting, their having to stay on their feet lest Seamus not be able to get up, once down. When he came near to faltering, he hooked one arm around her neck and got the whiskey from his pocket. "There's enough for two."

"Save it. It might make me sick anyway."

"And the heart of a mother lion."

"Oh, shut up, Seamus."

"Mush!" he cried, and clasped her shoulders again.

Julie thought of the lion rampant, the weather vane on the tower of the Stone Ring.

It was a long time before he spoke again except to call the "One-two" by which they coordinated their steps. Then: "Julie . . .

235

I don't think I can make it, love, and I've got to piss."

"Does it take two hands?"

"Three."

They were saved by the need to laugh, even if they were scarcely able. He relieved himself, and then before they took the next step, he said: "When we reach where the old road circled—remember? —couldn't you drive the car up and I'd wait here for you? I think it could make it. You just don't want to be timid with it."

Little did he know that her only experience of driving was from a summer at Amagansett, New York, when Jeff let her take the wheel on the country roads. "Refresh me on the gearshift," she said.

"You'll need nothing but low until we get out, and lean heavy on the petrol so it won't stall on you."

40

. . .

"Just let me pass out in the backseat," Seamus had said, "and then don't stop till you get to the hospital at Donegal."

That was the way it happened. The sun was at their backs by the time she turned onto the road overlooking Donegal Bay, and by then she could say that she knew how to drive a car. She called to Seamus now and then, but although he moaned at times, he did not answer. She experimented with the car lights in advance but she did not need them. Though fading, the daylight was still sufficient when she pulled up at the emergency entrance to the county hospital. Seamus was in the X-ray room before anyone came to her. The nurse brought her tea and biscuits. And McNally's wallet, from which she was to provide the hospital with such information as they needed. "And you're to get onto the telephone for him to his 'daily woman' and ask her to take care of his dog. There's an orthopedist coming down from Sligo. You're not to worry."

"When can I see him?"

"Let him rest. He's under sedation, but the last thing he said was, 'Tell her she'd better go to the Gardai with the story right off.' "

41

...

"We were wondering about you, Mrs. Hayes," the young policeman said. "Inspector Superintendent Fitzgerald inquires every day from Dublin if we've heard."

"He knew where I was going," Julie said. "There is no police station in Ballymahon."

"But they're on the telephone line, surely."

"I should have phoned," she admitted.

"You'll be staying in Donegal town for a time now, won't you? I'll inform the inspector superintendent. At the Abbey again, is it?"

"Yes, sir." She'd been gone almost a week, but she was given the same room by a desk clerk who remembered her. "Is there anything new on the Sligo murder, sir?"

"Not that I'd know of, Mrs. Hayes. It's all inquiry from there and very little disclosure. I must call through to Special Branch on the discovery you and your companion made. The coffins, now, wouldn't be of an archaeological nature, would they?"

"No, sir. Plain wooden coffins."

"Hard to come by these days. It's a Special Branch matter, sure. What were you doing there in the first place, if I may ask?"

"Exploring," Julie said, knowing that she would have to tell the story many times to officials with more than local authority. The town Gardai, she suspected, rarely had to deal with violence that was

238

not in the nature of a traffic accident or an after-hours donnybrook.

"You're an American," he said, explaining her curiosity to his own satisfaction.

After several attempts Julie reached McNally's housekeeper by telephone. The woman was convinced he had been in a car collision and gave a determined, mournful account of how recklessly he drove and how she had foretold that this would happen. There seemed little point in trying to tell her what actually had happened. In fact, it seemed better not to try. Julie promised that either she or Seamus would call again in the morning.

She was at her dinner when the two detectives arrived, one an Inspector Costello of the Special Branch and the other, Sergeant Lawrence Carr, the Dublin Murder Team man who had been present during her interrogation by Inspector Superintendent Fitzgerald in Sligo. She ordered coffee for them and soon joined them in one of the lounges not open to the public that night. Carr's warm smile was reassuring. Inspector Costello looked like a seasoned footballer—big shoulders and a knotty jaw that was crisscrossed with scars. The surprise about him was his voice: low and cultured. He had what Julie thought of as a university accent.

Both men listened without comment to her story. Costello's first question: "And you did not look into the newly installed boxes?"

"No, sir. One of them was marked *Caution*, and I was feeling pretty cautious by then anyway."

Costello made a sound that might have been sympathy. "What led you to so desolate a place, may I ask?"

"It isn't far from Ballymahon, and it was where Mr. McNally had once gone himself to interview my father."

"And it's to search for him that you are in Ireland. Is that so?"

"Yes, sir."

"And his name, Mrs. Hayes?"

"Thomas Francis Mooney."

Inspector Costello nodded.

"Did you find him?" Carr sounded genuinely concerned.

"No, sir. He's been gone from Ballymahon for seven years and is presumed dead. His boat was washed up three days after he disappeared at sea."

"The interview between him and the writer, McNally," Costello said, "it would have to have taken place before his disappearance." He paused, then: "Tell me, would your father have been known among his own as Aengus?"

"Yes, Inspector." She was not going to sort out what to tell and what not to tell this man who knew more about the IRA and its splinters than she would ever know.

"And who is it says they presume him dead, Mrs. Hayes?"

"His widow, my stepmother, and I suppose the other people in the village."

"Are you impatient with me? Please don't be," the brawny detective said in a gentle purr.

"I didn't mean to be."

"The name of the widow?"

"Edna O'Shea."

"The painter." He sounded as though he'd now put everything in order. "Is it not remarkable that nothing of hers hangs in Ireland? Her work is well thought of in Britain. I wonder what it tells us about ourselves."

Julie was surprised, almost suspicious.

He went on, "We shall have a forensic team arriving in Slievetooey in the morning, and they'll go up from there. I wonder if they'll see everything that you saw, Mrs. Hayes. Or will someone have tidied up after you? And for whom was the mine laid, and by whom? They could not have been expecting you. Troublesome questions. Could I have a drop more coffee, Mrs. Hayes?" Then: "Sergeant Carr, you're wanting to get on to the murder of Edward Donavan, I know." He settled back in the booth, his coffee cup and saucer in hand.

"I am," Carr said and took out his pocket notebook. "The inspector superintendent sends you his concern and greetings, Mrs.

Hayes. If he'd not something greatly important on his agenda, he'd have flown down from Dublin himself." He glanced at an open page in the notebook. "Do you know a Kevin Bourke in the States?"

Julie drew a quick breath. "Yes, sir. He runs an electrical equipment shop in New York."

"A friend of yours?"

"An acquaintance really."

"Why would a mere acquaintance hire a private security operative to convoy you through Ireland?"

"He wouldn't." She could be sure now that the Gray Man had indeed been in the employ of Sweets Romano. Long ago it had been Kevin Bourke who first got Romano's phone number for her; it was the very beginning of her relationship with the underworld figure. Bourke was a West Side man, a Saint Malachy's parishioner. He would not want to be used by the gangster, but he was weak and vulnerable and therefore available to Romano, who never did anything—charitable or savage—in his own name.

Carr waited, blinking his eyes as though to quicken her explanation.

Finally she said, "The Murder Team must know by now from the New York police who really hired Mr. Donavan, even if he used Kevin Bourke's name."

"Ah, but we don't know that at all. The only information they gave us concerned yourself, the matter of your having been criminally assaulted, and with your alleged assailants having disappeared while awaiting trial. This was very new to us. Mind, I'm not saying we'd expect you to bring forth that information as though it was merely your purse that was stolen. But murder shatters privacy. And it should provoke cooperation. We expected the New York police to find and question this Mr. Bourke for us. A routine accommodation among jurisdictions. But we were handed off to the district attorney's office, where they promised 'to get back to us.' Well, they haven't got back to us yet."

She had to decide on the instant whether to try to hold in trust Lieutenant Marks's information, his preparation of a case against

Romano to take before the Grand Jury. She was still riding the tiger. She would try to tell them her own story only.

"Okay. I think Mr. Bourke was being used as a front by an underworld character known as Sweets Romano. Romano's a terrible man, really, and yet . . ." She shook her head, disgusted with herself for the qualification, the *and yet*. "I'm not going to try to explain or justify my association with him. I can't. It's years ago, but I went to him a couple of times for information—okay, for help for someone. Ever since then he's seen himself as a kind of protector, and now maybe even an avenger. His henchmen are suspected of having roughed up the men who attacked me—strike that, who allegedly attacked me. But that's not proven."

"Ah, now I begin to understand," Carr said. "Both the prosecution of the crime against your person and the investigation of this underworld figure come under the district attorney. Am I right?"

"Yes, sir."

"Not proven," Carr said thoughtfully. "Couldn't you be more specific, Mrs. Hayes?"

"Sergeant Carr, I don't feel at liberty to be any more specific."

Carr looked at her for a few seconds and then changed his tack. "For a man who takes so much power into his own hands, your 'godfather' made a weak choice of Irish representative in Ed Donavan. Or would he have left the choice to Kevin Bourke?"

"No way," Julie said. "Mr. Romano knows who he hires. And he is not my godfather."

"Bad form on my part. I apologize."

"It may be that the real job Mr. Donavan was hired for was to find the indicted rapists if they were hiding out in Ireland. Romano may have thought I came to Ireland to look for them."

"And is that the case, Mrs. Hayes?"

"No, sir. I came for the reason I told Inspector Superintendent Fitzgerald. But I saw one of the men at the Wolfe Tones concert in Donegal the night after I left Sligo."

"Huh!" Then: "What are their names?"

"Frank Kincaid and James Donahue."

"I do have that somewhere . . . information out of New York. You saw but the one?"

"Both are here, I feel sure."

He sat back and drew a long breath as though adjusting himself to a new start.

Inspector Costello, the Special Branch man, said, "If I may ask, could it be that Joseph Quinlan is the defense attorney for those two buckos?"

"Yes, sir. They're represented by his firm."

"When does their trial come up?"

"Not until spring," Julie said.

"And in the States they'd be out on bail meanwhile, and easy targets for Mafia justice."

There was more to it than that if Kincaid and Donahue could be useful witnesses in the case Marks was preparing against the mobster, but Julie merely said, "That's what a lot of people over there think happened to them when they turned up missing."

"So we have two American giants with what we might call international interests trying to outwit each other over a pair of miscreants. And their forces seem to have been brought together in Sligo on the occasion of Roger Casey's funeral. Who could have predicted that?"

"Mr. Quinlan was there himself, in person," Julie said. "Roy Irwin interviewed him the night before, remember."

"Which would seem to have started the conflagration," Costello said, and then to Carr directly, "Forgive me, old man. I've intruded."

Carr turned to Julie. "We've been able to put together an itinerary for Mr. Donavan from the time of your arrival in Ireland." He reached for a dispatch case at his feet and from it drew a looseleaf notebook with tab markers. "It coincides, by the way, with your own account of your activities."

"That's nice," Julie said tartly, for she sensed something of approbation in his words.

"You could be thought to have led a man to his death," Carr said sharply. So much for the smile in his voice.

"I suppose I could," she said, "and for all I know I may have done just that. Am I responsible for Mr. Romano? Okay. Let's say I am. But for the timing of Roger Casey's death? Or that Richard Garvy wanted me to interview his grandmother, who lives in Sligo?"

"There, now, you're overwrought," Carr said, all kindness again. "Shall I go over our profile of the victim so that we three know a little better the man we're talking about? Forty-seven years old, invalided out of the Gardai Special Branch a year ago. In private security service between bouts of lung trouble. That, by the way, owed to chemical poisoning from an explosion. He was a bachelor, lived with and supported his sister, who attended his business accounts. You would think she might be of great assistance to us. Only on matters extraneous to this case. Ordinarily he operated in family or civil matters. In this operation he carried his notes, all information, on his person. And his assailants stripped him even of identification. They lifted his car, and it has not surfaced yet. He employed an associate, Thomas Riordon, to back him up in stake-outs or shadow assignments he could not manage alone. Riordon accompanied you to Wicklow."

"He did?" Julie had not seen anyone she suspected of following her. He'd have stayed on the bus and doubled back at the next stop, or followed her by car to the church and eventually to the house of her Great-uncle Crowley. Had he inquired at the pub of those old men about her visit among them? Those silent old men? He might have learned from them of her quest for Thomas Francis Mooney. "Sergeant Carr, what were the Gray Man's instructions to his assistant?"

"Well questioned, Mrs. Hayes. It's the key to his own assignment. Riordon was to report on where you went, whom you met with and in what kind of neighborhood. He reported your Wicklow people as working-class. He was to intervene if he felt you needed protection. And it did not matter if you spotted him. But if you questioned him, he was to deny even knowing of your existence until that moment."

"As he did himself in Sligo," Julie said.

"So we noted. Mrs. Hayes, were the men who violated you in New York working-class?"

"Blue-collar, yes."

"But you would not say that of the lady you visited in Ballina?"

"Oh, no," Julie said. "Who followed me there?"

"Donavan himself. But he phoned his Sligo hotel booking from there, picked up a carry-out lunch, and went on ahead. The lunch container was found in the waste bin near where he parked his car in Sligo. It would be extremely useful if we could find out what first alarmed him at Sligo. Both his sister and the assistant insist he had no premonition of personal danger in this assignment. I might say here he was paid a handsome retainer—out of which he provided a holiday for his sister. Payment was made in the form of a bank transfer from an account in the name of Kevin Bourke . . ."

"Is that how you got onto Kevin Bourke?" Julie wanted to know.

"We had two sources on him, the bank and information provided by Special Branch. Inadvertently, if you'll forgive my saying so, Inspector Costello. We have been able to reconstruct his modus operandi in this case: It was his practice to ring a New York City number—collect—and ask for Kevin Bourke. The call was not accepted, but the number from which he telephoned was taken, and someone, presumably Kevin Bourke, phoned back within minutes. Riordon confirmed Donavan's practice of reporting the day's information to his client from a public kiosk every evening.

"Now here's the maddening bit: Special Branch was monitoring calls in and out of Sligo that night, and they wiped out Donavan's call as having no political content—a private matter, in other words. Someone at the exchange, however, remembered the name Kevin Bourke and the calls to and from New York. The Dublin exchange has reported a similar pattern of calls earlier. But with no billing, there is no record of the number. So, you see, Mrs. Hayes, without your information, we'd still be looking for daylight in a very dark corner."

Julie recognized Romano's practice in the telephone rigmarole.

He never took a direct call, always called back. She could almost hear that velvety voice: "Romano here." She asked, "Did you try to reach Kevin Bourke at the number listed in the Manhattan phone book?"

Carr laughed. "You *are* sharp. It took us much too long to come up with that simple idea. By then, apparently, word of Donavan's death had crossed the sea. Mr. Bourke has been out of town since we first tried the number."

Julie had never known the man to leave his shop, morning till night, except for a funeral, and then he would close up. It was a one-man operation. His only travel was to and from the Willoughby Apartments on foot. Where Mary Ryan also lived. In spite of all, Julie felt a twinge of homesickness.

"Shall we go back now and pick up Donavan from his arrival in Sligo—from the time he put in at the Lupins Hotel, parked his little car in the courtyard, and went in with his bageen to claim his booking? Everything was in order, apparently. He sat down to a public tea and awaited your arrival. Why didn't you see him in the lounge, Mrs. Hayes?"

"I entered from the other side of the room, and it was crowded. There was a lineup at the phone. Anyway, I didn't," she said impatiently.

He raised his hand placatingly. "Hardly a man in the room but knew you were on your way to the Garvy house on John Street after your use of the telephone. Donavan went out shortly after you, and we have no sighting of him in the next two hours. Are you sure you had none yourself?"

"Not until I returned to my room from the state funeral the next day."

"And him entirely dead by then. Was he at Greely's, where most of the night's action was taking place? He must have been, since you were. He must have followed you to and from the Garvy house before that. Did it alarm him that you stopped at Greely's and asked for Maisie Craig? He'd have known her by reputation, a strong supporter of the IRA. Did he see Irwin get roughed up? We're still missing two critical hours in the man's life. About six o'clock, with

246

no one having seen him return to the hotel, he came down the stairs, his wee bag in hand, and asked at the desk that you be given the room he was vacating." The Murder Team detective sat back and folded his arms. "Something had occurred between four and six that altered his plans. It was a fatal alteration."

Carr referred again to his notebook. "He went out to the car, unlocked the boot, and put his bag in it. The chef was having a cigarette outside the kitchen door and watched him go along to the street the back way. There's a kiosk alongside the 'Ninety-eight memorial, and it was probably from there that he made his call to New York. We catch sight of him once more alive: He's alone at the bar, lingering over a beer that he didn't drink. Who was he waiting for? Why was he there? Did he think he was safe there, or what? Why didn't he go into the dining room and have a meal? Afternoon tea was his last meal. The newspaperman Roy Irwin saw him leave the lounge about eight-thirty in the company of a man he swears he can identify as one of those who lifted the tape of his interview with Quinlan."

Carr swung around on Inspector Costello. "I can't believe Special Branch did not have a man or two in the hotel bar that night. I'll even allow whoever was there didn't know Donavan from the service. But he was a conspicuous figure, we're all agreed, and your boys are paid to use their eyes. Have your people nothing more to offer on the man he was seen with?"

With a sad downward tug of his mouth that deepened the scars on his chin, Costello said, "I think you've already been given whatever's coming your way."

"In other words . . ."

Costello held up his hand, "Don't be putting other words into my mouth, man. I think you've made remarkable progress, and I'm going to build now on the foundation you've both laid down. If you'll indulge me. Mrs. Hayes, it goes without saying, does it, that Romano is a rich man?"

"Fabulously," Julie said. "He has an art collection that any museum could be proud of."

"Does he? And is there anything of Edna O'Shea in his collection?"

It took Julie a second or two to respond. "I don't think so. Not to my knowledge . . . no, no. That's wild."

"As you say, wild, but so are any number of possibilities. Where does his money come from?"

"Real estate, nightclubs, prostitution, pornography, gambling . . ." Julie thought back to the numerous sordid affiliations of which she had heard. "Now I've got to say that it's all hearsay as far as I'm concerned."

"What would you say to firearms, to the kind of munitions terrorists might want?"

"I could be wrong," Julie said, "but it doesn't feel like a Romano thing to me."

"But he would know whose thing it was in 'the family'?"

"Oh, yes. There's not much going on either in the family or out of it that he doesn't know."

"Then I think we can put in place one piece of the puzzle and fit others around it: how Romano came to employ Edward Donavan and not any other of a number of private operatives registered in Dublin. The ONI has attempted to purchase arms through the Mafia. We know they have made contact. Mr. Romano would have gone to the family branch with the Irish connection to recommend a private eye. They in turn would have rung up their ONI connection. And the ONI man, always on the alert for something that might prove useful, recommended Edward Donavan, a man of proven weakness, shall we say, someone in much the position to them as Kevin Bourke is to Romano. They knew they could break him, and probably did. I think they got what they wanted from him. Information they could use."

"Did they have to kill him?" Julie said finally.

"They must have thought so. Even they don't kill without reason. It is axiomatic among their community: If they can break a man, thereafter anyone can break him."

"What you're saying is, the information they got from him cost him his life."

"To be more specific about it, the use to which they intended to put that information cost him his life. He was alive for fourteen hours, remember, after leaving the bar. I don't think it took that long to persuade him. I think there was consultation among their top command about what could be done with the information.

"We've got to keep in mind that Donavan seems to have had nothing on his mind save his job until he got to Sligo. Even for a couple of hours after he got there, and he must have known from the moment he walked into that hotel the affiliations of some of the men who were on hand there. Yet he sat in the open drinking tea and nibbling biscuits. You, Mrs. Hayes, were his only concern. But something was happening among the hierarchy of revolutionaries that met in the back room of Greely's Bookstore. We can be reasonably sure a majority of the represented groups voted to refuse the ONI participation in their council and, most particularly, representation at Casey's funeral. They were an angry lot by then and, like a bunch of football touts on a rampage, they mussed up Irwin and took the tape of the Quinlan interview from him, and when they spotted Donavan, they got onto him and thereupon discovered something that gave them a new lease on life."

"What?" Julie and Carr said the word simultaneously.

"You, Mrs. Hayes. You became the focus of that lot's hope for survival."

42

...

"You were made secure—a room where you were bound to stay the night," the Special Branch man went on. "That seems important to me. Then he went out and placed his New York call. It would be very useful to know if the contents of his report to Kevin Bourke differed from those he had made previously. Is it possible, Mrs. Hayes, for you to be in touch with your benefactor?"

"No!" Julie cried before he could go further. "I cannot and I will not."

"I'm not sure about the *cannot*," Costello said, "although if the circumstances had been slightly altered, that might well have been the case. I suspect that when the ONI broke him down that night, they discovered you the perfect kidnap subject. Let's look at our 'givens': The ONI are desperate for funds, indeed desperate on all counts. You are a columnist for a well-known New York newspaper. The first thing you do, arriving in Sligo, is visit the relative of a famous American actor. More notoriety. You are under the security care of a man whom the ONI may have themselves handpicked for the assignment. In any case they took his own log of the case from him. Some among them likely knew the power and the wealth, if not the name, of Sweets Romano. If he was willing to pay so well for your protection, would he not pay a king's ransom for you?"

250

"I don't know," Julie said. "Maybe not. Inspector, let's say you're right on all counts. Why didn't it come off? Why wasn't I kidnapped?"

"That's the question of the moment, certainly," Costello said. "I would hazard a guess that they had to get in touch with their commandant. They may have been instructed to await a better place, a better time."

"Or would they have found out my real mission in Ireland, looking for someone they knew as Aengus?"

"That's a possibility, but I doubt it. Aengus was IRA. It's true, this lot is a breakaway from the Provos, but they are young and hard, and they identify with international terrorism. The only dead heroes they honor are those they can avenge: I've heard that was said of them in the meeting before Roger Casey's funeral."

"Do you know who said it?"

"I do. Joseph Quinlan. Which has its own touch of irony; if you remember, he closed his oration with Padraic Pierce's famous rallying cry in 1915 at the grave of O'Donovan Rossa. How does it go? '. . . The fools, the fools—they have left us our Fenian dead . . .' "

Sergeant Carr said the rest with him: " '. . . And while Ireland holds these graves, Ireland unfree shall never be at peace.' "

The two men were looking at each other across the table. It was a fleeting instant, but in it Julie sensed the sorrow of men who identified with the cause and despised its most passionate advocates.

They were all silent and thoughtful until Sergeant Carr said, "In your scheme of things, Inspector, could Donavan have had in mind to warn or protect Mrs. Hayes? Might he have gone to her room for that purpose?"

"In that case his captors would have first had to release him. They had but two options if the kidnap plan was to go forward: They had to kill him or take him with them."

"The plan didn't go forward, and they killed him anyway," Julie said.

"And tore into three parts a play by Seamus McNally to make sure it was known that they had been there."

"My God!" Julie said. "Is the cave where Seamus and I—could they have taken it over? Could I have gone on my own to the very place they might have hidden me?"

"I have been waiting for you to make that suggestion, Mrs. Hayes," the Special Branch man said. "It is a distinct possibility."

43

...

"Here I was thinking to be trussed up like a Christmas goose," Seamus said, "and they're not even feeding me from the bottle anymore. I feel like a fool. 'Let me pass out in the backseat': Did I say that?"

Julie grinned and nodded.

"And all I've got is a hairline fracture in the vicinity of where I'd have a tail if they hadn't cut it off some billion years ago. Did you go to the Gardai?"

"Yes, and then last night men from the Special Branch and the Murder Team came to me."

It was getting on toward noon when she finished telling him everything there was to tell, this time holding back nothing, but touching very lightly on Costello's theory of a kidnap plan.

What exercised McNally most was the presence in Ireland of Kincaid. "You could have told me you saw the bastard that night," he said when she was done. "It would have saved me some frivolous thoughts about why you'd changed your mind about you and me."

"Something very interesting, Seamus: The police last night didn't ask me a single question about them after they learned Joseph Quinlan was their lawyer. I think they're counting on him to take them out as quietly as he brought them in."

He gave a grunt of pain as he tried to change positions. Then: "Doesn't it make you feel you've been had in some way?"

"Yeah," she snapped.

"Ah, love, I don't mean that way: I was thinking of the tender care the justice system lavishes on monsters."

"It's better this way. I want them safe until their trial. I just don't want to have to see them until then. When can you go home?"

"Tomorrow if I let them convey me in something called an ambulette."

"They don't trust me to drive you!" Julie cried.

"It's the car they don't trust. Will you take it in hand and follow the ambulette? What an obscene word. It sounds American."

Julie laughed.

Then he said earnestly, "You didn't take seriously the idea of their trying to kidnap you?"

"I think the danger of that is past—if it ever existed. There's been plenty of opportunity, here in Donegal—in Ballymahon."

"Does Special Branch actually think the cave was taken over by the ONI?"

"They'll try to find out in the cave this morning."

"Ach, that'll be the last you or I ever hear of it," Seamus said. "But then, it might have been the last ever heard of us, come to think of it. A bloody round-robin, isn't it?"

"Seamus, could I borrow the Nissan this afternoon? I want to go to Rossnowlagh. Is that how you say it?" She had stumbled over the word.

"The friary?" He gave the name Rossnowlagh its Gaelic pronunication. "It's desolate in winter, rough winds now, but grand in summer. Lovely gardens, and a glorious view of the ocean and the strand."

"I've had that," Julie said. "It was a priest from there who went to Ballymahon and said Mass for my father when he disappeared."

"You like saying the words *my father*, don't you?"

Julie nodded.

"Take the car and come back safe. I'll need the both of you."

As Seamus had foretold, she found the Franciscan friary high on a windswept plateau overlooking the Atlantic. The gnarled trees along the entrance drive bent away from the sea like old rheumatics.

A Brother Charles came to talk with her, both of them sitting in a back pew of the very modern, very chilly chapel. In his brown robe and with bare, sandaled feet, tonsured, he looked out of place —or time—but in manner he was at ease with her. A young face, yet deeply creased, weathered. His cheeks were very red. "It would be *Father* Daniel, if he said Mass, and if as you say he was tubercular, he'd likely have come from a city—Dublin or Derry or Belfast— where they still make room for the old diseases. I was in Derry last winter and I couldn't hear my own voice at the altar for the hacking and coughing in the congregation. I could smell the sickness. It was called consumption in my mother's time, and I grew up with the strains of it still running through the family.

"We're chiefly a convalescent home here for overextended Franciscans," he went on with a smile that creased his whole face. "We send an occasional parish substitute, if called upon. Even Ireland is running short of priests these days. Now I do remember Father Daniel O'Meara. I knew if I talked on, it would come to me. Very devious the ways of the mind: If you wait for a thought, it may never come, and if you run on without it, there's a good chance it'll catch up with you.

"Father Daniel was a fine man and a great teacher, but it was said of him by the higher-ups that he was more political than Holy Orders required of him. And when he developed the trouble in his chest, they were glad to pasture him in the clear air of Rossnowlagh. And if the truth be told, he wasn't a day past recovery when the directors here cheerfully shipped him back to Dublin."

"Adam and Eve?" Julie said.

"Saint Mary's. Aye, that's Adam and Eve."

"That's where my father went to school."

"To Daniel O'Meara, I shouldn't wonder. He's getting on—if he's still alive, and I think he is. And you're wanting to know if your father is still alive. What was it again Father Daniel was supposed to have said?"

"That he might have beached the boat himself and vanished."

"And you're wanting to know why he said it?"

Julie nodded.

"The best I can suggest, then, is that when you're in Dublin, you go and ask him yourself."

44

...

The car sped past her as she followed the ambulette at a safe distance. They were all going north on the main highway and had reached midway in the ascent to the bridge over Barnsmore Gap. The Blue Stack Mountains were falling out of sight, blurring in the rearview mirror. She paid little attention to the speeding car: The ambulette driver had set a leisurely pace. She was turning phrases in her mind that might freshly describe the wild beauty around her. Stay simple, Jeff would say, let the event set the scene for you. She could do with fewer events. Or could she? If the reporting of events was to be her business. From *items* to *events*: Could she make a transition? Her father had tried to write, tried and tried. The afternoon Edna O'Shea left her with his notebooks, she had closed them after numerous attempts to read a few pages consecutively, not wanting the sadness of it. Or afraid of contagion? Or of claiming an inherited disability by way of escape? Escape to what? Back to items? And were items so bad? Some of the best writers were gossipmongers. It became the stuff of fiction. Come on, Julie: It is fiction.

The ambulette braked suddenly, and Julie slammed her foot on the Nissan's pedal. The shoulder belt sawed at her neck. She stopped within a couple of feet of the forward vehicle. It picked up speed again. Ahead of it the same car that had passed her raced over the hill and out of sight. She was fairly sure it was the same car. It would have pulled to the side of the road and then, as the ambulette was about to pass, darted out again. From then on she left more space between her and the hospital vehicle. It was some three miles on, well past the Gap, that the ambulette disappeared from her sight around a curve. She started to speed up and came near to colliding with a car that shot out from behind a thicket and drove parallel within inches of sideswiping her. When she accelerated, so did the other car. Two men. Then she saw that they were masked, the driver hunched over the wheel, peering ahead. The one nearest her, in the passenger seat, rolled down the window and motioned for her to pull off the road. She tried to pick up speed; then she thought to pull toward the shoulder and veer back at them, but they wouldn't give any space between the cars. She clung to the road. An oncoming car gave her hope, but the driver blasted his horn and swerved off to avoid the car driving in tandem with her. Surely he'd stop or give an alarm? Wouldn't the masks be noticed? The tandem car edged closer until contact occurred; they bounced apart; the steering wheel shimmied in her grasp, and she careened toward another smack. When it came, the other car slightly ahead, Julie gave way and jolted off the pavement. The Nissan struck the guard rail. The motor died, and the car bucked to a halt. The attack car stopped long enough to discharge the passenger, then streaked ahead and U-turned. Julie just managed to lock the door. She put her foot on the starter. The motor didn't catch. The man pulled at the door handle, then pounded on the window. He would soon find something to smash it with. But what he did was pull off the mask and shout at her, "We're not going to hurt you! I swear to God!"

Kincaid.

She trod again on the starter: a grinding whirr. Even as the other car crossed the road and parked in front, bumper to bumper. There was no sign of the ambulette. It had not turned back. Seamus would not have seen what happened. She had watched them strap him into place before they left the hospital. Julie reached across to lock the other door, but the shoulder belt delayed her until the man yanked open the door, pulled off his mask, and climbed in beside her. Donahue.

"Unlock your door or he'll smash it in. We're not going to hurt you."

"Go to hell," Julie said and again trod on the starter. Again a futile whirr. And how far would she go with him beside her? A car approached. Donahue grabbed her hand when she was about to lean it on the horn. Kincaid waved at the passing car in neighborly fashion.

Donahue thrust himself across her and flicked open the door lock. There was something sickeningly familiar in the unwashed smell of him. His lank, dark hair fell in a clump across his forehead like a dead mouse. "For Christ's sake, Frankie, open the door. Can't you do anything for yourself?"

Kincaid opened the door and started talking at once. "All we want is to tell you something. We never wanted to hurt *you*," Kincaid pleaded. "Never." He was sweating, and yet the wind was cold. He was still running scared, Julie realized, quite as wildly as he had been the night she saw him at the Wolfe Tones concert.

And he spoke the truth, small honor to them. Poor old Missy Glass was meant to be their prey. She could not look at either of them, but her panic fell away. "What do you want to say to me?"

"Not here. A place people won't be gaping at us. And where they won't be coming back right away to look for you."

"Where?"

Donahue gave an order: "Bring the Ford, Frankie. I'll turn this job around for her." To Julie: "It's not far. You can even phone your friend on the way and tell him what happened. I swear you'll be all right."

Kincaid added, "I swear it, too. I want you to see my mother when you get home."

Oh, God. Julie glanced at Kincaid and thought of how he resembled a Cabbage Patch Doll—he who had played ticktacktoe on her naked body with his switchblade. She turned her head to look full at him: watery eyes, a slithering tongue over wet lips, and a growth of beard to match the new red crop on the top of his head. She could taste her loathing. "And if I won't go with you?"

"Christian charity: That's all we're asking of you."

"No kidding." Then: "If you can start the car for me, Mr. Donahue, okay. But I'm going to drive."

There was no conversation between them, only his directions and not many of them, for the dirt road was crossed but once, with a public house, the Fox and the Hart, at the intersection. She declined the offer of a phone call from there. She did not want to enter the building, to give Seamus's number aloud, to advertise her vulnerability.

The cottage, some twenty miles' drive from where they had left the highway, was thatched, newly whitewashed, and had but one door and two windows. Fire, the smoke wafting around it, glowed in the hearth like a red, rheumy eye. A very old woman was ladling water from a bucket into the kettle when they entered. Nothing was said to or by her. She had grown small in age, Julie thought. Kincaid explained that she did not speak English. A clothesline, hung with blankets, separated the room into two parts. The cottage would be where Kincaid and Donahue had been hidden away in Ireland. It smelled of smoke and damp clothes and human rot. Smoke-filtered sunlight shone through the front window. Donahue led the way to a scarred porcelain-topped table, around which were three crude chairs. He parted the heavy curtains over the back window, and the light seemed to focus attention on a bunch of artificial flowers in a jug in the center of the table. "I bought her them when I was in Sligo," Kincaid said.

The sensitive type. Julie said nothing.

The old woman shuffled to the fireplace with the kettle. There was an alcove alongside the fireplace and in it a bed. When the old one had hung the kettle on the bracket, she proceeded to the alcove, climbed up on the bed, and drew a curtain across to close herself in.

"My God," Julie said, "won't she suffocate?"

Kincaid said, "She goes in there all the time. Unless she's sitting on the stool poking the fire and rocking and crying. Sometimes it gets weird, like she was trying to freak us out. She doesn't mean nothing by it, but Jim and me, we sing when she starts in. We must've sung every song we ever heard—lullabyes, country, 'Yankee Doodle,' 'God Bless America,' oh boy, you better believe it. But she ain't violent or anything, and we take good care of her. Jerry Devlin—he's our . . ."

When Kincaid paused, not having the word he wanted, Donahue provided one: "Our keeper."

"Anyway, he bought her a transistor radio once, you know? And what did she do with it? She took it outside and dug a hole and buried it. She wouldn't believe it wasn't a bomb." He seemed unable to stop talking.

Julie got her question in while he drew a deep breath. "Are you going to tell me what you want from me?"

Both men were silent then. They looked from her to each other and then down. They were sitting, their shoulders sloped, their hands out of sight beneath the table. Kincaid's were fidgeting: She could hear them rasping against one another, then she heard the wheeze of the old woman's breathing behind the curtain. Shoes and all in there, Julie thought. Finally Donahue said, "You came looking for us, right?"

"Wrong," Julie said. "If I had my way, I'd never have to see either of you again in my lifetime."

"You want us in hell, right?" Kincaid this time.

"Okay."

"Maybe what's happened to us ain't hell, but it's pretty close. Me and Jim aren't like we were that morning when we did that to you. We don't want to be excused or anything. Pigs. Animals. It was like we went crazy, you know?"

"I was there," Julie said.

"It was the booze we had, and some guy put something in it. We'd gone to a bunch of porn movies and got ourselves hotted up . . ."

"Look, Mr. Kincaid. You can tell this all in court. I may even have to be there. You said something about Christian charity—where does that come in? If you've got any of it, you'll let me go."

"Yeah, yeah. You're right, and like Jim says, it's all bullshit anyway. Excuse me. We did what we did and we were going to take our punishment if it wasn't for our families and Mr. Quinlan. And we wouldn't've had to get beat up to do it, either."

"That's bullshit too," Julie said. She would never forget the night she left Seamus in order to view these men in a lineup and to share Detective Russo's despair when she couldn't and Missy Glass wouldn't identify them.

"Okay. When we thought we could get away free—who wouldn't? That don't mean we weren't sorry or ashamed of ourselves. If it wasn't for Jim being in it too, I think I'd've killed myself."

Julie drew a deep, audible breath. Her eyes were stinging from smoke, and she rubbed them. "Can't you leave the door open?"

"That makes it worse, more downdraft or something," Donahue said. "It won't be so bad when the fresh turf catches. . . ." To his partner: "Stop explaining, Frankie. Just tell her and get it over with. Do you want me to do it?" To Julie: "He's a craw thumper. Do you know what that is?" He beat at his breast to illustrate the *mea culpa*.

"Yeah."

He took over then. "I'm not saying we'd've turned ourselves in if the goons hadn't threatened to ship us out in cement if we didn't. . . ."

The goons, Julie thought. Then: Wait a minute. These two had denied to Lieutenant Marks that they'd been assaulted at all. Why were they admitting it now? She interrupted him: "Why tell me this? Why didn't you tell the Grand Jury or the district attorney?"

"Mr. Quinlan wouldn't let us. I wanted to, but the thing was, I saw the driver of the car that night up close. A little guy—you'd've almost thought he was a midget. He jumped out and started kicking us and spitting on us. But Mr. Quinlan said I couldn't be sure of seeing anybody under the circumstances. I was to stay with my original story—me and Frankie having a fight—until he said different."

Julie understood. She knew Romano's driver, Little Michael, a man not over five feet tall and very slight. His was a lifetime loyalty to the boss, and Michael would himself have been outraged on her behalf. To put him on the scene was a perfect Romano link.

She did not want to hear any more. "Why can't you tell all this to a priest or somebody and leave me out of it? What am I doing here? If I'd been going to turn you in, wouldn't I have done it the night I saw you in Donegal? I don't want to know why you attacked me. I don't want to know why you would have attacked that poor old street woman if I hadn't come along when I did."

"Just calm down and I'll try and tell you." Donahue pointed at the curtained alcove. "That old lady in there—that's our penance, ma'am. Frankie and me aren't going back. We're going to stay here till she dies. And take good care of her. She'd be put away if it wasn't for us. And she will be if they extradite us. Back home—if they got us and put us on trial and called in the psychiatrists. . . ." He shook his head. "We did something crazy, like perverts. Now, you aren't going to believe this, but *we didn't want to do it*."

"Oh, Christ," Julie said.

"I told you she wasn't going to understand." His lips were drawn tight. Sweat rose beneath the mouse of hair on his forehead. His eyes, screwed up, seemed even smaller.

But something in what he had said provoked her curiosity: the suggestion of psychiatrists. "You didn't want to do it," she said. "And so?"

"So we did every stinking thing we could."

"You sure did," Julie said, and for the first time participated in whatever it was they were trying to communicate. "What does Joe Quinlan have to say about your staying here?"

"He doesn't know yet. And he didn't exactly bring us over here himself, like by the hand. He talked to us just the once. You'd've thought he'd want to know everything. But he didn't want to know anything. It was like he told *us* what happened. Like he believed everything my mom and Frankie's mother and the priest told about us. The people we've met over here—they're his cousin's family, and they think he's a whole bunch, Mister Big, he's God! He keeps them alive, see, when there's flood or famine or the sheep get sick, and their biggest thing is a united Ireland, maybe a United States of Ireland. I could tell you a lot of things, but I learned to keep my mouth shut."

"What do they think about you two?" Julie asked and remembered that Edna O'Shea had wondered the same thing.

"They don't know about you. They think we're being seques-

263

tered so's we can give evidence in a big trial coming up."

Julie would as soon they stayed in Ireland and let the Irish cope with their penance or their plunder. She doubted it could happen. Quinlan would whistle, and they would respond, whether or not they chose to. "I'm back at the same old question, what do you want from me?"

"We want you to say you forgive us," Kincaid said instantly.

She was stunned. Then she thought of what seemed a subtle, even a devious distinction: They didn't ask her to forgive them, but to *say* she forgave them. But she soon realized that she was wrong. The distinction was her own.

"The old lady in there won't last very long, and the handouts we get from plastering and spraying whitewash, they don't come to much," Donahue explained. "We've taken an oath or I'd tell you what else."

"You've joined the IRA," Julie said, not needing to hear more.

"I'm not saying, and nothing's happened yet. But I was good in high school chemistry," Donahue went on, "and Frankie wants to hang in with me. Maybe we can do something and make up, see?"

Like killing people outright, Julie thought. Nor could she believe that any revolutionary movement would trust such partisans as these. Possibly a mortician might be useful to them.

"What else can I do for you?" she said with ironic intent.

"If we don't come home in the spring," Kincaid now took over, "go and see my mother for me. You can tell her everything."

"And do you think she will believe me?"

"I wrote her a letter if you'll take it. That's what I wanted to ask you, will you take it to her—you know—if something happens to me?"

Jim Donahue shook his head. "It won't make any difference to anybody."

The wretched Kincaid stared at his partner across the table, stuck out his weak chin, and said, "It will to me."

45

...

"Of course it hurts!" Seamus shouted, and Julie was glad that she had not been the one to ask the question. "It hurts because they kept me strapped to a bloody ironing board when I should have been sitting up normal and looking about me."

"I only asked because you're in such a temper and they left something to give you for the pain." The housekeeper screwed up her mouth and gave a little toss of her head.

"I appreciate your solicitude, Mrs. O'Gorman. But if you'd make us a hot toddy, I'd appreciate it more. The hour's at hand. And don't be afraid to tilt the bottle, love."

Mrs. O'Gorman left the room, a model of dignity, holding in much of herself with her elbows. She was built along the lines of a large carrot, broad at the top and tapering down. She was ruddy-faced, a reluctant smiler, and wore her gray hair braided and twisted around into a peak on the top of her head as though it might add to her stature. From the moment she had opened the cottage door, top half, Then the bottom, one hand on the dog's collar, Julie had doubted her welcome. Both Mrs. O'Gorman and the great black and tan hound dog had hovered near the bedside since her arrival. The dog, on Seamus's command, had finally curled up on his blanket beneath the double window.

Seamus, as soon as O'Gorman could be heard clattering in the

265

kitchen, reached for Julie's hand and pulled her toward him. "To hell with the bastards and their mockery of contrition. You're here, and that's all that matters. Will you give us a kiss? I'm dying to know if we can do it after all the bum starts."

Julie got up from the chair and leaned down over him, her thigh on the side of the bed. There was no other way, really, him flat on his back. It was their first long kiss, and grew longer and deeper, and when Seamus put his hand to her breast, she made a little sound at the shock of pleasure.

On the instant the dog leaped up onto her back with a growl that mounted in fury. He caught the shawl of her heavy sweater and shook it as he might have an animal he had by the neck. Julie twisted away and covered her head with her arms. Seamus shouted and cursed the animal and got up in the bed to grab him. Mrs. O'Gorman came running, shouting also, and flailed her apron in the air.

Seamus by then had the dog by the collar and turned it over to the housekeeper, who dragged it outdoors, at once soothing and scolding it.

"The jealous brute," Seamus said. "Did he get his teeth into you?" He was sitting on the side of the bed, a long flannel nightshirt tucked between his legs. "Come and kneel down and let me have a look."

Julie pulled off the sweater and allowed him to examine her neck and shoulders.

"Nary a mark," Seamus said, "but I can hear your heart thumping. Or is it my own?"

Julie got up and pulled on the sweater, not looking to see the extent of its damage.

Mrs. O'Gorman was standing in the doorway. "I've put him out," she said.

"Will you take him up home with you and keep him for a few days?"

"He won't stay, and you need him here."

The implication to Julie was that he did not need her.

"Look at you sitting up there," the woman scolded him. "You'll be crippling yourself for life."

266

"On the contrary," Seamus said and slipped off the bed and onto his feet. "I've been misdiagnosed by the sawbones." He hobbled across the room and took a bathrobe from a hook behind the door. "We'll have our toddies in the lounge, Mrs. O'Gorman."

It was a large cottage named after the Swilly River, which it overlooked. Seamus had added onto it himself so that it was not authentic, as he explained, "but a hell of a lot more comfortable than it was in its authenticity."

Julie tried to memorize it—the large fireplace in the lounge or living room, the musical instruments. Seamus played the flute—"I'm not James Galway, but I can tootle a pretty tune." There were books everywhere, and the floors were covered with the woven carpets of Donegal. She took in everything she could, for she knew that she would not be long a guest at Swilly Cottage after all, perhaps not even the night. There was a sad inevitability to her feeling of imminent departure. That Seamus understood her need to go was implicit in his saying, "I was hoping to show you the far, far hills that are very near to here, and the village Richard Garvy is coming over to see before we go into rehearsal. But you're a writer. You know it's more a state of mind than a place on the map. And when you see it on the stage, you'll say you've been there, and so you will have been, don't you see?"

"I do see," Julie said.

"I've a copy of the play for you."

She did not remind him that she already had one, bought that first morning in the bookstore in Donegal town.

They had their toddies and an early dinner of poached salmon Mrs. O'Gorman had brought already prepared from her own house.

"It's twice poached, you know," Seamus said, "once from an English lord's demesne and once in a pot."

The dog barked incessantly, as though she had not already resolved to go, and Seamus was wincing with pain before the meal was over. Julie spoke to the housekeeper. "Seamus says you can arrange a car to drive me back to Donegal tonight."

"My son's in the livery business. I'll ring him up now."

"Your haste is indecent," Seamus growled. "Bring me back a pill when you come."

"That's why I'm in haste," Mrs. O'Gorman said, the last word.

"I'm sorry it's come out this way," Seamus said when she was gone.

"It's better that I finish up one part of my life before starting another," Julie said.

"I like that," he said and grinned like a boy with the promise of his favorite treat if he took his medicine.

Back in the same hotel room she had vacated in Donegal town that morning, she read again the inscription Seamus had written in the revised typescript he had given her of *The Far, Far Hills of Home*: "For Julie—with love that is and is to be."

46

Father Daniel O'Meara in his brown robes and sandals was a towering old man, and the cold, murky office, its windows smudged with the dust of Dublin, seemed to vibrate with his coming. He had heavy jowls and thunderous eyebrows over eyes so searching they could purge a sinner for life, Julie thought. But the large mouth told of humor, and his deep voice filled the room. His first words when he had moved her from the desk to where they could sit side by side, gave her pleasure: "Now, where have we met before, Mrs. Hayes? I know I recognize you from somewhere."

"I don't think so, but from someone maybe. Do you remember Thomas Francis Mooney? He was my father."

The priest pulled at his nose, taking a second or two before he murmured, "Mooney, is it? I do remember him as a lad. I taught him—a bright little fellow with fine, wide eyes like your own."

Julie could tell that the priest was groping his way through surprise. "I wasn't trying to take you unawares, Father Daniel. I've been in Ballymahon with Edna O'Shea for a week. She recognized me for his daughter, but I don't think he even knew of my existence. I should tell you that I know you said Mass for him when he disappeared."

"Yes, well. So I did. Is that why you came to see me?"

"It was something you said that she repeated to me: You said he might have beached the boat himself and vanished."

"Why did she tell you that, I wonder? Sheer speculation on my part."

Julie suspected that unless she told all she knew, she would learn little from him that was new. And it would be unwise to throw the cover name Aengus at him, with all its political implications, without preparing the way. "Father Daniel, do you have time to listen if I were to tell you how I got to Donegal in my search for him?"

"I have made a friend of time, Miss Julie. It had become too formidable an enemy. Tell on."

How odd that he should call her Miss Julie. He and Sweets Romano.

So again Julie told the story of her search for her father, the tale growing longer with each telling, with each new episode of discovery. She wound up with her visit to Rossnowlagh, saying that Brother Charles had told her that her father might very well have gone to school to him, Father Daniel, for politics as well as history and algebra.

"Not a reticent man, Brother Charles. Well, I forgive him as he forgave me my chauvinism. How did you find Miss O'Shea?"

"Through the cashier at Greely's Bookstore in Sligo."

The priest's jowls quivered when he chortled. "I was inquiring after her health actually. An idle question. What did you think of Maisie Craig at Greely's?"

"I didn't meet her. Another woman spoke to me. It was the night before Roger Casey's funeral, and Mrs. Craig was at a meeting."

"Wielding the gavel as though it were an ax. And did you and Miss O'Shea take to each other, having that uncommon man in common?"

Julie nodded. "She's very special, Father."

"Oh, she is that."

They were speaking of someone, Julie realized, who had seemed, at the time she mentioned the priest, to have scarcely known his name, as though it was accidental that he had been the one available to come from Rossnowlagh to say the Mass. Whether or not Edna

270

O'Shea knew it, the priest and her father were not strangers. "Is Frank Mooney alive, Father?"

The priest made a little face as though the direct question pained him. "I see I must tell you now—I was your father's confessor."

She smothered the vulgar word that leaped to mind, but she could not stem bitter sarcasm. "Well, you could not have confessed a dead man, could you?"

"I did not say when I served him thus, and I understand your anger to have come this far and have me take the Fifth, you might say."

"But if he were dead, you *could* talk to me, couldn't you?"

"Am I not talking to you?"

Julie thought about that. "Is it that I'm not listening to you, Father?"

He smiled and touched her hand—a brief pat—and she thought again of the Crowley hands. "Much better," he said. "I can accept you as his daughter and I do. I wonder if it would not be useful if I were to tell you the story of myself. I came here to school as a boy—a poor boy of the neighborhood. The country was in turmoil at the time. What rebellion had failed to achieve, reprisal hastened. The more rebels the British shot after the Easter Rising, the stronger the people's support for the martyrs' cause. And the young found purpose to their lives, and alas, to their dying. I was no exception. I revered and followed a poet whose name has been deliberately excised from the chronicles of rebellion and the civil war that followed it. It was after a particularly bloody assassination—or it might even have been before it, perhaps during its planning—that he dropped from sight. Rumor had it that he was himself destroyed in the explosion, but no part of him was identified among the mortal remains taken from the waters. He was never named among the heroic dead—of whom, you may have discovered, we often seem more fond than of the living. . . ."

When he paused, Julie realized she had been all but holding her breath. Her neck was stiff, her nerves taut.

"I knocked around a bit without an anchor," the priest went

on, "latching on, where they'd let me, to the literary wing of the republicans. When the cause was lost, or in abeyance, as I've come to believe it still to be—until union is achieved—I came back to the Franciscans. Because I wanted an education, I convinced myself and others that I had a religious calling. The Lord is not particular whether you enter by the back or the front door. I was on my way to become a priest. I had gotten as far as subdeacon orders when I was sent to Rome for a year. It might have been to Rome or New York, but I went to Rome, and do you know who it was there who taught me —and in Latin, mind you—Christian ethics? A Franciscan brother, the forgotten republican hero of my youth."

Fact or fable? Both. Julie drew a deep breath. Her mind teemed with questions, but before she could frame the first of them, the old priest rose from his chair, responding to a bell he said was for vespers.

In the end all she said was, "Thank you, Father Daniel."

It was a warm day, Indian summer, and as soon as she found a bench along the Liffey quays, she took her notebook from her carryall and entered the story almost exactly as he had told it. She had a good memory and she knew what she had heard . . . Rome or New York.

Was her search ended, and if it was, would it ever be truly ended? And must it be? This was much the question Edna O'Shea had asked her: What would we know of him if we knew the truth that would be better than what we know now?

47
...

It was her second day back in Dublin, and having decided to return to New York within the week, she phoned Tim Noble. He seemed less than excited at the prospect. New York was going to seem very dull to her, he suggested. Then he asked, "What about the character who was shot in your bed? The boss thought you'd file something on that. Where were you when it happened?"

"At a funeral."

"Lucky it wasn't your own." Amazingly, no word seemed to have reached New York on what had happened to her and Seamus McNally. "Are you going to bring me a present?" Now he was trying to sound cheerful.

"Of course."

"Are you sure you have the right size?"

"Bastard."

"Julie, the priest at Saint Malachy's called with a message for you. . . . Wait now till I dig it out of my drawer. . . ."

She waited, something like fear in her throat. But Tim would have said outright if it concerned Kincaid and Donahue.

He came on the phone again. "Here we are. He said you'd know what he was talking about and you might want to know it while you were over there: The information you hoped to get from the Chancery Office doesn't exist. The transaction simply could not have occurred. Does it make sense to you?"

"I do know what he's talking about. Thank you, Tim."

The whole annulment legend was pure fantasy. Perhaps there was a divorce somewhere down the years. It was one more thing she did not have to know.

In the early afternoon she phoned Roy Irwin's home. His wife answered.

"Where are you?" She sounded surprised to hear Julie's voice.

"Back in Dublin."

"Ach, and Roy in Donegal. He went down this morning with the Murder Team to Slievetooey. . . ."

"Slievetooey," Julie repeated, searching her memory for why the place name was familiar.

"The bodies of two men were found in a cave where there'd been an explosion," Eileen went on. "They're thought to be Americans. Another reason Roy went down; he was hoping to find you."

"Tell him I'm back in the Greer Hotel if you hear from him," Julie said. "They were killed in an explosion?"

"No, love. The explosion occurred days ago, but Special Branch found the bodies when they went to further examine the site. Each with a bullet in the back of his head. Where will it end, you wonder, where and when will it end?"

48
...

And what's to become of the old woman in her bed with the curtains drawn? Julie's first thought. Her legs were rubbery when she went out from the public phone in the Trinity College lodge after talking to Eileen Irwin. She had expected that, something might happen to those two—and not for an instant did she doubt they were Kincaid and Donahue—but not this. They were not that important. Except to one man, a New York gangster who didn't know they intended not to show up to testify against him.

She did not find a bench in Parliament Square and she very much needed to sit down. Students everywhere. Laughter and earnest conferences on matters nearer to life than to death. She would not have wanted them to die. Not that way. Christ! It was that old woman she was thinking of. Why not of Missy Glass? Why not of their mothers waiting for word much like this, but not from Ireland? She thought of Kincaid's letter she had wanted to throw away but hadn't. Finding no place to sit down, she followed a young couple who went, hand in hand, up the steps and into the chapel. At the altar an afternoon service was in progress—High Church Anglican. In which she herself had been baptized. She entered a far pew and sat wondering why her feeling was primarily of grief.

When she returned to the hotel, Detective Sergeant Lawrence Carr was waiting in the lobby. Her first fear was that he was going to ask her to go north with him, possibly to identify the bodies.

"Just talk," he said. "We can use your room if you like and leave the door open for propriety's sake."

When they had settled in, he said, "They're your buckos, all right. A man named Devlin came forward and identified them. There will be some notification of kin going on before their names are given out, but I'm afraid you'll be in for it, Mrs. Hayes. The whole story may break out into the open. What I'm to ask you here is whether you saw them again in Donegal."

"Yes."

When she had finished telling of her encounter with Kincaid and Donahue, he said, "The silly fools." Then: "But they were caught between the devil and the sea, weren't they? Isn't it remarkable, the similarity in *hit* techniques between terrorists and gangsters? But sure, what is one but the other?"

Julie said nothing.

"Our lot try for the poetic symbol as well: Aengus's Cave."

She felt the chill run down her back, and of course that was what had most grieved her, the desecration of her father's place, which she had wanted to keep a shrine. No. Be honest, Julie: What you're grieving for is the death of a dream. Then she thought about what the detective had said—the poetic symbol—and remembered instantly her session with him and Special Branch Inspector Costello, in which one of them had said that the ONI were a younger lot, to whom the name Aengus would mean little. "Sergeant Carr, do you know who killed Kincaid and Donahue?"

Carr rubbed the back of his neck. "It's not likely the IRA, now, is it, them being so close to Quinlan? But I don't think the IRA would have embraced them if, as they told you, they intended to stay in Ireland."

"And the ONI?"

"There has to be a reason. We said it before of Donavan's death: Even our terrorists don't kill without reason."

"An exchange of favors, then, with Sweets Romano. We said that before too," Julie said.

Carr merely nodded, an uncertain gesture toward affirmation. "When do you plan to return to the States, Mrs. Hayes?"

"The day after tomorrow," Julie said.

Carr smiled, almost wistfully. "There's an Aer Lingus flight in the morning. Both Inspector Duffy and Inspector Superintendent Fitzgerald feel that it would be in your best interests if we could get you aboard the earliest possible flight. They both sent you their warmest regards and directed me to particularly thank you for your cooperation."

"Yeah," Julie said and got up. "I'll pack as soon as you leave, Sergeant Carr."

"I daresay you'll be glad to get home."

"I daresay."

49
...

It was the questions he had not asked that Julie mulled during the long flight home, chief among them whether or not she had found further trace of her father. She read her notes from the beginning. There was a terrible ending to one of the articles she had yet to write for the Sunday magazine, the story of rape and vengeance.

And of the search? Afterward she was sure she had known in her soul the—for her—heartbreaking story that appeared in the New York newspapers the next day with the dateline, Ballymahon, Ire.

> An internationally known artist, Edna O'Shea, was arrested yesterday as the leader of the outlawed Irish extremist group known as the ONI. Miss O'Shea had been under suspicion as a member of the Provisional IRA for some years. It is now suspected that she led the split from the parent group. The ONI, which stands for One Nation Indivisible, takes the intransigent position on the union of north and south, and is known to have ties with international terrorism. What led to Miss O'Shea's arrest was the confession of a suspected ONI member that he had taken part, on her orders, in the killing of two Americans hiding out in Ireland and under indictment in New York for felonious assault.